A TAPESTRY
of
SECRETS

Books by Sarah Loudin Thomas

A Tapestry of Secrets
Until the Harvest
Miracle in a Dry Season

A TAPESTRY

of

SECRETS

SARAH LOUDIN THOMAS

BETHANYHOUSE
a division of Baker Publishing Group
Minneapolis, Minnesota

© 2016 by Sarah Loudin Thomas

Published by Bethany House Publishers
11400 Hampshire Avenue South
Bloomington, Minnesota 55438
www.bethanyhouse.com

Bethany House Publishers is a division of
Baker Publishing Group, Grand Rapids, Michigan

Printed in the United States of America

Library of Congress Control Number: 2016931063

ISBN 978-0-7642-1227-7

Scripture quotations are from the Holy Bible, New International Version®. NIV®. Copyright © 1973, 1978, 1984, 2011 by Biblica, Inc.™ Used by permission of Zondervan. All rights reserved worldwide. www.zondervan.com

This is a work of fiction. Names, characters, incidents, and dialogues are products of the author's imagination and are not to be construed as real. Any resemblance to actual events or persons, living or dead, is entirely coincidental.

Cover design by Kathleen Lynch/Black Kat Design
Cover image by "theboone" / iStock photos

Author is represented by Books & Such Literary Agency

16 17 18 19 20 21 22   7 6 5 4 3 2 1

For Aunt Bess (1904–2006)
who taught me to listen for God
and then patiently waited
for me to do it.

CRAGGY MOUNT, VIRGINIA
JUNE 2008

WHY DID SHE AGREE to have lunch with Mark? He'd been out of her life for almost a year now. What had possessed her to say yes when he suggested meeting? Ella peered at her former fiancé over her menu, then refocused on the day's special when he caught her looking.

Honestly, she wasn't even attracted to him anymore. She'd once thought those dense, dark curls and square jaw were handsome, but what she'd once seen as chiseled just looked hard now.

"Don't you have Perrier?" he asked the server.

"We have bottled water," she said.

"Only still, though. Am I right?"

The server looked confused.

"Not effervescent." Mark spoke slowly as though talking to someone who wasn't very bright.

"Oh. Right." The server nodded. "Yes, only still."

Mark sighed. "Fine. Unsweetened tea for me, and Ella, do you still prefer yours sweetened?"

"Yes, please." She folded the menu and gave the server an apologetic look.

Mark dismissed her with a wave of his hand. "We'll order in a minute."

The server raised her eyebrows at Ella and headed for the kitchen.

"I was ready to order." Ella tried to tamp down her annoyance. Although she wasn't seeing Mark anymore, she could still be nice. Based on what she knew of him, he could use a few examples of nice in his life.

Mark leaned in. "We're in no hurry, right? Now that I'm an associate at the firm, I can afford a long lunch now and again. And you, well, artists set their own schedules, don't they?"

Ella bristled. She bit her lip to avoid speaking too quickly. Gran always said, "Sow in haste, repent in leisure." She tried to take that to heart. Words were hard to take back once spoken.

"Generally, that's true, but I do have a deadline I need to meet so I can't stay too long." That was almost the truth. She did have a self-imposed deadline that she had pretty well already met, but Mark didn't need to know the details.

Mark's face pinched, but then he smoothed it back out and smiled. "Fine. What looks good to you?"

Ella caught the eye of the server, who was approaching with their drinks. "I'll have the shrimp quesadilla special."

The server nodded and looked at Mark.

"Are the crab cakes made with lump crab?"

"I think so," she said.

Mark rolled his eyes. "Bring me the crab cakes."

As soon as she walked away, Mark shook his head at Ella. "Ten to one it's backfin." He smirked. "I could probably bring suit against them for false advertising."

Ella suppressed a sigh. What was she doing? "But you wouldn't waste your talents on a frivolous lawsuit."

Mark considered her. "No. I wouldn't."

"So," Ella began as she smoothed her napkin in her lap, "what have you been up to? Seeing anyone?"

Again, Mark looked annoyed. "Well, as I mentioned, I'm an associate now. It was down to Paul Warren and me, and Paul, well, he just didn't want it as much as I did. You've got to be willing to sacrifice to get ahead at Finley, Robertson, and Ellison."

"What did you sacrifice?" Ella chastised herself. That wasn't a nice question.

"Whatever I had to," Mark said. He watched the server approaching and narrowed his eyes at the plate she set in front of him. He poked a crab cake with his fork and opened his mouth as if to speak.

Ella jumped in. "Thank you so much. It looks delicious." She widened her eyes at the server, who darted a look at Mark and then scurried away.

"This is not lump crab. I was going to send it back."

"I've found that backfin can be more flavorful," Ella said, cutting into her quesadilla. "Why don't you taste it first? And anyway, we're here to catch up with each other. Let's not let the food be a distraction. By the way, has the name of the firm changed? Seemed like it used to just be Finley and Robertson."

Mark's mouth twitched as he examined her. "You should probably study the law yourself. You'd make a fine defense attorney. Yes, Mr. Ellison is the newest partner. I'm still getting a feel for him."

Ella sipped her tea. "I suppose that's one of the advantages of making my quilt hangings—no co-workers or supervisors to figure out."

Mark sneered, then caught himself. "You're a fine craftsperson. How's business, by the way? Still dreaming about running off to your family farm to live the artist's life?"

Ella bit the tip of her tongue, wishing she'd never confided her dream of building a studio near her family and creating quilt hangings that would carry the art of Appalachia to the wider world.

"Dreams are just that, I suppose." She wasn't going to defend her ambition to Mark. Not now.

Ella suffered through another twenty minutes of chitchat and did her best to enjoy her food, which was really good. She persuaded Mark that she honestly didn't want dessert and walked through the front door into the heat and humidity of June in southwestern Virginia with a sense of relief. But Mark wasn't quite done with her yet. He draped an unwelcome arm around her shoulders and pulled her against him.

"We should do this again." He stopped and turned her to face him. "I've missed you. I know you had your reasons for leaving, but I've changed. I'd like to try again."

Ella swallowed and used all her self-control to keep from twisting away from him and running for freedom. "That's quite a compliment, Mark. I appreciate it. But I really don't think there's a future for us." His face darkened, and she rushed her words. "Thanks for lunch. I wish you luck at the firm—I'm sure you'll be successful." She smiled and took a step back so that he had to release her. "After all, you're quite the eligible bachelor. I'm sure you'll find the right girl for you."

Mark's head drew back, and he sucked air in through his teeth. "Yes, well, I think I know which girl is right for me." He reached out and tweaked her chin. "We'll talk again."

Ella opened her mouth, but Mark had already turned and was disappearing around a corner. She watched him go as dread rose in her belly. Why oh why had she agreed to lunch today?

Perla got out the good sheets with the embroidered pillow slips. She flicked the fitted sheet over the bed in the guest room, letting it drift into place. She couldn't say why, but she had a feeling someone might come for a visit. And if no one did, it was still nice to use the good linens. Maybe she'd sleep on them herself. She smoothed out the creases and wished it were Ella coming. Perla worried about her granddaughter—maybe more than she should. She sometimes thought Ella was too willing to make sacrifices to please others. And when you got right down to it, there was only one opinion that mattered. A Bible verse popped into Perla's head: *"For they loved human praise more than praise from God."*

She shook her head. She'd never really tried to correct what she saw in Ella, even though she well knew how destructive it could be to spend too much time worrying over what everyone else thought of you.

She sat on the edge of the bed to rest a moment, reaching up to smooth a stray wisp of white hair back into its twist. Maybe it was time to share her own story. It was common knowledge that she'd had Sadie out of wedlock back in 1949, something no one raised an eyebrow at anymore. It had become an overlooked fact rather than the shame she once carried. What Perla had never shared—what she'd long assumed she never would—were the circumstances and the name of the man she once loved. She'd loved him and wanted to please him enough to risk everything and suffer the consequences. Of course, she wouldn't trade a minute of that pain now, but that was because God had been merciful enough to redeem her.

Perla finished making the bed and leaned against the headboard. She was so very tired. Normally the thought of visitors—actual or hoped for—energized her, but today she felt worn to the bone. Maybe it was thinking about her mistakes and dredging up those days she'd long put behind her. And such thoughts inevitably brought her around to Sadie. Should she try to tell Sadie the truth first? Sadie had refused to listen the one time she offered to share the tale. Her daughter said that Casewell Phillips was more than father enough for her and she didn't want to sully his memory with another man's name. Perla had felt shamed by her daughter and never mentioned it again, but maybe now was the right time.

Perla stood to go into the kitchen when a wave of dizziness washed over her. She braced against the bedside table, taking deep breaths and fighting nausea until the moment passed. That was the second time she'd felt like that—she should probably mention it to someone. Maybe she'd tell Henry when he came to get her this afternoon. Her son tended to worry less about her health than Margaret did. Perla smiled. Maybe that's why their marriage was so strong—Henry took things in stride while Margaret paid attention to every little detail.

But right now she had some details of her own to tend to. Like baking a caramel cake for supper with her son and daughter-in-law this evening. She'd worry about sharing her story with Ella and Sadie later. Right now she had more pressing things to do.

When Ella returned to her apartment after lunch, the phone was ringing and her message light was blinking. She spied her cellphone on the counter. She was forever forgetting to stick it in her purse when she went out.

Snatching up the receiver, Ella used her other hand to thumb at the keypad on her cell, trying to see if she'd missed any calls. She had. Six.

"Ella, oh thank goodness. Where have you been?"

"Mom? Is everything okay? Looks like I've missed a bunch of calls."

"Sweetheart, it's your grandmother." Ella felt like she'd been splashed with ice water. Mom never got worked up.

"What about Gran?"

"We're here at the hospital with her. Your dad went to fetch her over for the afternoon, and she . . . well, we're not sure what happened. It might have been a stroke."

"Is she . . . ?" Ella couldn't think of what word to use.

"We don't know much at this point. They said we can go in and see her soon, which seems encouraging. Your father is talking to your aunt Sadie right now. I think she's planning to come."

It must be serious if Aunt Sadie was driving in from Ohio. She only came once or twice a year as a rule. Ella wanted to ask if Gran would be okay, but couldn't bring herself to put something like that into words. Instead she asked, "Should I come?"

"It's up to you, but I think it would be a good idea. Oh, Henry's waving me over. I'll call you again after we see her."

Ella dropped the phone back into its cradle and considered her options. She could sit tight and wait to hear more, or she could throw a bag together and hurry home. An image of Mark saying they'd talk again floated into her mind. She remembered the primary reason she decided to break up with him and found her decision suddenly easy. She hurried to her bedroom and considered what to pack.

⋘⋙

Ella pulled into her parents' driveway and sat for a moment, staring at the white farmhouse she'd known her entire life. She had the strangest feeling something was different, but she couldn't say what. She assured herself that everything was going to be okay. Mark would forget about her all over again and Gran would be fine. She shook off the strange feeling and opened the car door, appreciating the cool breeze even on a June evening.

She pasted a smile on her face and put a bounce in her step, but no one came out to greet her. Normally Dad would rush out, with Mom not far behind. She opened the rattling screen door and called out, "Anybody home?"

Her mother poked her head around the corner from the kitchen. "Oh, Ella, thank goodness. You can come with me to the hospital. I was about to write you a note, but felt terrible about not being here when you arrived."

Fear shot through Ella. "Is Gran worse? Where's Dad?"

"He's at the hospital—he simply won't leave Perla's side. Will you drive me over there? I know you just got out of the car—"

"No, that's okay. I can drive."

They climbed back into the car, Ella's luggage still in the trunk, and headed to the hospital in Clarksville.

"So tell me more about what happened," Ella said.

Her mother took a deep breath and let her head fall back against the seat. Ella noticed, maybe for the first time, that her mother was more than a little gray.

"Henry went to get Perla and found her . . . unresponsive on the kitchen floor. He called for an ambulance, and they got there right away. Now we're just hoping for the best."

Ella gripped the steering wheel and tried not to speed. She had so many questions, but looking at her mother's exhausted expression, she resigned herself to riding in silence the rest of the way to the hospital. She thought she saw Mom's eyes drooping a bit at one point, but then she jerked and sat upright, rubbing at her face. She gave Ella a weak everything-will-be-all-right smile, but Ella wasn't buying it. At least not yet.

Brook Hill, West Virginia
April 1948

PERLA WALKED OUT ONTO THE PORCH of her aunt and uncle's house. She needed some air and a moment to herself. Coming to help out while Uncle Chuck was laid up with a broken leg had sounded like a good idea when her mother suggested it, but was turning out to be more difficult than she anticipated. Uncle Chuck was a terrible patient, forever trying to get out and work the farm, and Aunt Imogene—often described as "high-strung"—seemed determined to live up to the label.

At least spring had finally come. After a long, harsh winter, the deep purple buds of the lilac bush at the end of the porch were about to burst open. Perla closed her eyes and leaned into the branches, hoping to catch the sweet scent on the verge of release.

"Howdy."

Perla jumped a foot and whirled toward the voice. A young man who couldn't be any more than Perla's own eighteen years stood with one foot on the ground and the other braced against a step.

"I've come to help," he said in a voice deeper than Perla expected. And for a moment she thought he meant to help her in particular.

"Help?"

"Cousin Imogene sent Ma a message saying she couldn't keep Chuck in bed and needed someone to see to the chores, so he can put his mind to rest as well as his leg."

Perla smoothed the apron covering her simple cotton skirt. She hoped she looked presentable. "I'm a fair hand with chores. Not sure why we need anyone else."

The young man shrugged. "I'm not saying you do or you don't. I'm just following orders."

Imogene walked onto the porch with a hand shading her eyes as though the light were too much for her. "That you, Sonny?"

Perla saw a flicker of annoyance cross his features. He glanced at her and then back to Imogene. "It is. Ma sent me to help out."

"Humph. Is that what she said." Imogene's comment was a statement rather than a question. "Well, we can work you sure enough. Perla does a fair job, but there's always more than one person can do on a farm."

Perla bristled. If Imogene helped, there'd be more than one. She opened her mouth, then snapped it shut when she saw a look of amusement on the man's face.

"Come on in then. Perla's got supper on and she cooks like she has an army to feed." Imogene disappeared inside.

Perla let her shoulders sag. Why did that sound like criticism? Maybe she was being too sensitive. She started for the door when Sonny stepped forward to open it for her, making the springs creak.

"My name's not Sonny," he said. "That's a pet name my mother uses."

Perla looked at him sideways. "Well then, what is your name?"

He gave her a sly grin. "Maybe I'll see if you can guess it."

Perla flipped her yellow braid over her shoulder and flounced through the door. "Maybe I don't much care to know it."

Perla tried to process what was happening to her. For a moment she thought she was back on Chuck and Imogene's farm that fateful summer. But no. She'd been reaching for the glass cake stand with the cover when her right hand began lowering of its own volition. She'd watched it droop like it belonged to someone else, but then her right leg seemed to give out. It hadn't hurt; she'd just felt surprised to find herself on the floor. Henry came in after that—she wasn't sure how much later—and when she'd tried to explain, her words didn't make sense. Henry did a double take and grabbed the phone. She knew he was calling 911 and tried to tell him she'd be fine if he would only help her up, yet the words wouldn't come.

Now she was at the hospital where doctors and nurses kept peering and poking at her. They'd put her in that awful machine that made her feel trapped, but coming out hadn't been much better. She couldn't move, couldn't speak, couldn't ask questions, and didn't know where her family was. She closed her eyes—well, the left one anyway—as the right one wasn't cooperating and had been drooping closed since her hand gave out. There wasn't much she could do at the moment other than pray. She asked for what comfort God could afford and must have slept after that.

When Perla awoke, she lay in a bed with beeping machines attached to her. The smell of rubbing alcohol burned her nose. She opened her eyes, although the right one continued to droop. Henry, Margaret, and Ella stood around the bed with stricken looks on their faces. Perla tried to lift her right hand, but it wouldn't cooperate. She found the left one more amenable and reached out to grasp Ella's hand, looking into her granddaughter's blue eyes—so much like her own.

"Bllphtt, murrgh."

Oh dear. That wasn't it at all. Perla tried again, but much to her horror the sounds she made were no better than a newborn baby's blather. Ella's hand tightened, tears welling up in her eyes. Perla willed herself to speak slowly, clearly, but it was no good. She couldn't do it.

"It's okay, Gran. The doctor said you—" she hesitated— "that you had a stroke. Dad must have found you soon after. They say your chances of making a full recovery are really good."

Perla thought she might suffocate under the horror of her granddaughter's words. A stroke? Merle Donaldson had a stroke and had to be institutionalized. Oh, to be able to ask questions, to get someone to talk to her. She wanted to thrash and cry out, to demand someone tell her exactly what had happened and what would happen next. She swallowed—even that was hard to do—and did her best to look her questions at Ella. She felt like she could almost see the jumble of words fly through the air and hoped somehow her granddaughter could sort them out.

Ella smoothed Perla's hair with her free hand. "You're getting the best treatment possible. They say the most dramatic improvement will likely happen over the next few days and then you should keep improving over the next few months. If everything goes the way they hope, you might even be able to go home soon." Ella's eyes seemed to reach deep inside Perla to the place where words flowed smoothly before they hit a jagged shoreline of confusion. "Either way, I thought I'd stay with you for a while." She laughed softly. "I've been wanting to get away lately so it's a win-win situation."

Tears flowed down Perla's cheeks. She hadn't even known she was going to cry until she felt the moisture. Yes, Ella needed to know her story—she could sense how important it was. She'd tell her, too. Just as soon as she could.

❧

Ella insisted on spending the night at the hospital with her grandmother so that Dad could go home. The nurses were kind, providing extra pillows and blankets for the chair that folded out into a semblance of a bed. Gran, of course, had nothing to say about anything, though Ella could tell she was grateful to have someone there. She moved her makeshift bed as close to Gran's as possible without being a hazard to the nurses. She kissed her grandmother good-night and settled down to pretend to sleep.

Even with the overhead lights off, it wasn't dark. Light filtered in from the hall, and there were lights on the machines hooked up to Gran. There was a low, steady beep that Ella tried to tell herself was soothing. And the smell of . . . Ella couldn't quite identify the mix of medical and cleaning odors, but what it boiled down to was *not home*. She wished for a bar of Dove soap to wash her hands and face—Gran always used Dove. Maybe she'd find some tomorrow.

A nurse crept in, checked Gran's vitals, gave Ella an apologetic look, and slipped back out with a little wave. Oh well, she hadn't expected to sleep. Without meaning to, she let her thoughts wander back to Mark.

She probably should have seen Mark's true colors sooner than she did, but she'd been so smitten at the time. She finally recognized how important status was to him when he competed for a spot as clerk with the chief judge of the Virginia Court of Appeals. He'd spread rumors and half-truths about the young man he was up against. Chad was his name. Then when Chad died in a mysterious drug overdose, Mark became a shoo-in. He wanted Ella to celebrate with him on the same day as Chad's funeral, and Ella knew then she needed to end the relationship.

Mark didn't take it well. She rubbed her arm, remembering how the impression of his fingers lingered as dark bruises.

She'd taken the coward's way out. Instead of being up front about what really bothered her, she claimed Mark's lack of faith meant they weren't suited for each other.

Ella rolled over, trying to find a more comfortable position. She might have even quoted that Scripture about being "unequally yoked." Although what she'd said was mostly true, her intent had been to get out of the relationship without a lot of fuss. Jesus was just a convenient excuse.

She sighed and sat up, too uneasy to sleep. She hoped that, in spite of Gran's illness, a visit home might give her the distance she apparently still needed from Mark, and—she smiled in the dark—as an extra bonus she hoped it would provide inspiration for some new art quilts. In the past, the beauty of the farm with its abundance of earth, sky, and water would set her mind to spinning with images of rich corduroy, soft linen, and slippery satin.

She eased out of bed and pulled a plastic chair close to Gran's side. She leaned her head against the cool sheet near her grandmother's hand. She closed her eyes and felt Gran's fingers tangle in her hair.

Gran sighed. And then, against all odds, they both slept.

Perla opened her eyes—well, she opened her left eye and hoped her right would get the idea. She was surprised to have slept as long as she did. She even felt somewhat refreshed. A nurse bustled in and fiddled with things, then made notes in a computer. Ella, who had moved back to her bed at some point, sat up and watched with interest.

"How are things looking this morning?"

"Her vitals are good. The neurologist and rehab folks will

stop by this morning, and Mrs. Phillips here can start down the road to recovery in earnest."

Ella smiled and it was like the sun coming out. Perla felt her own lips curve in response, although she could tell the right side wasn't coming along for the ride. Thank goodness she couldn't see herself. She must look a fright. And her hair—oh, she didn't even want to think about her hair.

Ella stretched and stood up. "Let's get you pretty for company," she said.

Perla had always been a bit vain about her hair. A pale yellow when she was younger, Casewell said it looked like spun sunshine setting off her sky-blue eyes. And now it was a pure silvery white. She'd never resorted to permanents or hair color like so many women approaching eighty. But her fine, thinning hair was likely sticking straight up now.

Ella pulled a hairbrush from her bag and gently smoothed Perla's hair. She usually wore it in a low bun at the nape of her neck, but it was obviously down at the moment. Ella worked out the tangles and plaited it, patting the finished product where it lay across Perla's shoulder. Then she fished out a compact, powdered Perla's nose and cheeks, and dabbed some lip gloss on her mouth.

Perla would have laughed if she could. It was silly, putting makeup on an invalid, yet she was grateful and somehow the simple act of being made presentable gave her the courage she needed to hear whatever it was the doctor would tell her today. She put her good left hand on Ella's arm and squeezed.

"You're welcome," Ella said.

The doctor came in soon after. Perla was surprised to see Sadie trailing in his wake. Her daughter must have arrived late the day before. The pair were deep in conversation, and Perla wasn't sure if that was a good thing or not. Sadie could be . . .

daunting. But then the doctor smiled, and his faded blue eyes crinkled at the corners. Maybe Sadie hadn't worn him out yet.

"Good morning," he said. "Don't you look lovely?" Perla pinked, even though she felt silly about being flattered. "I'm Dr. Endicott."

Perla worked her mouth, and he held up a hand. "No, no, that's all right. Speech should return, but it will take some time. Be patient. What you're experiencing right now is aphasia. Probably expressive aphasia, which means you have trouble speaking and finding the right word, but you can still think clearly." He hitched his pant leg and sat on the edge of her bed. "We'll set up a therapy regimen for you. The most dramatic improvement is typically seen right away, so we'll start you as early as this morning." He winked at her. "You'll earn your lunch today."

Based on breakfast, Perla considered that lunch might not be worth earning, but she nodded her agreement just the same. It felt like her head was listing to the side. She supposed that might be the aftereffects of the stroke.

The doctor patted her hand and stood, facing Ella. "Depending on how she does, moving her to a rehabilitation facility is always an option."

Perla felt alarm rise and spread through her like spilled milk. He was talking about a nursing home. She darted a look at Ella, who made eye contact and then refocused on the doctor.

"I feel certain Gran will do what's needed here and then we'll take her home to continue working with her. Aunt Sadie and I"—she darted a look at her aunt—"will be happy to stay with her as long as needed. I don't think she'll need to go to a . . . facility."

Perla exhaled a stuttering breath. Ella understood. She would be fine. All she had to do was focus on getting better. And avoiding a nursing home was all the incentive she needed.

Dr. Endicott smiled and nodded. "You do look like capable

women. Perla is lucky to have such a supportive family." His brow wrinkled slightly. "Of course, you ladies need to be aware that you're also at increased risk for stroke—it's often hereditary." He looked to Sadie. "What about your father? Does he have any history of heart disease?"

Perla stilled inside and out. She focused on Sadie, who visibly stiffened at the question. She watched her daughter remove a bit of imaginary lint from her sleeve.

"I wouldn't know. I only ever knew my stepfather."

"Ah." The doctor pondered that. "Well, if you know"—he glanced at Perla—"or can find out your biological father's whereabouts, it wouldn't hurt to look him up and learn his medical history. Stroke isn't something you want to take lightly."

Sadie pursed her lips. "I'll take that under consideration."

3

ELLA WOKE IN HER CHILDHOOD BEDROOM, feeling rested for once, under the quilt Gran had given her for her sixteenth birthday. After spending most of three days in the hospital with Gran, she was glad for a night back at her parents' house. Her grandmother was making strides, and with Aunt Sadie planning to stay for at least a month, Ella was needed less. Ella stretched and rolled to her back, staring at the familiar cracks in the ceiling.

While Gran could move her right side now, it was going to take months of therapy to recover fully—or as fully as could be expected. Speech was slow in coming, yet she'd been able to utter a few simple words the day before. One of those words was "Go," after Ella said she thought she might spend the night back on the farm. Gran had given her a stern look, but Ella knew it was pure love.

As she came more fully awake, she realized there was a racket going on in the backyard. Dressing quickly, Ella followed the smell of coffee and bacon into the kitchen, where her mother was scribbling on a notepad. There was no sign of Dad.

"Oh, Ella. Good. I was leaving you a note before I go to the hospital to sit with Perla. There's bacon in the oven. Do you want me to fry some eggs to go with it?"

Ella smiled when she saw the mug with a tea bag waiting on the counter. She'd never learned to drink coffee, so Mom usually kept her favorite tea on hand. She picked up the kettle simmering on a back burner and poured water into the mug. "No thanks. I'll make do with just bacon." She opened the oven door and grabbed a strip, munching as she dunked her tea bag.

Mom made a derisive sound. "Breakfast is the most important meal of the day."

Ella held up the bacon and raised her eyebrows. Mom huffed. "What's with all the noise this morning?"

Mom rolled her eyes. "With the few words she's mastered, your grandmother made it clear she expected your father to go on as if nothing has changed, so he decided it was time to tear down that old chicken coop out back. Will and a friend of his are helping."

"What?" Ella darted to the window and craned her neck to see. "Why would they do that?"

Mom laughed. "It's practically falling down. Your father kept patching and fixing, but he finally realized it was time for something new. They moved the chickens to the barn and should have a new coop up in short order."

"But the chicken coop's always been there," Ella protested. "How many times have I gone out there to gather the eggs?"

"I don't know how many times it was, but I know you usually complained about it." Mom gave her a questioning look. "Why are you getting worked up about the chicken house?"

Ella thumped her mug down on the counter. "I'm not getting worked up. I'm just not so sure it needed to be torn down. 'Waste not, want not'—isn't that what you always say?"

Mom snorted. "I say a great deal—interesting that you

remember it now." She gathered her bag and keys and spoke over her shoulder on the way out. "I'll be back before supper."

Ella waited until her mother drove away, then scooted outside to see what was happening with the now nearly dismantled chicken house. She didn't see her brother or her father, only a man with dark hair showing beneath a baseball cap. He was wearing a green T-shirt that pulled taut across broad shoulders as he stacked bits of lumber and chicken wire. He stood and smiled, and Ella did a stutter step. Or was that her heart?

"Hey there," he said. "You must be Ella."

Ella reminded herself she was mad about the chicken house. "I am. Who are you, and what are you doing?"

The smile eased into a more serious expression. He slipped his hand out of a worn leather glove and stuck it out. "Seth Markley. I'm cleaning up after this mess."

Ella blinked and took his hand. He'd answered her question, but she realized he hadn't come close to giving her the information she wanted.

"But why did you tear it down?"

Seth furrowed his brow. "Your father and brother asked me to help them with it."

Unexpected tears stung Ella's eyes as she looked at the remains of the chicken coop that had been part of their family farm since before she was born. She stomped her foot. "My great-grandmother gathered eggs from that chicken house."

"Well, that explains a lot," Seth said with a slow grin. "There was a good fifty years' worth of chicken mess crusted on those roosts. I think that's all that was keeping it standing."

Ella felt like he'd insulted someone or something precious to her. She stiffened her spine and looked him up and down. He might fill out a T-shirt nicely, and those hazel eyes made her wish she'd met him somewhere else, but enough was enough.

"It was a perfectly good chicken house, and you—"

"Hey punkin, you come out to give us a hand?"

Ella turned to see her father and brother approaching with a handcart and a tarp. "Dad, how could you tear down the chicken house?"

He dropped the tarp onto the cart and wrapped an arm around her shoulders. "Ah, my favorite daughter, the sentimental one. I forget how you hate change."

Ella shook her head. "I don't hate change. I just don't see why you had to tear down the chicken house."

He planted a kiss on top of her head. "Because it was about to fall down, and while I lean toward sentimental myself, your mother, ever the voice of reason, helped me see it was time. Shoot, there were holes in there big enough for two foxes and a weasel to waltz in together and help themselves. And I didn't trust the floor with the weight of more than two chickens at a time."

He shifted to look Ella in the eye. "The new coop will be even better. We'll build it right here where the old one stood. I'm even going to salvage some of the nesting boxes that are still in good shape."

Ella felt her annoyance slip a notch. Her father always knew what to say. She looked at the rotten boards encrusted with, well, *mess* was a good word for it. She lost more of her steam.

"I'm sorry, Daddy. I didn't mean to get all worked up about a chicken coop."

Dad winked at her. "That's all right. It's been a stressful few days. Now, do you maybe owe an apology to Seth? When I walked up, looked to me like you had him pinned down pretty good."

Ella flushed and glanced at Seth, who was busy watching an old crow perched on a fence post. Her brother, Will, watched the exchange with something like amusement. She wanted to stick her tongue out at him, but instead said, "Sorry about that, Seth. Guess I was kind of taken by surprise."

Dad squeezed her arm. "Good enough. C'mon, we've got work to do and you're more than welcome to pitch in."

Ella stuffed her hands in the pockets of her cutoffs and looked down at her bare feet. "I'm not exactly dressed for it. Guess I'll go work on a quilt piece."

"That's the ticket," Dad said with a wink.

Ella sighed and wandered back to the house. She glanced over her shoulder as she opened the screen door. Seth was watching her. She ducked her head and disappeared into the cool of the house.

Perla dabbed a little lipstick on her mouth and tried to smile. The right side still sagged, but if she tilted her head . . . Oh, but she was a vain thing. She patted her hair, admiring the way Ella had twisted it into a chignon. It looked nice. She still wasn't sure she was ready to go back to church, but she supposed the die was cast now. Ella and Sadie had taken turns staying with her around the clock since she came home from the hospital—helping with rehabilitation exercises, making sure she ate the awful prescribed diet, and dispensing medication. They both deserved an outing, and Perla was feeling a bit of cabin fever herself.

Ella appeared at the bathroom door, Sadie not far behind, and offered her grandmother her arm. Perla had a walker, something she hated. Vanity again. She wanted to tell Ella to leave the contraption behind. Taking a deep breath, she managed two words. "Go. Own."

Sadie made a face. "Mother, you're going to have to do better than that. The speech pathologist said we shouldn't let you take shortcuts. Try again."

Perla felt annoyance rise. Sadie always had a bossy streak, and she wasn't in the mood for it on this lovely summer Sunday when she was finally leaving the house.

Ella patted Perla's hand where it gripped her arm—probably a little too tight. "I put your walker in the backseat of the car, but maybe if you hold on to me or Dad, you won't need it."

Perla gave her granddaughter a grateful smile. It was almost as though she could read her thoughts. She remembered how Ella always seemed to understand everything when she was a child. She'd even known what that old bird dog of Henry's wanted when he wagged his tail or whined. Sadie rolled her eyes, but didn't press the matter. Perla felt a little thrill of triumph that she immediately regretted. This shouldn't be a battle of wills. But then she and Sadie hadn't really seen eye to eye ever since . . . well, probably since Casewell died. Somehow Perla felt as though the secret of Sadie's parentage stood between them. And now there was the question of Sadie's health; knowing her father's medical history could help her make good decisions. Surely it was time to tell her daughter the truth.

Perla squared her shoulders as best she could. Life was a journey, and she was determined not to let this stroke business sidetrack her. She needed to get her voice back so she could tell Ella and Sadie what they needed to know.

4

ELLA WAS SURPRISED by how excited she was to get back to Laurel Mountain Church with Gran on her arm. She'd been here as recently as Easter, but it felt different now. She'd been feeling more and more like her old self since coming home and this was part of what she needed to regain her footing. The one-room church with its steeple pointed heavenward was something that would never change. Here was her firm foundation.

Helping Gran up the steps one at a time, she felt proud that she was the seventh generation in the Phillips family to sit in these pews—a descendant of the founders. Looking around, she was surprised at how small the congregation was this morning, maybe twenty in all. Ella remembered the pews being full when she was a child. Probably sixty or seventy people would crowd in to hear Reverend Archibald Ashworth preach. But he'd retired the summer before, and Mom said several pulpit supply pastors had filled in until they sent someone new to take over. Dad talked like the church might not last much longer if something didn't change. But Ella wasn't worried—Laurel Mountain Church was a fixture in Wise. This wasn't a falling-down chicken coop; this was the lifeblood of the community.

"His name is Richard Goodwin," Mom whispered in Ella's

ear. "He's been here three months now. I think the turnout is pretty good because folks are still curious about him." She flicked her eyebrows. "We have yet to see if he's going to be able to gain ground, though. He's supposed to be rebuilding the church."

Pastor Goodwin stepped up to the pulpit as the congregation settled in. Ella marveled that twenty people was considered a good turnout. The pastor was youngish and looked like he should be playing tennis or sailing a boat. Ella thought he looked too . . . what? Affluent? He just didn't quite fit here.

Ella didn't pay much attention to the service, but rather basked in the familiarity of the place and the comfort of having her grandmother here and on the mend. For now, the only thing anyone expected of her was to sit and at least pretend to listen. It was a relief.

Reverend Goodwin finally wrapped up his sermon and invited the congregation to stand for the closing hymn. Sometimes Ella struggled to focus on Scripture or the message, but the traditional hymns held her attention. Mavis Sanders banged away at an old upright piano while the people sang from worn hymnals.

The church featured two front doors, which confounded more than one bride marrying into the local community, and since Pastor Goodwin could only stand at one of the doors to shake hands, Ella made sure Sadie had Gran in hand before slipping out the second door. She headed for the cemetery and went straight to her grandfather's headstone with its unique inscription. Casewell died long before Ella was born, and she'd heard all her life what a good man she missed out on knowing.

Lost in bittersweet ruminations, Ella jumped when someone spoke.

"Your mother said you came out here, and I wanted to make it a point to meet you," said Reverend Goodwin. "I hope I'm not disturbing you."

"Oh no—just visiting family." Ella waved a hand at the stones around her.

"It's nice to remember where you come from." He smiled. "I'm Reverend Richard Goodwin, but you can call me Richard." He grimaced. "Actually, please call me Richard. I can't seem to get any of my congregants to call me anything but Pastor."

"Calling you by your first name probably seems too familiar to them. Don't worry. I hear it took Archie a good five years before they really embraced him when he first came forty years ago. I think that's why he stayed—too hard to break in a new congregation."

They stood with Casewell's gravestone between them. Ella became acutely aware of the way the sun gave Richard's light brown hair blond highlights. His gray eyes didn't quite go with his hair color, creating a vague feeling of dissonance. Seeing him in the pulpit, she would have thought he'd tower over her, but now, standing so close, she could see he was only a few inches taller.

They both spoke at once. Richard laughed. "Go ahead."

"I was going to ask where you're from, since your ancestors aren't laid out at our feet." Ella winced. Did that sound irreverent? But if Richard thought so, he gave no indication.

"I'm from Connecticut. My family is mostly gone now, and I was never all that attached to the place where I grew up, so I decided to make my way south. This area suits me." He scanned the cemetery, the church, and the valley beyond. His gray eyes appeared to turn the color of early morning fog. "It'll suit me even better once people warm up to me." Then he added, "Not that they haven't been nice. I just get the feeling I'm on some sort of probation."

"Of course you do." Ella laughed. "You are."

They stood smiling, silence mounting. It should have felt awkward, but Ella felt peaceful instead.

Finally, Richard said, "Your grandmother looks like she's doing better. I haven't been to see her since she doesn't really know me, but I'd like to visit if you think she'd welcome it."

"I think she'd like that. She's recovered a lot of her movement, but language is slow coming so she's not much for conversation. I'm sure she'd enjoy having a cup of coffee and listening to us chat, though."

Richard looked like a little boy who'd been offered a puppy. "I'd enjoy that, too. I'll plan to come by one day this week, if that's all right."

"We'll look forward to seeing you."

Did he sound eager or was Ella imagining things? Attraction sparked, but she quelled it. He was a pastor. And she'd managed to stay clear of any romantic entanglements since breaking up with Mark. Not that she hadn't thought about dating again; she just wanted to be extra careful after her last poor choice.

Ella turned back toward the parking area. When she stumbled over a footstone, Richard reached out to steady her. She was surprised at his large callused hands. Farmer's hands, she thought, and felt that spark again.

Richard walked her to Aunt Sadie's car and opened the rear door for her so that she could slide in behind Gran. "I enjoyed meeting you, Ella. I hope I'll see you back in church next week. If nothing else, it'll mean I've increased the congregation by one." He closed the door, stepped back, and watched the car pull out of the lot and drive away.

"I think you made an impression on the new pastor," Sadie said. "Mother, I'd ask what you think, but you'll speak in code."

Ella cringed, not sure why there was such tension between mother and daughter. She reached over the seat and squeezed Gran's shoulder.

"I think. Too soon. To tell," Gran said, reaching up to grasp Ella's fingers.

Ella laughed. Gran always did have a way of summing things up.

❦

"Those last pieces you did sold out fast. When will you have more for me?" Ella had finally returned the third call from Sylvia, the owner of the shop where she sold most of her art pieces. "It's best to strike while the iron is hot, and you're hot right now."

Ella wrinkled her nose. She usually loved talking about—and selling—her art quilts, but she hadn't been able to get anything to come out the way she wanted since that stupid lunch with Mark. "I've got a few things in the works, but nothing I'm ready to share . . ." Ella trailed off, not quite prepared to lie outright.

Sylvia made a *tsk*ing sound. Ella could picture the gallery owner tucking her silver hair behind her ear and tapping a finger against her lower lip.

"What about that dandelion piece I saw last time I was in your apartment?"

Ella pictured the half-finished wall hanging of an overlarge dandelion puff against an azure background. She'd wanted the flower to have a sense of lightness, an ethereal quality, but the thread wouldn't cooperate. She grimaced. "It just isn't quite right—there's something missing."

"What? The colors are great, and the composition is solid. Finish it off and I can sell it in five minutes."

Ella flopped down across her bed and stared at the ceiling. "Maybe next week." She pictured two squares at the bottom of her workbag with pastoral images—rolling meadows, cows, and trees. One featured bright sunflowers that were too happy for Ella's taste. "I guess I have a couple that aren't exactly inspired I could send you."

Sylvia snorted. "Inspiration is for people who don't have

34

bills to pay. Send me what you have." She hesitated a moment, as though deciding whether or not she had anything else to say. "Mark stopped by yesterday."

Ella froze. "He did? Was he looking for the perfect piece of country kitsch to add to his ultramodern kitchen?" She tried to make a joke, but unease settled over her.

"He wanted to see your work specifically. I told him I was out, and he asked if I expected you to come in anytime soon. Seemed like maybe he'd gone by your apartment a couple of times and when he didn't find you there thought to see what I knew."

"What did you tell him?" Ella could hear the strain in her voice and seriously doubted Sylvia would miss it.

"Just that you were out of town and I didn't know for certain when you'd be back. He gave me his number and asked me to call him when I got some more of your work in." She paused. "Are you two dating again?"

Sylvia asked the question lightly, yet Ella knew her friend cared deeply about her and really wanted to know. She petted the soft fabric of the quilt on her bed—the material had worn until it was like silk to her fingers. "No. He called me a while back out of the blue to have lunch." She sighed. "I probably shouldn't have agreed to see him. I may have given him the wrong idea, although I thought I was clear. I can't imagine why he's suddenly interested again."

Ella could hear Sylvia moving the phone around—it clicked against her earrings. "You know I was never a big fan of Mark's and I still don't trust him. You be careful. That man always did make me uneasy." Ella heard Sylvia's heels tapping across tile now. "Maybe you should stay put in West Virginia for a while. I know your family needs you, and you can work on your art anywhere. I can pack some things up and ship them to you."

Ella leaned off the end of the bed and hooked a hand through the straps of her sewing bag, dragging it up and onto her lap. "I do have some stuff here, but you wouldn't know what else to pack—"

"Wouldn't I? I'll gather it up this afternoon. You'll have everything you need plus a few things you didn't know you wanted before the week is out." Sylvia sounded so pleased with herself, Ella didn't have the heart to say no.

"Okay, okay. Maybe digging into some work will be good for me."

"That's my girl. Call me if you need anything."

Ella ended the conversation and stared out the open window, slumping on her bed like a cranky teenager. Her parents didn't have air-conditioning, and she craved the breeze slipping through the screen. The sky was that sort of gray that brought gloom without actually producing rain. Then a beam of sunlight pierced the leaden sky like a needle shooting through fabric and Ella jerked upright. She knew then what was missing from the dandelion piece. She dug it out, found a spool of silvery thread, and set to work.

5

PERLA SAW THE WAY Pastor Richard looked at Ella and hoped something might spark between them. As far as she knew, Ella hadn't really dated since breaking up with that Mark fellow, who always struck her as a little too smooth. She smiled. It might be nice to have a preacher in the family.

She thought back to the admiring look in Richard's eyes. She'd seen that look before. As a matter of fact, more than one man had looked at her that way over the years. Thank goodness Ella wasn't quite as naïve as Perla had been that summer of 1948. She hadn't dwelt on those days for a long time, but if she was going to tell Sadie and Ella about them, she should try to make sure she had it straight—think how she wanted to put it once the words in her head started flowing past her lips again.

She hadn't known his given name for a long time. It became a game between them. She'd call him Sonny and he'd accuse her of not having enough imagination to guess his real name. Chuck and Imogene called him Sonny if they called him anything at all. But mostly he stayed outside, working as though his life depended on it.

Perla came to admire him—how hard he worked, the pride he took in doing things right. The farm was neat as a pin. Fence mended, barn tidy, garden planted, animals tended to. Perla often worked alongside Sonny, hoeing the garden or minding the animals, and had come to look forward to their talks. She also noticed a restlessness about him that grew with each day that passed.

They were working in the garden one late April afternoon, Perla planting peas and lettuce while Sonny cleared rocks from the furrows.

"Do you have any brothers or sisters?" she asked.

"Three older sisters and a brother." He grunted as he pried loose a large rock half buried in the ground. "Elam, my brother, died over in France. I would have gone after him, but I was too young then."

"I'm sorry about your brother. I'm an only child so I can't even imagine how hard that must be."

"Ma took it hard." He was silent for a while, and Perla thought to change the subject, but then he spoke again. "Elam left a girl behind, too. She's the same age as me. Broke her up pretty bad."

"How awful." Perla sifted soil over tiny black seeds and patted it down. "I've never had a serious beau." She flushed. What made her say that?

"No?" He grinned at her, stretching out his back. "Can't see why not. Seems like your pa would have to chase 'em off with a stick."

Perla felt her braid slither over her shoulder as she knelt. She looked up at him through pale eyelashes. She might try flirting a little, but she'd never really known how. "Guess not."

"Probably you're so pretty they're scared of you," he said. And the frank admiration in his eyes warmed her more than the April sun ever could.

She cleared her throat. "What about your sisters? Any of them married?"

"Every single one. Got you'uns too." He bent to his work

again, sending up the scent of the soil as he hefted stones. "I'm an uncle five times over. Oldest one isn't but two years younger than me."

"Do you want children?" Again, Perla was amazed at herself. Such questions to ask a young man.

"I want at least six or seven—as many as I can get. How about you?"

He wasn't looking directly at her now, but she felt overwarm just the same. "I'd like to have a few—maybe not that many— but more than one. It's hard being just one."

Sonny laughed, yet it sounded harsh. "Just be glad you don't have to be responsible for anyone but your own self."

※

Ella woke in her grandmother's spare bedroom on another sunny Sunday morning. She'd opted to stay with Gran after Aunt Sadie returned to Ohio. There were therapy appointments, follow-up doctor visits, and ongoing treatments, all of which Ella was happy to coordinate. Plus there was plenty of time to work on her art—or try to—while Gran napped, read, or watched television. And although Gran still couldn't speak very well, Ella had a knack for understanding her.

"Do you still want to go to church this morning?" Ella asked after they'd finished breakfast.

Gran sat at the kitchen table finishing a second cup of coffee. She nodded her head.

"Just because I understand you doesn't mean you can give up talking," Ella teased as she wrung out the dishrag and hung it over the kitchen faucet.

Gran frowned, looking intently at the sink.

"What is it?" Ella asked, raising her eyebrows and trying to look innocent.

Gran frowned harder and pointed at the dishrag.

"Yes?" Ella slid into a seat next to her grandmother.

With a huff, Gran gripped her mug and began to speak. "Dish. Rag goes. Uh-uh-under sink."

"Oh, right." Ella got up to hang the cloth on a hook inside the cabinet door. "There we go."

Gran rolled her eyes, but she was smiling. "Looking for—ward to church."

"Me too. I'm going to go get ready now. Holler if you need anything."

Gran gulped some coffee. "Ha-ha-holler indeed."

Ella patted Gran on the shoulder and disappeared into the bathroom, thinking about how appealing the new pastor was and how it might be time to consider her options again. Of course, there was also that handsome Seth Markley to consider. She wondered if he ever came to church as she pondered what to wear.

Finally walking out into the family room in an outfit she hoped was attractive without being obvious, Ella found her grandmother sitting on the sofa. Gran patted the spot next to her.

Ella sat, and her grandmother handed her a small velvet box. Clicking it open, Ella found a narrow gold band with a small diamond nestled inside.

"Mine," Gran said. "Casewell." She cleared her throat. "Gave that-t-t me. Best day. Of my life." She smiled at Ella, a tear glittering in the corner of her eye. "Yours now."

Ella felt tears of her own rise. She had often admired the ring—especially as a child when all she saw was the way it sparkled. She noticed when her grandmother quit wearing it, when arthritis made it difficult to slip the ring over swollen knuckles. When she was little, Ella had imagined that it was a jewel beyond price. Now, as she slipped the band over her right ring finger, she realized how priceless it was. She hugged her grandmother. "I wouldn't trade it for a million dollars."

"I know," Gran said, and it was the clearest she'd spoken since coming home.

The two pulled apart, and Gran patted Ella's hand, now adorned with a family heirloom. Ella tried not to notice that her grandmother looked a little sad.

⌘

At Laurel Mountain Church, Ella slid into the pew that had been holding members of the Phillips family since its founding more than 150 years earlier. Mom, Dad, Gran, Will, and Will's girlfriend, Laura, made it a tight fit, especially since so many other pews were empty. Her grandmother's ring gleaming on her finger, Ella smoothed a hand across the well-worn wood of the pew in front of her. Generations of Phillipses surely had touched this exact spot.

A little girl rang the bell to call church to order. It once called folks from the hills and hollers to the churchyard for Sunday services, but now Ella supposed they rang it mostly in memory and in hopes of reminding those who didn't or couldn't come to church that God still dwelt among them.

After announcements and the opening prayer, Pastor Richard stood and began the service. He looked handsome in a black robe with a burgundy tie peeking out at the top. Ella thought the robe was a bit much for their little country church, but she couldn't deny it lent a certain grandeur to the proceedings.

Instead of focusing on the sermon, she mostly daydreamed about how one of these days she'd have a husband who'd sit beside her in church—or maybe even stand behind the pulpit. They would build a house and studio for her out on the ridge beyond Gran's cottage. They'd live there, part of one big happy family, carrying on the Phillips family tradition for another generation.

Now, if only she could find the right man to fill that role. . . .

After the service, Ella intended to get Gran in the car and whisk her back home, but as usual everyone wanted to stop and talk. Ella kept steering Gran toward the car, trying not to be outright rude, until Mavis Sanders cornered them. She leaned in close and grabbed each of them by an elbow.

"Perla, have you heard about the church being sold?"

Ella rolled her eyes. "Mavis, that's not going to happen. Someone's been telling you stories."

Mavis either didn't hear or didn't care. "I heard some big-city developer is planning to come in and run us off the land. He wants to build cabins or some such and needs the church property. He's been buying up land all around. Milton Samuels sold out, packed up, and moved to Florida just last week."

Ella didn't want to listen to Mavis tell tales, but at the same time felt annoyed that someone was spreading such silly rumors. "Gran, haven't you been saying Milton's been threatening to move to Florida for the past ten years? Maybe he finally decided it was time."

Mavis thumped her cane on the ground. "Humph. Or maybe some outside meddler talked him into it."

Ella felt fear tighten her belly, even though she told herself it was silly. "Maybe it's just a rumor. Do you know someone wants to buy the church property for sure?"

"Poke your head in the sand if you want, Ella Phillips, but my family helped start this church as much as yours did, and I'm not going to let some outsider come in and ruin everything."

Ella desperately wanted to spin on her heel and walk away, but she couldn't leave Gran. After a few minutes she managed to appease Mavis enough to get free of the conversation and tuck Gran into the passenger seat of the car.

"What do you make of all that?" she asked, trying to sound light.

Gran took a deep breath and closed her eyes. "Mavis gets the news first." She clenched her hands in her lap and scrunched her face. "Doesn't mean it's right." She exhaled, then tilted her head to the side. "Could be a grain of tru-truth, though."

Ella felt something like hysteria bubble up under her rib cage. "I know church attendance has been down, but surely it wouldn't make sense to sell. Richard just got here—they have to give him a chance."

Gran turned those cornflower eyes of hers on Ella. "God's in control," she said. Then she leaned her head back against the seat as though the morning had exhausted her, which it most likely had.

Ella felt bad that coming to church and hearing from Mavis had taken a toll on Gran. Even so, she was grateful for the scrap of information. If the church really was in danger, she needed to know. This was her family's heritage, and she would fight for it.

Perla kept her eyes closed as Ella drove them home. She felt exhausted. Going to church and focusing on uttering even a few coherent sentences had taken all the energy she had. She could feel the weakness in her right side—especially her arm—and knew if she tried to smile, that side of her mouth wouldn't lift high enough. Not that she had anything to smile about at the moment.

While Mavis Sanders couldn't resist spreading rumors, all too often her news turned out to be mostly right. Perla felt confident there was at least some truth to this one, too. Attending church wasn't important to people anymore. And although she liked him, she hadn't seen anything from Richard yet that made her think he would turn things around. Perla kneaded her right hand, trying to ease the weak feeling. Maybe what the church needed was a threat to its very existence. Maybe losing the church would finally wake some folks up to how important faith was to their little community. Maybe it would even get the attention of her own family.

Perla smiled and didn't worry about the right side of her mouth. Yes indeedy, sometimes a good dose of trouble was exactly what folks needed.

6

W E'RE HAVING A CHURCH PICNIC the Saturday before Labor Day. Will you bring Perla?"

Mom kneaded bread while Ella pretended to pay attention. Like she was going to learn to make bread. What Ella was really itching to do was be alone so she could work on a quilt hanging she'd started, one that depicted the church. She couldn't get the angle of the building right. She wanted viewers to feel as though they were looking up at the church even if the piece hung at eye level. Her perspective was off, and she longed to work on it.

"Did you hear me, Ella?"

"Yes, of course I'll bring Gran. Will it be the usual covered dish kind of thing?"

"It will, with a wiener roast, plenty of watermelon, and toasted marshmallows. I plan to take deviled eggs. Make sure your grandmother knows she's not expected to bring anything."

"Maybe I should bring something?" Ella had never been much of a cook, but she had the feeling her grandmother would consider it an unspeakable faux pas to arrive at the picnic empty-handed.

"It's not necessary. We always have too much left over. Instead

of bringing something, you might think about bringing someone."

Ella wrinkled her brow. "I am. Grandma."

Mom blew a wisp of hair off her forehead. "I was thinking
of someone like that handsome Mark you dated for so long. I
actually had a card from him the other day." She darted a look
at Ella, then went back to her bread in a way that was altogether
too casual. "He wrote to say how much he enjoyed that fried
chicken I made the time your father and I came down to your
apartment and he joined us for dinner." Another glance. "He
also mentioned how much he regretted letting you go."

Ella wondered if it were possible to feel your blood pressure
rise. "He *wrote* to you?"

"Yes, such a thoughtful young man. I always liked him."

"That's because you didn't really know him. I didn't know
him for that matter, and as soon as I got to know him that was
the end of that."

Ella was tempted to tell her mother how Mark had lied his
way into his law firm at the expense of Chad . . . whatever his
name was. She could also tell her about those few times when
Mark's anger had surfaced in some really ugly ways.

No. There was no reason to rehash all that. She was done
with Mark and that was all that mattered.

But maybe Mom wasn't quite done with him. "Sweetheart,
I can appreciate that Mark might not be perfect, but there's
nothing wrong with marrying someone who can take care of
you. I suspect he has a bright future ahead of him, and you
could be quite comfortable without having to worry about
your trust fund running out. Your grandparents weren't that
well-off."

Ella stiffened. Mom almost never talked about the trust fund
Grandma and Grandpa Hoffman had set up for Will and Ella. In
fact, she almost never talked about her parents, both of whom

died while Ella was still very young. This was no casual conversation. Mom was serious.

"Your art is beautiful, but I don't suppose you can make a living at it—not without that money set aside."

"I'm doing okay."

"Of course you are. But marrying well wouldn't hurt, either."

Ella felt her pulse pounding in her throat. "Are you suggesting I should marry Mark because he'll make good money and buy me a nice house? Is that why you married Dad?"

Mom plopped her ball of dough in a greased bowl, covered it, and set it on the back of the stove to rise. "Of course not. I loved your father and I want you to marry for love, too. I'm just saying there's nothing wrong with looking at the practical side, as well." She moved to the sink to wash her hands. "Your father and I had some lean years, and that sort of thing will put a strain on even the best marriage. I want you to have every advantage."

Ella released the breath she didn't know she was holding. "Okay, Mom. I appreciate your concern, but trust me when I say Mark isn't the man for me."

Her mother shrugged and dried her hands. "Fine, fine. I still say he's a nice young man, though."

Ella opened her mouth to reply, then closed it, opting to leave it at that. Some arguments weren't worth winning.

A few days later, Ella walked over to her parents' house to get a dozen eggs and a casserole her mother made for Gran, who had been home a full month now. As they stood in the kitchen chatting, Will showed up with Seth in tow. Ella felt a tingle of excitement when she saw her brother's friend come in the door, but did her best to suppress it. She hadn't made a very good first impression on him, and if she was going to consider romantic possibilities with Richard, perhaps she should limit herself to one guy at a time. She watched Seth take off his hat and run his hand through wavy hair. Then again maybe she shouldn't be too quick to lean in any one direction.

"Seth came to help me move that hog Dad and I are raising," Will said. "Anyone else want to help?"

Ella decided she might like to see this hog and laugh at her brother moving it, if not actually assist in the process. "I'll come with you," she said, trying not to glance at Seth as she spoke.

Her mother looked at her like she'd announced she was moving to China. She hoped neither Will nor Seth had seen the look.

The hog turned out to be docile and cooperative. In short order they'd walked her up a ramp into the back of Will's truck, where she settled into some loose hay and crunched apples, seemingly pleased with her lot in life.

"Ella, you want to see her on home with me? You're welcome to ride along."

Ella glanced at Seth, who looked back steady and level. "Be glad to have you."

Was that encouragement? Ella had no idea, but she wasn't in a hurry to get back to Gran's cottage, and she'd always liked helping Dad around the farm when she was little. This was kind of like that. "Sure," she said with a shrug.

Ella sat in the middle of the bench seat, Will driving, and Seth riding with one elbow crooked out the window.

"Why does the girl always have to sit in the middle?" she asked.

"Hey, sitting in the middle is the place to be," Seth said. "The driver has to drive, and if we come up on any gates I'm the one who has to get out to open and close them." He gave her a serious look. "I see a gate up there a ways. Want to trade?"

Ella laughed. "I suppose I'll allow you to continue being chivalrous. Goodness knows Will won't be."

Will snorted. "Got that right."

"Except where Laura's concerned." Ella dug an elbow into his ribs and watched him color.

He smiled and drove up to the gate that Seth did, indeed, open and close before hopping back into the truck. When he slid onto the seat he brought the smell of late summer with him—warm and woodsy with a hint of pine. Ella could picture him chopping wood, plaid shirtsleeves rolled up to his elbows. She gave herself a mental shake. Surely she wasn't developing a crush on this guy? Gran would call it unseemly to be attracted to two men at the same time.

At Will's place, he backed the truck up to the hog pen, and they escorted their guest down the ramp and into her new home. They leaned on the fence and gazed into the pen.

"Got her last spring and I'd say she's already more than two hundred pounds. Should top out at three hundred or more by November when we butcher," Will said.

An involuntary shudder passed through Ella. She'd grown up on the farm and butchering animals wasn't anything new, but something about it bothered her today.

She straightened and headed toward the house. "Let's go sit on the porch. It's not like that pig's going to do tricks or anything." She hurried up the rise.

The two men ambled up the hill and joined Ella, where she sat on a porch swing. Will grabbed a chair, leaving Seth with the choice of standing or sitting next to Ella. He opted to stand, leaning against the porch railing. She hoped she hadn't discouraged him in some way. Not that she wanted him to sit next to her, but still . . .

Ella pushed off with her toe, setting the swing in motion. "Weather's not too bad for August," she said. There, that was a safe topic.

"*Farmers' Almanac* says we'll have a hot spell in September,"

Will said. "Doesn't much matter to me so long as it turns off cold in time for a hog-killing come November." He grinned at his sister. "Remember the first time Dad let us come to one? Man, bleeding out a hog is something to see."

Ella felt her own blood drain from her face. Seth, who was watching her intently, straightened and said, "Hey Will, have you met Keith Randolph yet?"

"Who?"

"Keith Randolph—he owns the company that's looking to put a hunting preserve in on Laurel Mountain. He stopped by to get some advice on forest management. Seems like a good guy."

Ella stopped the swing and sat up straighter. "A hunting preserve? Is this Randolph fellow the developer Mavis Sanders was talking about?" She gripped the slats on either side of her. "The one who's trying to buy up the whole mountain and maybe the church, too?"

Seth held up his hands. "Whoa now, I don't know about all that. I guess he is a developer—has hunting properties in Georgia, North Carolina, and Virginia. But I don't suppose he'd want to disturb your church."

Ella leaned back in the swing again. "He'd better not. No way would we give up seven generations of heritage like that." She snapped her fingers and scowled at him.

"Get a grip, little sister. The man was just making conversation." Will tilted his chair back on two legs. "A hunting preserve could be a good thing. Too many folks around here have given up farming and just let their land lie fallow. I for one would like to see good use made of it." He turned toward Seth. "You think this Keith Randolph will take good care of the place? Manage the forest and the wildlife?"

Seth shrugged. "I only met him the one time, but I liked him well enough and I appreciate that he asked questions instead of jumping on in there like he knows everything." He rubbed the back of his neck. "And considering all those other properties, I'm betting he does know a good bit. Yeah, I think he'll probably do right by the land."

Ella snorted and then flushed when Seth looked at her, eyebrows raised. "Well I don't trust him," she said.

Will laughed. "You haven't even met him. Maybe he'll be the best thing to happen to Wise since Village Hardware started selling gas for two cents less than the station downtown. We could use a little something to stir this community up."

Ella kicked the swing off again, pushing harder than necessary. "Stirring up is exactly what we don't need. What we need is to appreciate what we have just the way it is."

She crossed her arms over her chest and tried not to stick her lower lip out. Seth appraised her with cool eyes, and Ella caught herself wondering what he thought of her. Not that it mattered. She told herself all that mattered was helping Gran get better and preserving the church.

Well. She might also consider getting a social life. She flushed under Seth's gaze. If nothing else, having a boyfriend would help her keep Mark at arm's length where he belonged.

7

ON THE SATURDAY BEFORE LABOR DAY, the whole community turned out for the picnic and hot-dog roast. Ella considered that if even half of them would come to church, they'd be full up. But it was probably uncharitable of her to think such a thing.

It was early when Ella parked near the picnic area along Laurel Creek. Normally she'd park in the pasture, but Gran was still unsteady so she stuck close to the tables. They left the food they'd brought in a cooler in the backseat for the time being. There was Gran's coleslaw, which Ella helped prepare, and Ella's three-layer coconut cake. She had to confess she was pretty proud of her effort and hoped it had survived the trip. She decided to wait and look when it was closer to time to eat. She couldn't do anything about it now anyway.

Ladies fussed with the food tables while several men selected slender branches and sharpened the ends for the hot-dog roast. There was also a contingent arguing over the best way to build and feed the bonfire so it would be perfect for cooking. Children ran around like wild Indians, as her grandmother would say, but then she had no notion of political correctness. Ella smiled to herself. Eventually, one of those children would get into trouble for setting a marshmallow on fire and threatening a sibling with it. She knew from personal experience.

Ella saw Richard walking toward them. He took Gran's arm and helped her to a chair in the center of things.

"Perfect afternoon for a picnic," he said.

"It is, and looks like a good turnout." Ella gave him her best smile, glad she'd worn a cotton dress that she hoped accentuated her waist and hid her hips. She had a sweater in the car, knowing it would likely be cool once dusk fell. Richard looked like he appreciated her efforts.

She gave him a once-over as well, thinking he looked kind of like a J. Crew ad with the sleeves of his button-down shirt rolled back, loafers with no socks, and hair lightly tousled. He settled Gran and stretched his arms wide, inhaling deeply.

"Man, the air around here is like breathing in vitamins." He tapped his chest with a fist. "Makes me feel vigorous."

Ella smiled and took a deep breath of her own.

Richard glanced at the activity around them. "I don't think we'll be ready to eat for a while yet. Perla, if you don't mind I thought I'd take Ella for a walk—work up an appetite."

Gran inhaled and put a hand to her chest. "That sounds good." She exhaled. "I'll be right here." She smiled like she'd won a blue ribbon at the state fair and Ella felt a stab of pride. Gran had come a long way in her speech therapy.

Richard put his hands on his hips and looked around. "Are there any trails?"

Ella wondered if he was picturing a paved park path. All she knew of was an old logging road on the far side of the swimming hole. They could reach it by picking their way across the creek on rocks or by walking downstream a little ways to the nearest bridge. She glanced at Richard's loafers, considered her own white canvas shoes, and suggested the bridge.

"Excellent. Let's explore."

Ella hid her smile. Walking the logging road up toward the Simmons place was hardly exploring, but then Richard had never been here before. Maybe it would be something of an adventure for him. Dad said the Simmons were moonshiners back in the day, although now Lisa Simmons Hartwell lived on the property with her husband, Stuart, and their three kids. They were into organic gardening and solar energy—quite a change from moonshine.

"We can follow an old logging road back into the hills a ways." Ella pointed to the trees rising beyond the creek. "Might even find evidence of an abandoned moonshine still."

Richard's eyes lit. "Do you think so? Does anyone still make moonshine?"

Ella laughed. "Sure, but it's mostly legal now. There's a distillery down in Summersville that's been making it for a while. I guess maybe a few folks still make their own, but it's hardly big business these days."

Richard shrugged. "Oh, well. Guess I'll have to settle for the beauty of the day and some good company. That should be adventure enough."

He took her arm and headed for the bridge. At the touch of his hand, Ella felt her pulse pick up—and not because they were walking at a brisk pace. She enjoyed the warmth of the sun on her face, the sound of water over stones, and the smell of damp leaves underfoot. Glancing at Richard as he strode along, head up and eyes taking everything in, she decided this was exactly the kind of adventure she needed.

Fifteen minutes later, the track narrowed enough that it was hard to walk side by side. Richard took the lead, chatting about the amazing diversity of flora and fauna in the mountains of West Virginia.

"Do you think we'll see a bear? Or maybe a raccoon?"

Ella peered around Richard to make sure they hadn't left the trail. "A deer maybe, but raccoons mostly come out at dusk. If we see one in the middle of the afternoon like this, we'd better steer clear. Might be rabid."

Richard shot her a look over his shoulder. "Rabies? Is that something we should be worried about?"

Ella shrugged. "I never have before. I think we'll be fine."

"Hey, what's that?" Richard darted into a rhododendron thicket and thrashed around. "I think I found an old still." His voice rose like he'd uncovered buried treasure.

Ella pushed branches aside—one flipping back and scraping her cheek—until she reached him. He stood over some twisted metal half buried in leaves and dirt. Ella kicked at it.

"What you have found is probably an old truck fender."

Richard grabbed the metal and tugged on it until it popped loose. He dropped the rusted piece of junk and crouched down to examine it more closely. He grunted. "Yeah, I think you're right. Thought we had something there."

Standing, Richard dusted his hands off and started pushing through the thicket.

"Where are you going?" Ella asked.

"Back to the trail."

Ella pointed in the opposite direction. "Trail's back that way."

Richard wrinkled his brow and looked both ways. "Are you sure?"

"Yup." She started working her way out. "Don't want to get lost in one of these rhododendron hells. They're called that for a good reason."

Richard followed her, although he kept glancing back over his shoulder. He seemed surprised when they popped back out on the trail and hesitated as though unsure of which direction they should go.

"I'm about ready to head back and see if it's time to eat," Ella said, starting back the way they'd come.

Richard trotted a few steps to catch up. "Sounds like a good plan." He shoved his hands into his pockets and looked all around. "Sure is gorgeous out here, but I guess it could be dangerous if you aren't woods savvy."

Ella looked at him from the corner of her eye. "It could be. Although if you walk another fifteen minutes up the trail, you'll come to a house. And even if you fought your way through the rhododendron you'd pop out over on the Rexroad Place. There are plenty of folks around. They just don't like to be on top of each other."

Richard nodded and whistled what sounded like a made-up tune. "So, Ella, I've been thinking that I might like to get to know you better."

Ella had been thinking about all the neighbors within walking distance, and she had to refocus to catch up with Richard's sudden change in conversation. Once she did, she felt a little thrill. Did he mean romance?

"And I'm thinking I can be up front with you now and ask the question that's most important to me."

Ella's breath caught. What in the world?

"Are you a believer, Ella?" He looked her in the eye and then went back to watching the trail. "I'm pretty sure you believe in God, but I'm not sure where you stand in terms of a personal relationship with Christ. The Bible is clear in advising us not to be 'unequally yoked' with unbelievers. I *think* you share my faith. But before we go any further, I need to *know* you do."

Ella had rarely felt this uncomfortable. Richard's words almost echoed what she'd said to Mark when she broke up with him. Of course she was a Christian. She'd grown up going to church and she believed in God. What a question—just because he was a pastor didn't give him the right to get all . . . all *religious* on her.

If he could ask her such a question, what must he think?

He obviously had doubts about her and her beliefs. Of course she shared his faith. Oh, maybe she didn't pray as often as she should and she didn't go to church every week—or at all when she wasn't at the farm—but who was Richard to judge? She was certainly more religious than a lot of people she knew.

Ella resisted the urge to snap at Richard. She focused on walking around some rocks in the trail, trying to buy time.

"Have I offended you?" Richard stopped and placed a hand on her shoulder.

Ella turned and looked at him. Those gray eyes were so incongruous—he should have blue eyes. She tried to find words for how she felt.

"I guess I'm a little surprised that you'd ask. You've seen me in church. You're getting to know me. Surely you can tell I'm a Christian."

Richard dropped his hand and started walking again. "I've found that there are plenty of people who say they're Christians who haven't spent a whole lot of time thinking about what that means. I want to know that your faith is as important to you as mine is to me."

"Well, yeah. I mean, I haven't gone to seminary or anything, but church has always been a big part of my life. Shoot, our family helped build Laurel Mountain Church." She glanced at Richard, who walked with his head down as though deep in thought. "And I pray. Maybe not as much as I should, but me and God, we talk." She put a smile in her voice and tried to laugh a little.

Richard looked at her and took her hand. "Good. Because I'm really enjoying spending time with you." His brow furrowed. "You aren't seeing anyone, are you? I don't want to be presumptuous."

Ella thought of Mark—she was doing her best *not* to see him. Then she thought of Seth, but they were little more than acquaintances. "No, I'm not seeing anyone at the moment."

His smiled deepened, and she marveled at how the color of his eyes seemed to shift with his mood. She caught a glimpse of the swimming hole beyond his shoulder, where water tumbled over stones to flow into the pool she'd swum in time and again growing up. As though for the first time, she heard the music of the water and could swear it was singing a familiar song, something she'd heard once before. If only she could remember . . .

Richard followed her gaze. "Did you ever go swimming there?"

Ella snapped out of her reverie and refocused on him. "Yes. We went a lot when I was a kid." She started walking again. "But I haven't been back here in ages."

Perla watched Ella and Richard return to the picnic area. They looked like they were having a serious conversation. She wondered again if the pastor had taken a shine to her granddaughter. She thought Richard was less likely to break her heart than that Mark fellow. Of course, there was no sense in trying to find the right person if you hadn't figured out how to be the right person. And Perla suspected Ella still had some figuring to do.

Now that Perla was finally gaining ground with her speech, it wouldn't be long before she could tell Ella her story and hopefully give her granddaughter some insight into the difference between fancying yourself in love and growing into the kind of love that could sustain you for a lifetime. She and Casewell had that. But she'd come by it the hard way, getting love horribly wrong before she got it right. It would be a blessing if she could save Ella that same pain.

Henry and Margaret arrived and set up chairs near Perla as Richard returned Ella to her family. He then excused himself to mingle with the crowd. As Richard walked off in one direction, Seth Markley approached from the other. Perla eyed him, thinking Ella was attracting young men like a birdfeeder attracts squirrels. Although, truth be told, Seth seemed to be drawn to the whole Phillips family, not just Ella.

Henry clapped Seth on the shoulder and pulled him into the group.

"Did you bring your appetite? Seems like all the women in Wise are trying to outdo each other." Henry waved toward tables made from plywood laid across sawhorses. They sagged in the middle.

"I plan to do my fair share," Seth said.

Ella jumped up from where she'd settled in a folding chair. "Oh, I almost forgot to get the food out of the cooler."

"I'll help," Seth said, moving to her side. Perla hid a smile as the two hurried off to get the cake and salad.

They reappeared as Richard stepped up onto a stump and invited them all to bow their heads. Perla closed her eyes and remembered another pastor praying in much the same way.

8

REVEREND ANDERSON PRAYED before they ate dinner on the ground the first Sunday Sonny came to church with Perla. Aunt Imogene had one of her sick headaches, and Uncle Chuck refused to let his neighbors see him hobbling around on a crutch, so Perla determined to go to the Methodist church on her own. She felt a little nervous. Although she'd been to church with Imogene several times, she'd hardly been anywhere all by herself—ever. As she set out, tugging her gloves into place and carrying a basket of food, Sonny loped across the yard to join her.

"Out for a Sunday stroll?"

Perla sniffed. "I'm off to church, thank you very much."

"Oh-ho. Gonna get you some Holy Spirit." His hazel eyes danced. "What's in the basket?"

"We're having dinner afterwards. I made chicken and some biscuits."

Sonny's eyes lit up. "Reckon I might come along then. I'll carry that for you."

Perla didn't want to give him the basket, but it was in his hands before she could think.

"You oughtn't to speak of holy things so disrespectfully," she said, adjusting her hat now that both hands were free.

Sonny watched her, something soft and warm in his eyes. "I expect you're right. Ma raised me better than that. It's just . . ."

"Just what?" Perla walked briskly now, hoping to have time to wipe the dust from her shoes after they arrived.

"Well, folks don't always live up to what you think Christians are supposed to act like. Sometimes they flat let you down."

He looked so sad Perla had an urge to reach out and touch his shoulder, but she resisted. "No one's perfect except Jesus."

Sonny snorted. "Now that's the sort of pious talk I'd expect from Cousin Imogene. There's imperfect and then there's hypocritical. Guess I've run into my fair share of that second sort of late."

"What do you mean?"

"Ah, nothing. I'm just talking." He skipped off the dirt road and plucked a branch of fire azalea growing wild in the underbrush. "My lady." He bowed low and presented her with the flowers.

Perla pinked and took the deep orange blossoms. "Do you always act the fool?"

"Every chance I get," he said with a laugh. Then he winked. "Some girls like it."

Perla felt her cheeks grow even warmer. She matched her pace to his and tucked the flowers into the basket in his hand. Surely it wouldn't do to arrive at church carrying them. Sonny grinned at her like he knew what she was thinking.

He behaved himself the rest of the morning. He sat with some of the other single men at church and participated like a regular member, proving that maybe his mother had raised him right.

After church, when the pastor asked them all to bow their heads, Perla snuck a look at Sonny. And what she saw chilled her. While everyone else bowed their heads in reverent prayer, he glared at the pastor like he wanted to do him harm. Perla quickly shut her eyes and tried to erase the image.

But here she was, sixty years later, the picture of Sonny's anger just as clear. Maybe clearer now that she knew exactly how he—and even she—had suffered at the hands of pious people.

❧

Ella was relieved to have a chance to close her eyes and be still. First Richard delighted her with the offer of a walk, then he confused her with talk of being a Christian, and now Seth was here being so very helpful. He'd lifted her cake from the cooler and balanced it on one large palm. He'd commented that he couldn't wait to sample it, and his simple statement had pleased her way more than it should have. Mark and his domineering personality felt a million miles away.

Midway through the prayer, Ella snuck a peek at Seth and then squeezed her eyes shut when she saw him sneaking a peek at her. She'd make a proper fool of herself yet.

When she opened her eyes again, Ella found Seth watching her still. "Want to jump in line with me?" she asked to hide her confusion. "If we don't get it started, folks'll hang back being polite all night. I gave up wanting to be polite when I saw Mavis's homemade macaroni and cheese."

They walked together to the head of the long table where they picked up plates and plastic utensils. They made it to the end of the line, plates overflowing, and Seth followed Ella to some big rocks near the creek. They settled, and she realized they hadn't gotten anything to drink.

Seth stood. "Can I get you tea or something?"

"Lemonade, please," Ella said, sampling the decadent mac and cheese.

Ella watched Seth walk toward the drinks table and fill two plastic cups with lemonade. He straightened and looked toward the pasture where the cars were parked. A Land Rover pulled in at the end of a row, standing out like a thoroughbred in a field of cattle. A burly man stepped out and waved at Seth, who tipped his chin since his hands were full. Seth waited as the man made his way over. They spoke a moment, and then the man filled a cup with tea and followed Seth back to where Ella sat.

"Keith Randolph, this is Ella Phillips," Seth said, and Ella tried to keep the shock from showing on her face. Will and Laura joined them, giving her the distraction she needed to gather her wits as Seth continued his introductions, adding, "Keith here is hoping to make some improvements and preserve underutilized land up on Laurel Mountain."

Ella felt her face tighten, even though she was determined to remain polite. Seth handed her the lemonade. She didn't thank him, but instead took the cup and found a level spot on the ground at her feet.

"You're that developer buying up property." Ella set her plate down beside her cup and stood, hands on hips. "What exactly are you planning to do with all that 'underutilized' land?"

Keith took a swig of tea. "Hunting preserve. Folks'll trip over themselves for the chance to hunt a pristine area like this. There are some farms up around there, but a lot of the forest is untouched, and I've rarely seen so much wildlife. Deer, bear, turkey, grouse—might even be a mountain lion." He looked so eager, Ella almost liked him in spite of his plans.

"And what about our local history?" She wasn't backing down no matter how much he looked like a little boy at Christmas.

Keith cocked his head. "Well, I've run into places where land is significant to certain people groups before. We were able to make concessions that satisfied all the parties involved."

Ella snorted. "That sounds like something a lawyer would say."

Keith laughed. "Guess I've spent my fair share of time around them, too. What I'm trying to say is, I always aim to honor the heritage of a place when I build. I have a lodge in Georgia with a fine collection of American Indian artifacts. Down in South Carolina we have a Lowcountry theme with sweet-grass baskets and information about the Gullah people." He leaned toward Ella. "What do you suggest we honor here?"

Ella blinked twice in rapid succession. "I . . . well, I suppose local arts and crafts, maybe the Scotch-Irish history, mountain music—that sort of thing. But without all of the hillbilly nonsense."

Keith nodded, and Ella half expected him to pull out a pad of paper and start taking notes. This guy was smooth. She shook her head to clear it. "The main thing is that we preserve the church and the cemetery. It's been there for more than a hundred years, and the families that started it still attend."

Keith held a hand up, palm out. "I wouldn't be interested in buying the church property unless the members were interested in selling it. Shouldn't be a problem there."

Ella still didn't trust him, but she relaxed enough to notice Gran watching them while making shooing motions toward the food table.

"My grandmother is indicating that you should help yourself to some food," she said with a laugh. "Goodness knows there's enough to feed Wise for a week."

"Come on, Keith. Laura and I will introduce you around," Will said. "And if you want the ladies to warm up to you, you'll eat at least a bite of every dish over there."

Keith eyed the groaning table. "I've had worse assignments," he said and followed the couple to the food.

Ella resettled onto the rock and picked up her plate. Seth sat beside her and reclaimed his food, as well. They ate a moment in silence, Ella thinking and Seth letting her.

"Can he be trusted?"

Seth shrugged. "As best I can tell. He seems straightforward enough, and I haven't heard anything to make me cautious."

Ella made a soft humming noise. "I might have to do a little research on your Keith Randolph."

Seth might like this Keith fellow, but Ella wouldn't trust him as far as she could throw a bull by the tail. Although she had to admit his question about what he should honor had set her mind to whirling. What if there were a visitors' center in a historic cabin on this hunting preserve? She knew of one that needed saving. They could showcase farm implements, household tools, maybe even clothing. There could be a garden outside with herbs that her ancestors would have used for medicine as well as cooking. An heirloom quilt on the bed—or even better, set up on a quilt stand as though someone would return at any moment to stitch away.

Ella felt Seth watching her. She needed to stop daydreaming. Keith hadn't said he wouldn't buy the church property, only that he wouldn't buy it unless it was offered. Ella couldn't imagine anyone offering, but it still seemed like the developer was hedging his bets.

"You about ready to go toast some marshmallows?" Seth asked.

Ella realized she'd been a poor dinner companion. "I'm sorry, I've been sitting here brooding over that development. You must think I'm awful."

A slow smile spread across Seth's face. "Nope. Just attached to your family and your history. Seems like those are good things to me." He looked at her parents sitting nearby. "Your family's really great. If I had that kind of legacy, I'd want to preserve it, too."

"Where's your family live?"

"I mostly grew up in Madison, South Carolina. My mom's from South Carolina and Dad's from Bethel, West Virginia, but

I'm adopted. I've always wished I knew who my real ancestors were." He stood and offered a hand to pull Ella to her feet. "You're lucky you know your history."

Ella took Seth's strong, warm hand and for a moment wished he'd tug her on up and into his arms. But that was silly. Maybe she was drawn to him because of the way he admired her family and understood how important her history was to her. She released his hand and straightened her shoulders.

They headed for the fire that had largely died down now, making it perfect for toasting marshmallows. Dusk settled around them like a piece of worn flannel, soft and not too heavy. Lightning bugs sparked here and there, and the children, already too full of sugar, abandoned the fire to chase them. Ella joined Seth, and he handed her a sharpened stick already loaded with two marshmallows.

"I assumed one wouldn't be enough," he said.

Ella grinned. "Right now I'd say two won't be enough, but I may change my mind after I eat them."

Seth held his stick over the coals and carefully turned it to brown the marshmallow on all sides. Ella stuck hers over a section that was still flaming—she liked them charred. She watched the concentration on Seth's face, noting how the fire reflected in his hazel eyes, making them glow. Just then the end of her stick burst into flames. She screeched, whirled the stick around, and blew on it with all her might. In short order she had one mostly black marshmallow and a second still white.

Seth took her stick and handed her his with a perfectly toasted marshmallow on the end. He ate her ruined dessert before she could protest. She smiled sideways and ate what he offered.

"Too bad we don't have some chocolate and graham crackers," someone said from the far side of the fire.

Ella squinted and saw that Richard had joined them. "I don't think we've ever made s'mores at the Labor Day picnic."

"Could be time to start a new tradition," Richard said, walking around the fire. "I'll be sure to remember next year."

"Might not want to tamper with tradition," Seth said. He didn't sound pleased, but Ella couldn't think why he'd care.

She forced a laugh. "I'm all for tradition, but I can't see turning down a chance to eat more chocolate."

Richard took her elbow. "I was talking to your grandmother. I think she might be about ready to call it a night."

Ella handed her stick back to Seth. "I suppose it is getting late. Thanks for dessert, Seth. I'll see you later."

She could see his smile in the flicker from the fire, but his eyes now looked utterly black and somehow it made him seem sad. She squeezed his arm and let Richard lead her over to where Gran sat, sweater snugged around her shoulders, visiting with the other ladies around a camping lantern. She looked back once to wave at Seth, but he was staring into the fire, apparently lost in thought.

9

THAT SUNDAY SETH CAME TO CHURCH with Will and Laura. They slid into the pew in front of the one where Ella sat with her parents and grandmother. Seth wore stiff new blue jeans with a white button-down shirt. His boots were polished, and his hair was missing the dent from his ball cap. He looked a little uneasy as they settled in for the opening prayer. Ella thought to move up and join the threesome, but decided they would look too much like paired-off couples, so she kept her seat. Will made a face at her while Seth nodded with a serious expression.

Throughout the service, Ella snuck glances at Seth. He seemed to relax once the opening prayer was over and they moved into the first song. He had a nice baritone and sang as though he genuinely enjoyed it. Ella caught herself smiling as she watched him, then forced her focus back to the hymnal in front of her.

> "I am weak, but Thou art strong;
> Jesus, keep me from all wrong;
> I'll be satisfied as long
> As I walk, let me walk close to Thee."

She stole another glance as they launched into the chorus. Seth closed his eyes and lifted his face as though singing only for his own pleasure—or God's—as though he'd forgotten there were people in the pews around him.

> "Just a closer walk with Thee,
> Grant it, Jesus, is my plea,
> Daily walking close to Thee,
> Let it be, dear Lord, let it be."

Watching him, Ella felt as if she were spying on something private, intimate almost. She looked away. Behind the pulpit, Richard sang as he flipped through the Bible, probably to find the Scripture he planned to read. She peeked at Seth one more time as the song neared its end. He looked back at her, the hint of a smile curving his lips. She blushed and turned her attention back to the page. Now why was she flustered? The song ended, and they all sat and focused on Richard as he began his sermon. Ella tried to pay attention, but couldn't get the image of Seth singing out of her mind.

After the closing prayer, the handful in attendance made their way out front and stood around talking and enjoying the early September sunshine. The conversation focused mostly on how much land had been bought up around the church and how bulldozers had come in to begin work on what Mavis had heard would be the lodge.

"Going to make it out of logs. Not a cabin, though, much grander than that." The gray-haired pianist leaned on her flowered cane and lowered her voice. "The sort of place none of us could afford. Ritzy."

Richard finished shaking hands at the door and came to stand near Ella. He touched her arm in greeting, then tucked his hands in his pockets.

"How about you, Preacher? Ain't it your business to keep up with what's happening in the community?" Mavis squinted at him like this was a test.

"What's happening in the community?" Richard repeated.

Mavis made a face. "That developer buying up the land and likely bringing in highfalutin folks with more money than sense to make us feel inferior." She waved her cane all around. Ella wondered if she needed it or if she just liked having a prop.

"And a good thing, too," Steve Simmons said. "This is probably our only chance to get anything for this falling-down church with its bad plumbing and even worse wiring. It's a miracle the place hasn't burned down." He poked a finger in Mavis's direction. "If they had less money and more sense, they probably wouldn't want this land."

Mavis glared at him, then turned to Richard. "Well?" Mavis raised her eyebrows.

Ella saw Will and Seth ease up to the fringe of their little group. Her parents were getting the car, and Gran stood right next to Mavis. Although her speech was much improved, she seemed to have embraced quiet as her default mode. An expectant silence bloomed.

"Well, I suppose the thing to do is invite Keith Randolph—I believe that's his name—to church. He might be looking for a place to attend while he's here, and Laurel Mountain would be convenient."

Mavis blew air from between pursed lips. "Fine, fine, invite him to come sit and sing with us, but what are we going to do about his buying up all the land? He's practically putting folks off property that's been in their families for generations. He might even try to put us off the church property."

Richard wrinkled his forehead. "I thought he was paying a fair price. And I'm not aware that he's approached anyone about acquiring the church property."

"Give him time," Mavis said. "No respect for plain folk."

Steve waggled a finger at Mavis. "If this feller wants to pay a fair price for the church and land, it might be what we need to get a new start. Let 'em have it."

Mavis's chin dropped, and she looked like he'd suggested they all strip down to their underwear and dance around the cemetery.

Steve held up a hand. "I'm just sayin', that old building needs to be rewired and reinsulated. The roof leaks in places. It's too hot in the summer and too cold in the winter. And that bathroom we tacked on the back has a toilet that runs all the time, and the water's so hard it clinks when you run it in the sink." He looked at the others standing around and appeared to take courage from a few nodding heads. "I'm just sayin' if we can get a decent price for it, we could put us up a brand-new building down on the paved road. Maybe have a community room with a kitchen or something. Might get some folks back interested in going to church."

There were murmurs of approval. Ella felt like someone had just suggested she trade her grandmother in for a newer model simply because she'd had a stroke. She hadn't taken the idea of the church being sold seriously, but now doubt began to tickle.

"But the heritage and history," she blurted.

Richard held both hands up. "I can see this is a potentially divisive topic. Let's all go home, pray about it, and have a church-wide discussion in the near future."

Ella hoped Richard knew what he was doing, but thought he sounded like maybe he was trying too hard. She sensed someone behind her and turned to find Seth standing there.

"I'm not sure Richard fully grasps the situation," he said.

"Of course he does," Ella snapped. "But he's not going to jump to conclusions based on rumors and doesn't want us to, either."

Seth held both hands up. "Good for him."

Ella took a deep breath and decided to change the subject—she didn't want to even imagine a world without Laurel Mountain Church in it. "Did you enjoy the service? I know Gran is pleased to have a few extra here this morning."

"I enjoyed the singing," Seth said. "I like those old hymns." He looked at her as though he'd gotten a really good idea. "I've been a few times before and I might even come again."

Ella flushed—something she was prone to with her fair skin—and smiled to cover it up, fanning her face with the bulletin. "That would be good. I know it would make Gran happy."

"Just Gran?"

"Everyone I expect. We're all glad to have more folks coming." She glanced back at Richard, who was still trying to mediate between Mavis and Steve. "Might put this talk of selling the property to rest if we could get attendance up."

Seth touched her arm much as Richard had, but this time she felt like she'd scuffed her feet on the carpet and touched a doorknob. She forced herself not to jump.

"Will and I have a meeting with Keith to discuss forest management and regulations related to the processing of deer. I'll let you know how it goes."

Ella nodded, at a loss for words. Richard approached them as the group wandered off toward their cars.

"You're meeting the developer? Let him know we'd be happy to have him attend services here—get to know the community." Richard looked like the idea pleased him. "As a matter of fact, if you'll wait a minute I'll write him a note inviting him to come." Richard hurried back inside before Seth could say anything.

Shrugging, Seth watched Richard go. "Not from around here, is he?"

"Why do you say that?" Ella bristled.

"No reason. He's just . . ." Seth looked back at Ella. "Never mind. He seems like a good guy and his sermon wasn't half bad, either."

Ella started to say it was better than that, but found she couldn't remember exactly what the topic had been. She'd been too busy watching Will and Laura hold hands. Plus Seth had distracted her with his singing. She opted to remain silent as Richard returned and handed Seth a folded piece of paper.

"I'm sure this enterprise isn't as elitist as Mavis fears. Thanks for reaching out on our behalf and for coming to church today." He moved closer to Ella and placed a hand on the small of her back. "Hope to see you again."

Seth's gaze lingered on the spot where Richard's hand disappeared. About the time Ella began to feel uncomfortable, he nodded once. "Reckon I just might do that." He reached toward his head as though for a hat, then tugged at his ear instead. He nodded again and ambled off toward his truck.

"Interesting fellow," Richard said. "Friend of the family?"

"He and Will work together. I've only met him recently."

Richard made a noncommittal sound. "Your mother invited me to Sunday dinner. I told her I'd drive you home if that's all right with you."

Ella assured him it was as they walked toward his dusty Subaru. She slid into the passenger side and watched Seth pull out of the dirt lot—sleeves rolled up and a bronzed elbow crooked out the window. Not very dignified for a Sunday, she thought, even as she looked again, watching him drive toward the land under development.

Perla thought Seth looked surprised when she asked him to take her out to see the future hunting preserve. She'd stolen a moment to speak to him at church when she didn't think anyone was watching, or listening for that matter. She still didn't feel confident about her speech. But he agreed to take her on a tour readily enough. She found herself liking this young man—he was direct and plainspoken. He might even remind her of Casewell a bit.

Perla was waiting at the door when he pulled up on Tuesday. Ella had gone into town to run a few errands, and Perla hoped to be gone and back before her granddaughter returned. "Let me get my scarf and sweater," she said, grateful that she could sometimes speak a whole sentence without losing words or tripping over her own tongue.

She tied a gauzy scarf over her hair and slipped on a nubby beige sweater Liza Talbot knitted decades ago. She rubbed the fabric covering her arms, supposing it would last forever. Hoping it would.

They chatted as Seth drove over the winding country roads, although Perla let him do most of the talking. She was surprised that he shared a good bit of personal information, like the fact that he was adopted and had grown up in South Carolina where his parents still lived. They even talked about his work.

"Are you . . . close to your family?" Perla asked.

Seth shrugged. "I guess. I see them when I can, and they like to come up and do mission work at a place my great-uncle Ben started over in Kentucky." He frowned and stared out the window. Perla was about to formulate her next question when he spoke again—she was learning that silence often invited others to fill it. "My family isn't like yours. You're all right here, on the same land you've lived on for generations. Shoot, you folks have three generations practically living together now. My mom and dad were always looking for their next 'calling' so we moved around. Guess I'd like to know where my roots are the way you do."

He glanced at Perla as though realizing she was actually

listening. "Not that they aren't great. My parents are really good people. It's just sometimes . . . well, like everyone was saying about the church. Your family built that. I'd say that's pretty special—knowing where you come from that far back."

Perla reached over and squeezed Seth's arm. "It is." She wanted to advise him that it was certainly no more special than having parents who loved the Lord enough to follow where He led, but laying the words out like that one after another overwhelmed her. "Your family's special . . . too." It wasn't what she wanted to say, but it would have to do.

Seth smiled like he appreciated her efforts, puny as they were.

Soon they passed the church and crossed onto land that would be part of the hunting club. After driving for maybe ten minutes, they came to the area where construction had begun on a massive log structure. Seth explained that it would be the lodge, a sort of central spot for hunters to gather, eat, and socialize.

"This land belonged to Wes Cutright," Perla said. "His six children squabbled . . . after he died." She tried to remember how it used to look. "I suppose Mr. Randolph made them an offer—" Oh, what was that line from *The Godfather*?—"they couldn't refuse." She paused to form the words she wanted to say next. "Wes would like having hunters here . . . better than children fighting."

Bulldozers pushed dirt around, and some men were clearing trees off to the right. A man who appeared to be dressed a little better than the others peeled off and walked toward the truck. When he got close enough, Perla recognized Keith from the picnic. Seth lifted a hand and called out to him.

"Hey there, Keith. Brought Mrs. Phillips to see the show."

Keith peered in Seth's window. "It's some show. Want to take a closer look?"

Perla nodded, keeping her words to a minimum.

Keith walked around to her door and helped her down, then held out his elbow so she could take his arm. Perla gave him a good once-over before they started out—she'd only gotten a glimpse of him at the picnic. Keith was of average height with salt-and-pepper hair. He was thick, but not fat. He wore blue jeans and expensive-looking work boots that had plenty of dirt on them. His shooting shirt had patches and gussets, fancier than anything the men around Wise would have worn. And she was pretty sure he smelled of Bay Rum.

Keith squired Perla around the construction site as if she were an investor or potential member. Seth trailed along behind, saying little. When they returned to the truck, Keith handed Perla up as though she were a fine lady and the beat-up Ford Cinderella's coach. Perla held on to his hand for a moment.

"Come have dinner with us next Sunday," she said. "And you too," she added, including Seth. "We'll eat at Henry's—more room there." She released Keith and clapped her hands, finding her delight in the idea had loosened her tongue. "It'll be a fine party."

"Oh, I don't know about that, ma'am. I generally do paper work and get everything in order for the coming week on Sunday."

Perla frowned. "If God wasn't too busy to take Sunday off, then you shouldn't be—" she searched for the word and found it—"either." She patted Keith on the shoulder.

He hesitated, lowering his head and scuffing his boot in the dirt.

"My pork roast makes grown men cry." Perla smiled. "That's what made my . . . husband fall in love with me." She hoped he'd say yes because she'd used all the words she could find to persuade him.

Keith laughed softly. "Ma'am, I expect he would have fallen in love with you anyhow." He heaved a sigh. "All right then. Count me in, but don't be expecting any offers of matrimony."

Perla swatted at him.

Keith eased the door shut and stood watching as they drove away. Perla kept an eye on him in her side mirror, noticing how utterly alone he looked in the midst of all that activity.

10

ELLA FELT A STEW OF EMOTIONS. She was helping Gran make Sunday dinner for the whole family plus Laura, Seth, Richard, and Keith Randolph, whom she mentally referred to as *the enemy*. That made nine of them crowded around the table that barely stretched to seat eight. She fiddled with the place settings again. Someone would have to straddle a table leg and it would probably be her. Good thing she was wearing pants.

Gran was in her element. It was rare for her to cook full out like this, and it was the first time since her stroke. She put the pork roast on before they left for church, along with scalloped potatoes. Now she was sautéing Brussels sprouts Mom decided to grow this year while Ella dished the fresh applesauce they'd made the day before into a bowl and sprinkled it with cinnamon. A loaf of crusty bread sat waiting to be sliced, and Mom had made her fabulous chocolate cake. Ella eyed the kitchen counter—they could feed twenty with all this. She and Gran slipped out of church the moment Richard said his last amen. The rest of the crowd would be here any minute.

Adjusting the bouquet of cornflower blue asters in the center of the table, Ella saw a car come around the curve of the driveway—that would be Mom and Dad with Will and Laura in the backseat. A truck—that would be Seth with Keith—followed close behind. Richard would likely be a bit later since he needed to close up the church.

Ella considered that the men gathering around the table outnumbered the women by one. Who was the odd man out? Keith? Seth? Richard? She wasn't sure who belonged and who didn't.

"Ella, put that out." Gran indicated the dish of bubbling, creamy potatoes.

Ella set a hot pad on the table and topped it with the casserole as her parents walked in the door.

"Perla, what can I do?" asked Mom.

"Toss the salad." They'd all gotten used to Gran's staccato way of talking. She said it saved on words while she was replenishing her supply.

Mom reached for an apron as she came into the kitchen. Ella looked down at her own tweed pants and sweater, brushing at a spot. Probably wouldn't hurt for her to wear an apron either, but they seemed so old-fashioned. She noticed Seth and Keith, standing at the door and looking awkward.

"Where's Will?" she asked, moving toward them and leaving the kitchen to her mother and grandmother.

"Outside canoodling with that pretty girl of his," Keith said. He flushed and looked like he was afraid he'd said something wrong.

"Of course he is. He needs to go ahead and marry her," Ella said.

Seth smiled, his eyes crinkling at the corners. He moved closer, and Ella swore she could feel heat radiating from his skin. Or was that her skin that was suddenly too warm?

Richard breezed in, and his eyes narrowed when he looked at her standing there between Keith and Seth.

"Dinner's ready," Dad hollered from the dining room as Will and Laura entered.

Ella took a breath. She needed to get ahold of herself. "Guess we'd better go in."

Richard smiled and stuck his arm out, effectively blocking Seth. Flustered, she hooked her hand through and allowed him to escort her to the dining room. Dad was seated, and Will pulled Laura into a chair next to him while everyone else stood around looking uncertain. Gran stepped into the gap, shooing everyone into chairs. Ella found herself between Laura and Seth with Richard seated opposite. And she was straddling the table leg. Everyone settled and looked toward Dad.

"Richard, normally I'd ask you to return grace, but you've already done a good bit of praying this morning. Seth, how about you bless the meal?"

Seth looked like he'd been asked to stand on his head. "Me? Oh, well, I guess I could." Dad held his hands out, indicating that they should all join hands for the prayer. Ella slipped her fingers into Laura's hand on one side and then, feeling self-conscious, reached for Seth. He looked at their clasped palms before bowing his head and closing his eyes.

"Dear God, I thank you for this food we are about to eat. And I thank you for the people gathered around this table." Ella felt a quiver run down his arm. "Bless us, guide us, lead us in the paths you've laid out for us." There was a pause, and as it was bordering on uncomfortable, Seth said, "Amen." Everyone echoed the amen as heads came up and hands reached for food. But Seth didn't release Ella immediately, and for a moment she forgot to pull away. Then Laura passed the platter of pork and Ella let go to reach for it.

"Keith, how are you enjoying our part of the country?" Dad asked.

"It's beautiful," Keith said, digging into the potatoes. "I'm from Shelby, North Carolina, but it's more rolling down there. These mountains are spectacular."

Dad looked pleased. "That they are. Our family's been here for more than a hundred years so we're partial to it."

Ella reached for a slice of bread. "Of course, some of the land you're buying has been in other folks' families even longer."

Keith paused in his chewing, then resumed. He swallowed before he spoke. "And now we're preserving that land just as it is indefinitely. Seems like the folks I've dealt with prefer that to losing the land to the bank or seeing a trailer park go up." He scooped up some applesauce. "Seth here can attest to the fact that we're using good land-management practices."

"That's not the point," Ella said. "I'm talking about people's heritage, maybe even their livelihoods."

Keith opened his mouth, but before he could say anything, Gran interrupted. "Keith, do you have children?"

The developer exhaled long and slow. "Yes, ma'am. Two daughters. One's married and living in Raleigh, North Carolina, and the other just started the MFA program at West Virginia Wesleyan College. She wants to be a novelist or some such. That's a big part of why I came to West Virginia. I'm more likely to see her."

"Are you close?" Ella asked, trying to follow her grandmother's lead. Sunday dinner probably wasn't the right time to push Keith about his plans.

Keith looked at his plate. "I wouldn't mind being closer."

"And your wife?" Richard asked.

"We've been divorced better than a decade now." He shifted his attention to Gran. "This is about the best pork roast I've ever eaten. Maybe you weren't joking when you said your husband married you because of it."

Gran smiled. "Thank you."

Ella's father stabbed the air with his fork. "Hey, remember that time Dad and I ate a whole butterscotch pie—just the two of us?" He grinned, and Ella thought she could see the boy he once was. "That was some good pie."

"Seems you did that more than once," Gran said.

"Yeah, isn't it about time you made another one of those pies?"

Gran swatted at Dad with her napkin and the conversation moved into gentler waters, but Ella felt unsettled. She wanted Keith to . . . what? Maybe say he hadn't realized how important the land was and he'd build his lodge somewhere else. Then what would happen to the families who'd probably already spent the money he'd paid them? The hunting retreat felt all wrong, yet Ella couldn't figure out what was right. Her elbow bumped Seth's arm, and he jostled her back. She flushed and looked around the table. Richard watched her with an intensity he usually saved for preaching. Dismissing the tiny frown in Richard's eyes, Ella turned her attention back to her food.

After dinner the men disappeared onto the front porch to talk about the fall hunting season while Ella helped her mother and grandmother in the kitchen. Will and Laura opted to go for a walk—Ella saw them disappear on a trail that led into the woods. She kind of wished she were with them, maybe holding hands with, well, someone.

Richard walked into the kitchen. "Hey ladies, can I lend a hand? I'm not much for all that talk about the best spots to stalk a deer or flush some grouse."

Mom handed him a dish towel and said if he dried, she'd put things away. "Ella, why don't you go see who wants coffee?"

She might have imagined it, but Ella thought Richard looked disappointed. She gave him a flirty smile and stepped out onto the porch.

"Mom's making coffee—anyone want some?"

Keith, sitting on the steps, stubbed out a cigarette and tucked the butt in his shirt pocket. "None for me, I'd better be getting on home." He stood and stretched. "You ready to hit the road, Seth?"

"Sure thing. Just let me tell Mrs. Phillips how much I enjoyed dinner."

Seth squeezed Ella's arm as he walked past her into the house. It seemed so natural. She caught herself smiling before she looked up and saw her brother approaching with his arm around Laura. He was grinning like he'd won the lottery. He waved and called out. Ella nodded in response, even though she didn't know what he was so happy about.

"Get Mom and Gran out here," he said as they drew closer. "We've got news."

Laura was all rosy-cheeked and smiling. Ella felt a pang as she guessed what their news might be. The kitchen crew came out onto the porch, and Dad said to gather around because his boy had something to tell them all.

"We're getting married." The words burst out of Will like he couldn't contain them any longer. Laura blushed, and they wrapped their arms around each other. "I asked her and she said *yes*."

Dad stepped over and slapped Will on the back, then kissed Laura on the cheek with something approaching reverence. "Welcome to the family."

Mom and Gran clapped their hands and pried Laura away from Will so they could hug and fuss over her. Will grabbed Richard and asked if he'd perform the ceremony. Ella figured she'd better get in there with some congratulations of her own, but she held back just a moment. Not so long ago she was the one getting married. Now . . .

"You'll get used to the idea." Ella felt a hand on her arm and the tickle of Seth's breath against her ear. "It was kind of weird for me when my sister got married. Made me think about whether or not I . . . well, it just made me think."

He released her, and she wished he'd left his hand right there, warm and solid and comforting. Her smile wobbled a bit. "I was supposed to get married, but it . . . it didn't work out." She wanted to clap a hand over her mouth. She hadn't meant to confess that.

"I'm sorry."

Ella swallowed hard and felt the onset of tears. She certainly didn't love Mark anymore. Maybe didn't even like him. But she did miss the *idea* of a man she would marry. And she hated to be reminded that she'd gotten it wrong when she tried to choose someone to spend her life with. Seth's simple statement sank into her spirit, and she wished they could go somewhere and talk.

"Thanks." She forced a smile. "Guess I'd better go hug my sister-to-be."

Seth nodded and Ella felt her sorrow ease.

"Ella, will you be a bridesmaid?" Laura stood in front of her practically bouncing up and down. "My sister will be my maid of honor, but I'd love for you to be in the wedding, too."

"Of course," Ella said.

Of course she'd be a bridesmaid. She looked at this sweet young woman who for some unfathomable reason loved her brother. Who knew? Maybe being in a wedding would be fun.

As the congratulations and chatter continued, Ella noticed Keith standing on the periphery, hands jammed in his pockets, looking even more sad and alone than she felt.

Perla anticipated Will's announcement and watched Ella instead of the newly engaged couple. It was just as she expected. While Ella jumped in with her congratulations, the first look to cross her face was one of dismay. Perla suspected Ella felt as though Will were beating her in this particular game. Ella had never fully explained why she ended her relationship with Mark, but Perla suspected the young man had been a significant disappointment to her granddaughter. She longed to explain to Ella that loving someone wouldn't fix their problems, wouldn't magically cure what troubled them. She suspected Ella had hoped her love might wear away Mark's rough edges and when it didn't, well, she knew from experience how devastating that could be.

It was time to tell the truth. As her speech improved, Perla toyed with the idea of calling Sadie and inviting her for a long weekend so she could tell them both at the same time. It might even be easier to lay her own mistakes on the table if there were two hearts to see how she'd been forgiven. Yes, she'd call Sadie when they got home, and by this time the following week her youthful sins would be laid bare.

Perla knew she'd been forgiven and redeemed long ago and had thought there would never be a need to revisit her shame. But watching Ella's forced smile made her realize something— God could indeed use all things for good. Even foolish indiscretions. And while she'd long thought Sadie was the good to have come from her failure, she was now beginning to see how God could still use it. Old Testament Scripture talked about the sins of the father being visited on offspring even to the seventh generation. What if, in these days of grace, the sins of the mother could be used to bless her offspring for generations to come?

Perla smiled and slipped over to put an arm around Ella's waist. Who would have ever thought she'd be excited to confess her shortcomings?

11

PERLA CLOSED HER EYES and massaged her temples. Sadie would be here soon and she couldn't afford to have a headache now. She thought back to Imogene and her sick headaches. She'd never had much sympathy for her aunt, but this week she wished she could go back in time and say she was sorry.

Ella had gone back to Henry and Margaret's so that Sadie could have the spare room here. Perla was glad to have the house to herself that morning. Since coming home from the hospital, it seemed there was always someone underfoot. A little privacy was exactly what she needed as she considered how best to tell her story.

But right now she wished for someone to bring her an aspirin. No, not just someone. She wished for her mother. How could it be that she, a woman of seventy-nine, could still long for her mother?

She looked at the clock and saw that she had at least an hour before Sadie was due to arrive. Their relationship had grown more and more strained in recent years, and she hoped that with her finally revealing the identity of Sadie's father, the ice would begin to melt.

"'The truth will set you free,'" she whispered.

Glancing at the clock again, she decided there was time to take that aspirin and lie down for a bit. Maybe she'd try Imogene's trick of laying a cool cloth across her eyes.

⁂

Ella watched the Volkswagen Jetta putter toward the house, knowing Aunt Sadie was inside the car. Ella was eager for her aunt to arrive so she could find out what Gran was up to. She'd been acting mysterious all week, like she knew something Ella didn't. Maybe she'd finally share whatever was preoccupying her now that Sadie was here.

Sadie pulled up to the house and, a minute later, came inside. "I thought I'd come say hello before heading over to Mother's. You're welcome to come with me, Ella."

Ella hugged her buxom aunt, loving the enveloping feel of her arms. Sadie had always been on the plump side and leaning into her was like snuggling into a down comforter. At fifty-nine, her aunt called herself a permanent old maid, yet Ella couldn't help wondering why she hadn't found someone. She was smart, kind, and adorable with her ginger curls that hadn't turned gray so much as turned a few shades lighter. And she had the warmest brown eyes.

"I'd love to ride over with you. Gran said she was looking forward to having some time to herself today, so I haven't even called to check on her." She laughed. "It's probably the first day she's truly been alone in months. She'll either be anxious to see us or wishing she could have another day like this one."

Sadie stretched her neck like it was stiff from the drive down. "Mother has never been shy about letting me know what she needs. If it's time alone, I'm sure we can accommodate her."

Ella decided not to answer that. Apparently the tension she'd been noticing between her grandmother and aunt was alive and well. Best not to dig—at least not right now.

"I'll grab a sweater and we can head on over. I think Gran is making chicken and dumplings for supper."

They drove the short distance between houses and walked up to the door. Ella expected Gran to come out and greet them, but there was no sign of her. Maybe things were even tenser than she realized. They walked into the kitchen and still there was no sign of Gran, even though a pot sat on the back of the stove on low heat, sending up a wonderful, comforting aroma.

Ella gave her aunt a confused look and poked her head into the living room. No Gran. She peeked into the bedroom and then put a finger to her lips. "Looks like she lay down for a nap and is still sleeping."

"Oh, for heaven's sake, wake her up. I can't tell you how many times she let me know she didn't want to be treated like an invalid, so let's not start now."

Ella tried not to cringe at the annoyance in Sadie's voice. She tiptoed into the bedroom and laid a hand on Gran's shoulder. "Gran, we're here."

Her grandmother stirred and lifted a hand, a soft moan escaping her lips. Ella watched, alarm stirring in her belly. This wasn't right. One eye had opened, but the other side of Gran's face looked like it was sliding toward her neck. Like a hand was dragging it down. Gran groaned again and opened her mouth, but only gibberish came out.

Sadie stood in the doorway, looking peevish.

"Call 911," Ella said. "I think it's another stroke."

⚜

Something had wakened Perla. She lay in bed, eyes straining against the darkness, wondering what made her stir. Something rattled against the side of the house, and she slipped across the cool floor, nightgown clutched to her throat, to peer out the second-story window. At first she saw nothing. Then a shadow, darker than the rest, separated from the trunk of a sugar maple, and Sonny materialized in the side yard.

"I want to show you something."

Perla felt both scandalized and excited. She'd never before had a young man waken her in the dead of night and ask her to come out to him. She knelt at the open window so that her body was mostly hidden from view.

"I can't. It's not proper."

"Well, get dressed then. I'll give you five minutes and then I'm going without you."

She thought about telling him to go away, but instead she slipped a housedress on over her gown, wrapped a sweater around her shoulders, and stepped into her shoes. Feeling as though the blood in her veins was bubbling, she stifled a giggle. She mustn't let anyone hear her. Goodness knows she was old enough to do as she pleased, and for some reason running out into the dark to see what Sonny would show her was exactly what pleased her.

Though it was May, the nights remained cool. Perla could feel the dew wetting her shoes and ankles as she skipped across the yard to where Sonny waited. The lilacs were almost done blooming, but she could still smell a hint of their perfume on the night air. Stars sparkled overhead, and she had to swallow laughter down once again. What was it about Sonny that made her heart feel so light?

He held his hand out, eyes capturing the glint of the stars and throwing it back at her. She did laugh this time as she took his hand and followed him wherever he might lead her.

After about ten minutes of tripping through the dark, they came to Panther Run. Perla shivered, maybe from the cold, maybe from the thought of the wildcats the little tributary had been named after.

"No one's seen a panther round here in a coon's age," Sonny said.

She laughed again. "I should hope that isn't what you dragged me out here to see—a little spill of water and no wildcats."

"It's not such a little spill," he said, pulling her close to his side. "Looky there."

He pointed across the water to a still pool on the far side. Perla peered through the dark, trying to see something other than water and rocks and the roots of trees. The water stirred, then something shimmered, quicksilver in the starlight.

Perla gasped. "What is it?"

"Trout spawning. Rainbows." He laced his fingers with hers and it felt as natural as breathing.

"How did you know?" Perla turned her face toward Sonny and found him watching her rather than the fish. She swayed toward him and then caught herself and took a step away, releasing his hand.

"I just knew," he said, raising and dropping one shoulder. "It's like I can hear them sometimes."

Perla didn't know what to make of that. "It's beautiful," she said while watching the water. "But maybe I should go back in now."

His face slid into shadow, and she couldn't guess what he was thinking anymore. "Reckon so," he said.

They walked back to the house, not touching each other. Perla could see a hint of dawn in the east and hoped no one would be up yet. What had she been thinking? A whippoorwill called from the edge of the field. As she moved to step up onto the porch, Sonny caught her hand.

"I'm glad you came out with me. Sometimes I get more lonesome than I ought."

Perla smiled, hoping he could see it in the dark because she didn't know any words to ease lonesomeness.

"—caught it in time."

Perla meant to sit up, but she felt as though giant hands held her down. She opened her mouth to speak, then quickly shut it again when she heard the horrible sound that came out. Warm hands grasped her own and smoothed the hair back from her face. She felt like she was peering through a fog and couldn't quite make anything out.

"Just rest."

That was Ella. But there were other hands on her as well, and somehow Perla knew they belonged to her daughter. She could feel the frustration burning in Sadie's fingertips. She slid back into darkness, hoping the tide washing her out to sea might carry her back to 1948 and those days when she was still innocent and life was pure.

"It's much more serious this time," Dr. Endicott said, rubbing his hand over tired eyes. "I'd hoped with her improvement after the last stroke that we might be out of danger, but these things tend to be unpredictable." He looked embarrassed, as though he'd broken some rule by admitting he didn't know everything.

"She recovered quickly last time. What are the chances she can rebound like that again?" Sadie was all business, writing in a little notebook she'd pulled from her purse.

Dr. Endicott sighed, and Ella wished she had the nerve to give him a hug. He was wrung out. Anyone could see that.

"I really can't offer a prediction at this time."

Sadie made a face like that was an unacceptable answer. "It took a great deal of effort on the part of the family to work with her last time. Are we looking at something similar? I'm not sure how long I'll be able to stay, and clearly she'll need assistance for some time to come."

Dr. Endicott straightened his shoulders a notch. "A rehabilitation facility is always an option. Of course, she'll need to stay here for a while. If she fails to improve as rapidly as after the last stroke, we can look at alternatives to returning home."

Ella felt like she'd better jump in. The last thing Gran wanted was to go to some rehab clinic or nursing home. "What should we be doing for her now?"

"Being here with her is good. Touch her, talk to her, let her know you're close. Often stroke patients can still think clearly even when they have a hard time articulating thoughts."

Sadie opened her mouth, but Ella spoke ahead of her. "So just love her?"

"I can't think of a better prescription," the doctor said. "I'll be back around in the morning. We should know more then."

Sadie pursed her lips and tucked her notebook in her bag. While Ella loved her aunt, she was skeptical that she was going to be much help at the moment. She seemed to be carrying some sort of grudge that kept her from connecting with her own mother.

12

ELLA BRUSHED AND BRAIDED Gran's hair. "There—you look like a girl with your hair plaited." Gran grimaced. Clearly she wasn't buying the compliment.

They could finally take Gran home. After a week in the hospital, the doctors agreed that Gran's gradual recovery might pick up if she were back in familiar surroundings.

"I still say we're likely biting off more than we can chew. The hospital has a perfectly lovely rehabilitation floor where Mother can have the proper care instead of relying on people to come to the house. Honestly, we're inconveniencing these professionals." Sadie didn't make eye contact with Gran as she spoke, just bustled about the room, checking in cupboards and drawers for any last personal items.

"I've been paying close attention when the therapists come in so I can help, too," Ella said. She squeezed Gran's hand and it was like she could feel Gran's fear tickling her fingertips. "Gran just wants to go home. I honestly think she'll do better there."

"Well, I can only stay so long if I want to keep my job. I'm already pushing my supervisor's patience to the limit."

Ella smiled at her grandmother, who now looked frightened. "It's okay. I plan to stay. I can do my work from anywhere."

And that's when Ella knew for certain that she would stay—at least for the time being. There wasn't anything back in Craggy Mount pulling at her, and the thought of not running into Mark around town was a relief. Plus she felt really and truly useful, like she had a purpose.

Sadie harrumphed and marched out to the nurses' station. She bustled back into the hospital room and plopped down in a chair with a puff of breath. "There's no hurrying those doctors and nurses. No argument persuasive enough, no offer of assistance tempting enough. They will operate on their own schedule and that is that."

Ella smiled at her aunt's way of talking, feeling the earlier tension ease both in herself and Gran. She had a notion Sadie had spent so many years trying to sound educated in order to head off hillbilly stereotypes that her language had simply evolved into something from one of her dusty old novels.

"So long as we're home before dark. Right, Gran?" Ella patted her grandmother's hand and felt the fingers move in response. "Gran wants to see the sun setting over the pond before she goes to sleep tonight."

Sadie huffed. "Why do you say such things? As if you could know what Mother wants."

Ella shrugged a shoulder and smiled into Gran's eyes. The gleam she saw there told her she was right about the sunset. Why argue with Sadie about it? Her aunt was unsettled enough.

"So the school's going to let you have another month off?"

"They said they would. Goodness knows I've accumulated enough leave and have never taken a sabbatical before. But I don't trust them not to try and leverage this into early retirement. I'll be sixty soon and I'm sure they'd like to install a newer model." Sadie's mouth tightened as she looked out the window. "Perhaps one with fewer unknown health risks."

A nurse clopped into the room in a pair of clogs, her scrubs covered with pictures of kittens. Ella wondered what had ever become of white uniforms and caps.

"We're almost ready to transport you, Mrs. Phillips. Have you been practicing getting in and out of the wheelchair?"

Her voice was bright and chirpy. Ella saw annoyance flash across the side of Gran's face that was still mobile. Gran hated being at the mercy of others, and while she could move with assistance she still had a long way to go before she'd be doing something as simple as walking across the room.

"She's been doing really well," Ella said. "But she still needs a little bit of help." She flashed a grin at her grandmother. "Soon enough she'll be on her hands and knees in the yard, dividing those lilies that are trying to take over."

Sadie rolled her eyes, but Ella was pretty sure Gran couldn't see her daughter. She just sent her gratitude to Ella through her unwavering gaze.

⸙

She would give almost anything to be able to sit up, swing her legs over the side of the bed, and walk out of here. If only to show Sadie she could. Perla clenched her left hand, but even that was a poor effort. Her return to the little gray house couldn't come soon enough. It seemed that if she lingered much longer, Sadie would have her institutionalized.

The way these people pawed at her and fawned over her, as though her mind were as crippled as her body. Oh, she could think just fine and she'd done little else since waking up and realizing what had happened. But she couldn't voice those thoughts. Not one bit.

Perla looked at her daughter. She'd heard her worries about losing her job and her frustration at being needed to help care for an invalid parent, and it wounded her very soul. If it had been Casewell lying here, Perla had a feeling Sadie would have sacrificed anything. She remembered the day she first peered into Sadie's brown eyes and knew she could never give her up no matter how inconvenient a child out of wedlock might be. She still loved Sadie more than her own flesh, but somehow they'd lost that early connection.

Sometimes it was easier to love someone who wasn't related by blood. Perla wondered if Sadie needed to know who her father was so she could forgive him, maybe forgive them both. She thought she saw some of Sonny in their daughter—laughing one moment, moody and dark the next. And so utterly committed once he made up his mind to fight for what he wanted.

Suddenly, Perla longed to blurt out his name, to give her daughter a way to look up her medical history, if nothing else. But now she had no idea how to share the name, much less the full story. Speaking was beyond her, and learning to write with her left hand might take months. Sadie needed to know now just as did Ella. Why had she waited so long? What if she had another stroke and died before she could tell them?

Perla had long ago laid down the weight of her sins, but now she felt a new weight pressing on her. It was the heaviness that came with a longing she feared might forever go unfulfilled.

Although Ella spent her nights with Mom and Dad, most of her days were committed to Gran. She'd taken over the kitchen table to work on her quilt pieces and spent a lot of time just sitting with Gran and rambling on about life. Gran seemed to be grateful for the conversation. Somehow it didn't feel all that one-sided. It was like Ella could hear what her grandmother was thinking most of the time.

One night, after arriving at her parents' house, Ella realized she'd left her cellphone at Gran's. She jogged the short distance between the houses in the twilight and breezed through the front door. "Aunt Sadie, have you seen my phone?"

Sadie looked at Ella like a possum caught in the nighttime glow of the porch light. Her hand froze in the box of papers sitting on the kitchen table in front of her, and Ella thought she saw her swallow unnaturally.

"Where did you leave it?"

"Maybe with my quilting things." Ella drifted through the kitchen and found her phone under a pile of blue-and-green scraps Sadie had pushed aside. "Whatcha doing?"

Sadie deflated. "Mining for secrets."

Ella slid into an empty chair at the table and looked a question at her aunt.

"I want to know who my father is." She pulled a stack of papers and cards out of the box and sifted through them. "I always told Mother it didn't matter—insisted I didn't want to know. No one could ask for a better father than Casewell Phillips." A tear welled, which Sadie brushed at the way she would a fly. "But that doctor got me thinking when he asked about my father's medical history." She turned sad eyes on Ella. "What if I have a double dose of genetic predisposition towards heart disease and stroke? I haven't taken care of myself the way I should. What if knowing who my father was could save my life?" She sighed and rubbed the bridge of her nose where her reading glasses pinched. "Or maybe it's just that it looks less likely than ever that Mother will tell me. I thought I didn't want to know, but now . . ."

"I can see why you'd be curious," Ella said.

Sadie cocked her head to one side. "When Papa was alive, I hardly ever thought about my biological father. And then that January when he died, I swore I'd never betray Papa by trying to find another father." She picked up the next item in her stack.

"But I can't help wonder whose brown eyes these are. Whose curls? Why do I struggle with my weight when Mother has been slim all her life? Do I have brothers and sisters, someone who looks like me? So many questions."

Ella fished an old letter out of the box on the table. "So you're looking for clues?"

"I am."

"Any luck?"

Sadie leaned back in her chair. "No. As best I can tell from the boxes in the attic, Mother saved every scrap of paper anyone ever gave her. I've been going through them of an evening after Mother is asleep. But none of them mentions my father."

"Do you know anything about him?"

"I assume he was from somewhere other than Wise or Comstock. Mother and I lived in Comstock with my grandparents for the first five or so years of my life. Then, as Mother says, when it became clear the town would never forgive her, we moved here to live with your great-aunt Delilah and her husband, Robert." Sadie smiled. "Such good people."

"Are either of them still alive?"

"Delilah is. She and Robert sold the store and moved to South Carolina to get away from the hard winters. I got a Christmas card from her last year. She's living in some sort of retirement facility or nursing home now that Robert's gone. Goodness, she must be well into her nineties now."

"Maybe we should go talk to her. She might know something about your father."

Sadie blinked at Ella. "That's not a terrible idea. I suppose I could call."

Ella tilted her head and smiled at Sadie. "People are so much more likely to talk about things in person. Plus I've never met Aunt Delilah and I'd love to."

"Who will watch Mother?"

"Mom, Dad, Will, Laura—we'd only be gone a few days." Ella leaned into the idea, getting excited. "We can say that coming so close to losing Gran has made us realize there's not much time left to see Aunt Delilah. No need to tell them why we're going . . . Mom can get uptight about things like this."

Sadie let her shoulders drop and laughed. "Maybe you do know what people are thinking. Goodness knows you have my number right now. Yes. Let's go. It's exactly what I need."

Dropping her stack of papers back in the box, she rubbed her hands over her face. "We'll give Mother at least one more week at home and then we'll go. I don't want her to know what I'm doing. At least not yet."

Ella started to ask why not, but remained silent. She guessed maybe she knew why not.

They thought she was sleeping, but instead she was lying here, heart splitting in two. Pride. Pride and vanity had kept her from telling Sadie about her father, insisting that she know her history. And now she couldn't tell and ease the ache her daughter clearly carried. What kind of mother was she? The thing her child wanted most in the world was on the tip of Perla's tongue, but she couldn't make it go any farther. She felt hot tears trickle down onto her pillow. She could probably work up the strength to wipe them away with her left hand, but decided not to even try. She needed the anointing waters of forgiveness, and for now tears were as close as she'd get.

Perla closed her eyes and relaxed. The therapist told her meditation would be good for her mind, might heal the stroke-damaged parts that wouldn't let her speak. Anointing waters . . . that was what she'd felt once upon a time.

Sonny jumped up from the porch step where Perla suspected he'd been sitting for a while. Two fishing poles leaned against the railing, and he had a wicker creel slung across his chest. His broad chest, Perla noted.

"It's high time I took you fishing," he said.

Perla glanced back over her shoulder. Chuck was snoring over a day-old newspaper while Imogene was laid out in the back bedroom with the shades pulled down. Now that it was late May, she was meant to be getting tomatoes and corn in the ground. She'd planted the beans, squash, and cucumbers with Sonny's help the previous week, so he knew she didn't have time to waste.

"The garden can wait. Shoot, it might even frost again, and you know Chuck'll be glad for some fresh fish for supper."

Perla smiled in spite of herself. "Tell me your real name and I'll go fishing with you."

"Puddintane, ask me again and I'll tell you the same."

Perla threw her head back and laughed. "Fine, let me get my shoes."

She skipped back out of the house moments later, breathing in the spring air that tasted like sugar and smelled like green things pushing up through fresh soil. Sonny looked like she'd handed him a package tied up with a big bow.

"You look sweet as a spring lamb," he said.

Perla felt her cheeks pink and raised a hand to hide behind. "Go on now. Let's get to fishing before the sun climbs too high."

They raced to Panther Fork, where Sonny seemed more interested in seeing her fish than wetting a line himself. After thirty minutes or so of not even a nibble, Sonny laced a worm onto his hook and threw it out. Almost immediately he pulled in a fine trout.

"Beginner's luck," he said, laying his catch on some moss in his creel. "You try again."

While Perla was happy to enjoy the soft day, the warmth of the sun on her face and arms, and the purl of the water over stones, she kind of wished she could show off by catching a fish or two. Sonny reeled in a second fish while she pondered where to cast her line.

"How do you do that?" she asked.

He shrugged. "Guess I've been doing it awhile now."

"Show me."

Sonny's eyes gleamed as he looked at her standing there on the bank. She felt stripped bare under his gaze, but chose to lift her chin when what she wanted to do was duck away from those piercing eyes.

"If you're such a good fisherman, show me."

"All right." He laid his fishing rod down and stepped behind her, wrapping his arms around her waist to place his hands over hers on the reel.

Perla froze like a fawn left by its mother. She almost forgot to breathe. Sonny spoke near her ear, making a wisp of hair flutter against her cheek.

"See that spot right over there?"

She gave a jerky nod and tried to focus on the water.

"I've got a feeling there's a trout right there wondering what he's going to have for breakfast. If we can drop that hook directly in front of him, I don't see how he'll be able to resist."

As Sonny spoke, Perla could almost see the fish, lazy in the pool, tail barely moving, waiting to see what might drop in for a meal. Sonny drew her arms back, and together they cast the line so that it dropped right where he said. After a moment, Perla felt a tug on the line, followed by a sharper pull.

"Set the hook," Sonny whispered, releasing her.

His sudden absence took her so by surprise that Perla jerked the line, effectively setting the hook. She reeled in the best-looking trout she'd ever seen.

"There you go. Ain't nothing to it."

Perla let Sonny remove the fish and lay it beside his own. She kept her line in the water another twenty minutes without any results. Finally, Sonny tried again and after catching a fourth trout deemed it plenty for supper and flopped down on a grassy hummock under the tender blossoms of a multiflora rose. He leaned back and pulled his straw hat low over his eyes. Perla settled next to him, tucking her skirt around her knees.

"Do you miss home?" she asked.

He stilled. "Some things, I guess."

"Will you go back soon? Chuck's supposed to be out of his cast in another week or two." Perla gathered fallen petals, one by one, into her skirt.

"I'm not sure." He hesitated. "The thing is . . ."

"What? You can tell me."

"I didn't come here so much because Chuck and Imogene were in need of me. It was more because, well—" he raised up on one elbow and looked at her—"I'm married."

Perla felt as if someone had sprayed her with creek water. "Married?" Her voice sounded like it was coming from the bottom of a barrel.

He sat up all the way and leaned his arms across his knees. "You might say we got hitched without the proper blessing—either from her folks or mine." He rubbed a hand across his eyes. "I'm supposed to be forgetting about her, and she me."

Perla was so taken aback she wasn't sure how to respond. "Are you . . . ?"

"Am I what?"

"Forgetting about her?"

He ducked his head so that it was almost between his knees. His voice came back to her muffled. "I've tried. Might be she could do better than me. Her family sure thinks so." He turned pleading eyes on her. "No. I haven't forgotten."

Perla's stomach clenched. She hadn't taken time to consider what she'd come to feel for Sonny—she still didn't know his proper name, for goodness' sake—but now that she knew he was married, she realized she'd been feeling something a great deal more than friendship.

"I'm sorry," she whispered.

"Me too," he said, and she had the notion he was sorry for more than being separated from his wife.

13

RICHARD STOPPED BY on the Saturday Gran progressed to sitting up in bed. Sadie and Ella propped her up on a mountain of pillows and helped her into a sky-blue bed jacket just before someone knocked on the front door. Ella saw panic flash in Gran's eyes, but she composed herself and smoothed the coverlet with her good hand as Sadie went to see who had come calling. Ella raised her eyebrows, and Gran gave a slight nod before Sadie reappeared in the doorway.

"Pastor Richard has come to see how you're doing. He says he'd be happy to come again if you aren't prepared for a visitor."

"Gran would be delighted to see Richard," Ella said, feeling something like anticipation herself.

Sadie's mouth tightened. "Perhaps Mother should try to tell me that herself."

Gran made a beckoning motion with her left hand and tried to smile, but her face still wouldn't cooperate. Ella hated to see the sag in her grandmother's mouth, but wouldn't let anyone see how much it bothered her. Especially not Gran.

"Mrs. Phillips, aren't you looking well?" Richard entered the room with a level of ease and comfort that surprised Ella.

Maybe that was something they taught in seminary. "Ella." He took her hand and looked genuinely glad to see them both.

Ella stood and offered him her chair, moving to sit at the foot of Gran's bed. Sadie excused herself, saying she had a phone call to make.

"I'm hearing good reports from Henry and Margaret," Richard said. "Sounds like you're progressing nicely."

Gran scrunched the left side of her face and made a sound that Ella was pretty sure she hadn't meant to let slip. She was also pretty sure Gran had a strong opinion of people talking about her when she wasn't around.

"Gran's not up to talking yet, but the therapist is really proud of how well she's doing with her physical therapy. Monday she starts with the speech pathologist."

Richard nodded and patted Gran's arm. "That's wonderful. I miss hearing you sing at church." He turned his attention to Ella. "And what about you? Have you decided to stay in Wise for a while?"

Ella shifted, hooking her knee up on the coverlet. "For the time being."

Although she was enjoying being at the farm and was glad she could help Gran, she felt like she was running away from something. Maybe Mark, but maybe something else she couldn't quite pinpoint. She'd always had that dream about living on the farm and creating beautiful art while her adoring husband chopped wood or something. But that didn't feel quite right anymore, either.

"Well I for one am awfully glad to have you around." He looked at Gran sideways. "You have a lovely granddaughter, and I'm hoping she might be willing to have lunch with me one day this week."

Ella had to take a moment to sort out that comment. Was Richard asking her on a date? Gran looked more amused than pleased, and Ella had the thought that this was an odd way to ask someone out. Gran patted the coverlet to get her attention and nodded.

"Umm, lunch. This week. Sure, that sounds nice."

Richard crossed one ankle over his knee and leaned back like a man well pleased with the state of the world. "Excellent. Perla here is on the mend, next Sunday's sermon is almost finished, and now I have a lunch date to anticipate. How's Thursday at noon?"

Ella smiled and hoped it looked genuine. "Sure, Thursday will be great."

He uncrossed his legs and took Gran's good hand in his. "It's a pleasure seeing you look so well. Would you mind if I pray for you?"

Gran squeezed his hand and nodded. Ella bowed her head along with the other two.

"Dear Lord, thank you for watching over Perla and seeing her home safely from the hospital. Please continue to heal her body and spirit and bless those who give their time and love to watch over her. I pray this in Jesus' name, amen."

Ella echoed his amen and then stood to escort Richard to his car.

He paused outside the front door. The October sky was that perfect shade of blue that made Ella long for yards and yards of fabric dyed to match. It was a hopeful color, and as Ella considered the man standing before her, she felt a measure of that kind of hope. She wasn't entirely sure she liked the way he'd asked her out, but he was obviously a good man to whom she felt a certain attraction. Yes, she just might let herself hope a little.

"I'm looking forward to our lunch," he said, tucking his hands in his pockets. A shock of blond hair fell across his forehead, making him look boyish and uncertain. "I wasn't sure I'd get you to myself so thought I'd better go ahead and ask in front of your grandmother. Plus I really hope she approves of us seeing each other. I'd like to honor your family."

Ella felt a surge of pleasure at that. Finally someone who understood the importance of family.

"Thank you. I'm looking forward to it, too."

He fished a set of keys from his pocket. "I'll pick you up—here or at your parents' house?"

"Here," Ella said. "That way you can say hello to Gran, as well."

He grinned. "Good plan. I'll see you Thursday."

Ella waved him off down the dirt road and turned to see Aunt Sadie standing in the open door. She had a wistful look on her face.

"He's a nice young man. You could do a lot worse."

Ella pinked. "It's just lunch with a friend."

"Ah," Sadie said with raised eyebrows, "I thought it was something else."

Gran, Sadie, and Ella settled into a more or less smooth routine, and while Gran was definitely improving physically, Ella suspected her struggle to speak was beginning to take a toll. Gran got frustrated and cried easily, which her speech pathologist said was perfectly normal. Still, Ella worried that her grandmother would get discouraged and maybe even depressed as she fought to communicate. It was as if she had something of deep importance to tell them and simply couldn't find the will or the words to get it out.

After her second speech-therapy session, Ella entered the bedroom to find Gran laboring over a notepad, pencil gripped in her left hand, tears dripping from her chin. Ella stepped closer to see what Gran was writing. The print was barely legible, but Ella squinted and read it aloud.

"Must talk. Not working. Ask doctor." She sat on the edge of the bed and looked Gran in the eye. "Are you hoping there's something more they can do for you? Some other therapy or medicine?"

Gran closed her eyes, weariness washing over her face, and nodded her head.

"I'll talk to the doctor, Gran, but I think they're doing everything they can, and you've just started the speech therapy. We're going to have to be patient."

Gran stabbed the pad with her pencil, scrawling the word NO. Ella nodded. "I understand. If there's something more we can do, we'll do it." Tears of her own rose, and she willed them away. "Hang in there, Gran. Even if you never get your voice back, we'll still love you just the same."

Gran hung her head and let it swing a little side to side. She circled the NO on her notepad.

"There's something in particular you want to tell us, isn't there?"

Perla nodded, sorrow settling like a cloak over her shoulders.

"Well then, we'll have to get you talking."

Ella kissed her grandmother on the temple and urged her to relax back against her pillows. She set the notepad and pencil on the bedside table and smoothed the coverlet over Gran's legs. "Rest awhile. You've had a long day."

Gran closed her eyes and nodded.

Ella stepped out of the room and found Sadie standing just out of sight, arms crossed tightly over her chest.

"You humor her too much," Sadie said.

"She's trying so hard—she needs encouragement, I think."

"She needs to try harder. I don't know what it is she thinks she has to tell us, but I know there are some things I mean to ask her." Sadie uncrossed her arms and stalked to the window where Ella had the feeling she wasn't even seeing the blaze of autumn color. "And this time I'm going to let her tell me everything."

Ella spent Thursday morning working on the quilt piece of the church on her grandmother's Formica-topped kitchen table. She was laboring over a border inspired by "Grapes and Vines" by Marie Webster, experimenting with three-dimensional techniques. She wanted the silky green leaves to look like they were fluttering, and the fabric wouldn't cooperate. She made an exasperated sound and leaned back in her chair, rubbing her eyes.

"Need a hand?"

"Thanks, Aunt Sadie, but this is kind of different from the quilting you're used to."

Sadie made a harrumphing sound and pulled out a chair. "Just because the quilts I helped Mother make were for practical use doesn't mean they didn't require skill."

Ella stretched her neck. "I'm not saying they didn't. But you probably didn't spend a whole lot of time trying to figure out how to get a sense of movement in your nine-patch or log-cabin patterns."

Sadie picked up a threaded needle and made a series of small stitches along the edge of one of Ella's leaves. She tied off the thread and then added a few more stitches a little further along. After one more series she snipped the thread and sat back. "How's that?"

Ella raised her eyebrows and leaned forward. It was just the effect she wanted. Sadie rippled the leaf in a way that made it look as if it were fluttering in a gentle breeze.

"I was leaving it loose so it could *actually* move. You stitched it on there so it gives the idea of movement." She looked at her aunt. "Where'd you learn that trick?"

"By making mistakes mostly." Sadie stood and patted her ginger curls. "Of course, your grandmother would have insisted I rework that. We weren't trying to create a sense of *movement*, just something pretty and warm." She poured herself a cup of coffee. "Now, shouldn't you be getting ready for lunch with Pastor Richard?"

Ella looked at the clock and jumped to her feet. "Oh my goodness. I was so involved, I didn't notice . . . Thanks, Aunt Sadie." She kissed her aunt's soft, powdered cheek and rushed into the bathroom where she tried not to panic.

What in heaven's name should she wear? Slacks and a sweater, a dress, a skirt, heels, flats—the options and their imagined implications were endless. She'd been working on the quilt in an effort to stop stewing, but all she'd done was delay the inevitable. She looked down at her worn jeans and her brother's flannel shirt. Well, not this at any rate.

Ella had three choices hanging on the back of the bathroom door. She decided to go with her standby black pants and a top with a fluttery neckline. Maybe she'd add some jazzy earrings or something. She'd dabbed on the smallest dash of lipstick when someone knocked on the door. No one ever knocked—they just walked in. It had to be Richard arriving ten minutes early. Better early than late, she supposed.

She ran her fingers through her hair and flew to the front door. Sadie sat on the sofa looking amused. Ella opened the door to a bouquet of yellow, orange, and red sunflowers. Richard grinned out from behind them.

"They seemed like the right choice for the season," he said. He was wearing khakis, brown loafers, and a sort of rust-colored shirt open at the collar with the sleeves turned back. She took the flowers and invited Richard into the kitchen while she dug out a vase. All she could find was a Mason jar, but that seemed appropriate.

"I thought we'd go to that burger joint that caters to the tourists," he said. "Unless you'd rather try the coffee shop. I hear they have great wraps and pasta salad."

"The burger place is fine."

Richard greeted Aunt Sadie and went in to speak with Gran while Ella considered putting her hair into a ponytail. She had the notion men liked her hair better down, but she knew she'd be tempted to fiddle with it. Then Richard reappeared and it was too late to change her mind.

Once in the car, their conversation flowed easily. Ella found herself marveling at how much she was enjoying her . . . she decided to call it an *outing* with a preacher. At the restaurant he ordered a blue-cheese-and-bacon burger, while Ella got chicken salad. After the waiter left, their conversation about growing up, interests, and mutual acquaintances continued to flow.

When they'd finished eating, Richard paid the check, then suggested a walk around town before he took her home. They walked in companionable silence, peering in shop windows and enjoying the crisp, fall afternoon. Richard took Ella's hand as she stepped over a pothole while crossing the street and didn't let go.

"So have you given any thought to returning to the farm permanently?" Richard asked. "I know you've stayed this long because of your grandmother, but might you decide you want to come back home for good?"

Ella tried to think how best to answer his question. "I'm not sure. There were several reasons I came home when Gran got sick." She thought of the get-well card from Mark to her grandmother she'd intercepted two days earlier. He'd even had the nerve to hint that he might come visit to see how she was doing. He was being sneaky in his persistent pursuit, trying to win over her family. "The longer I stay, the fewer reasons I can come up with to go back to Craggy Mount."

"Nothing pulling you back there?" Richard pointed to a park bench, where they settled in to continue the conversation.

Ella thought he might be fishing. "Not really. I have friends and the town is nice, but I'm already subletting my apartment and I think the girl staying there would be glad to have it permanently. I can't come up with a compelling reason to go back, and there are several to keep me here."

Richard gave her a hopeful smile and reached for her hand. He looked like he was about to say something important when someone spoke from behind them.

"Why, Ella Phillips, fancy finding you here."

Ella whirled around to see . . . Mark sauntering toward them. He came around to the front of the bench and stuck his hand out toward Richard.

"Mark Arrington. I'm a friend of Ella's from Craggy Mount. And you are . . . ?"

"Richard Goodwin. Pleasure to meet you."

Richard stood, and somehow it embarrassed Ella that he was shorter than Mark. She wished she were with someone who would tower over her ex. It occurred to her that Seth certainly would, but then she banished the thought.

Richard stuck his hands in his pockets and rocked back on his heels with a glance toward Ella. She quickly got to her feet, as well.

"What brings you to Wise?" Richard asked. "Although I can imagine seeing Ella is reason enough."

She felt a rush of pleasure at Richard's compliment, but it did little to soothe the anxiety building at seeing Mark here, so close to home.

"I'm an attorney, had some business over in Clarksburg and thought since I was so close, I'd pop over and see my best girl."

Richard's eyebrows shot up, and Ella's heart sank. Mark acted like a man staking his territory. She wasn't sure how to make it clear exactly how unwelcome he was.

"Well, Mark, I'm sure you need to get back to your hotel. Or maybe you're even driving back to Craggy tonight? Don't let us keep you."

"Oh, I'm staying for a day or two. No rush." A catlike smile spread across his face. "As a matter of fact, we could all go for coffee. Richard and I could get better acquainted."

Ella took an involuntary step back. "No." She drew a deep breath and let it out slowly. "No, I need to get back to check on Gran, and Richard probably needs to work on his sermon." There, that was a flicker of surprise.

"Pastor, are you?" Mark regained his footing. "I may have to stick around and hear you preach."

"We'd be glad to have you," Richard said. He took Ella's hand and tucked it through his arm. She was struck by how steadying the gesture felt. "But for now, we'll take our leave. Nice to meet you."

"Yeah, you too." Ella could feel Mark's eyes on them as they walked away. "See you around, Ella," he called.

14

ELLA AND SADIE WERE ENJOYING a vicious game of Scrabble on a TV tray in Gran's room when they heard a vehicle drive up and stop.

"Maybe that's Henry," Sadie said. "He mentioned he'd be over with more of your mother's canned stuff this afternoon."

Ella wished Sadie would be more careful to include Gran in conversation. She might not be able to add much, but she certainly understood everything and had an opinion. Even now Ella could see that she had an opinion. One that Sadie was lucky she couldn't express.

"I'll go see." Ella waggled a finger at Gran. "Keep an eye on Aunt Sadie. No peeking at my tiles."

She walked through the kitchen and flung the door open expecting her father. Instead, Seth stood there with one hand raised as though to knock.

"Oh. I thought you were Dad."

Seth looked over his shoulder. "No, it's just me. I, uh, wanted to talk to you, if you have a minute."

"Sure, come on in." Ella opened the door wider. "Do you want to say hello to Gran? I'm sure she'd love to see you."

"That sounds good, but why don't we talk first?"

He seemed nervous, twisting his ball cap in his hands. Ella

noticed the familiar dent in his hair, even as fear over what he might have to say insinuated itself between them. After her recent encounter with Mark, she felt edgy and uncertain.

"Okay." She waved him over to the dinette, where they each took a seat.

"I was talking to Keith the other day"—Ella went tense inside; she hadn't anticipated talking about the development—"and he was talking about needing someone to consult with his interior decorator. Now that the lodge is under construction, he's got someone doing up the inside and he doesn't think she knows enough about this part of the country to make it 'true to place.'" He made little quotation marks in the air.

"Seems like maybe you had some ideas when he brought it up at the picnic." Seth looked eager. "So I suggested he talk to you, especially since you're an artist, and he said that sounded great to him. He was going to call you, but I said I'd come talk to you about it first."

Ella leaned back in her chair. "Consult with an interior designer?"

Seth nodded. "I'm pretty sure he'll pay you."

Ella bristled, but then took a breath. Seth was trying to help and it was nice that he noticed she was an artist. Not everyone considered what she did to be art.

"I did have a few ideas. I guess maybe it wouldn't hurt to talk to this designer. At least I'd know they weren't going to junk the place up with little outhouses, corncob pipes, and mock moonshine stills."

"A hat rack with a couple of coonskin hats on it might be nice, though."

Ella must have let her horror show. Seth held up his hands. "Just kidding. I'm sure you can do much better than that."

Ella felt her lips twitch. "Although Mason jars with handles might be just the ticket in the bar."

"Now we're talking," Seth said, slapping the table.

"What are you kids up to out there? Ella, if you don't come finish this game, I'm going to consider it a forfeit."

Ella smiled and stood. "Aunt Sadie, do you remember Seth? He works with Will."

"Nice to see you. Do you play Scrabble?"

Seth raised his eyebrows. "I've been known to give my parents a run for their money."

"Excellent. Now we can play three-handed, although I really believe Mother could make it four if she'd try."

Seth followed them into Gran's room. Ella saw her grandmother watching them with what she'd come to think of as her eagle eye. The right eye still didn't fully cooperate, but the left one seemed to make up for it. And the message she was getting just then was that Gran wanted to play.

"Seth, I think you've given Gran a little extra pep. Looks like we'll be playing all four sides after all."

"It's about time," Sadie said, but Ella thought she sounded a little softer. Like maybe she really was glad to see Gran trying something new.

Perla found herself liking this Seth fellow more and more. He knew all those sneaky little Scrabble words worth lots of points, while Sadie relied on her extensive vocabulary. As a result he was whipping all three of them and doing it with grace and good humor.

While she'd been glad to see Ella spending some time with Richard, she thought it wouldn't hurt her granddaughter one little bit to go see a movie or some such with Seth. He clearly liked her. She'd even seen him slip Ella a vowel when she was stuck. She watched Seth lay down three tiles and score forty-eight points. She would have smiled, but didn't trust her mouth to cooperate.

And now that she thought about it, Ella seemed to like Seth right back. She kept fiddling with her hair, and her cheeks were rosy. Yes, Perla surely knew the signs. She also knew how dangerous it could be to fancy yourself in love too soon. Better that Ella have several beaus and not settle on one anytime soon.

They wrapped up the game, and Perla let Ella know how tired she'd grown. It was the strangest, most blessed thing, the way Ella seemed almost able to read her mind. And when she attempted to speak—which had gotten a bit better but still had a long way to go—her granddaughter understood her with ease. If only she could convey something as complex as what had happened during the summer of 1948.

As Sadie packed away the game, Ella helped Perla get comfortable. She could get around now if she really needed to, but it was such a chore. She felt trapped in a body that wouldn't listen to her. Some days she wanted to yell at her hand to do as she said, to scold her foot into following her directions. But she'd have to speak to do that.

Seth stepped over and laid a work-roughened hand on her shoulder. "I've enjoyed my afternoon with you ladies. And it's good to see you so pert, Mrs. Phillips. I hope you won't mind if I come again."

Perla smiled before she forgot that she couldn't, but Seth didn't flinch, just smiled in return. She nodded to let him know she'd be glad to see him again. She looked at Ella and then back at him, hoping he'd understand her encouragement. He looked surprised, but then winked at her and squeezed her shoulder.

"I'll be seeing you, and soon."

"Good," said Perla, mentally scrambling for what came next. "Bye." That was it. She felt pleased with herself.

Once the room was empty, she sank back into her pillows and did the breathing exercises her therapist had shown her. Somehow it freed up her mind and she found she could make connections that escaped her otherwise. Yes, there it was. Pert. Seth wasn't the first man to call her that.

⚜

"You're looking mighty pert." Sonny had avoided her since confessing that he was married, but then on Sunday morning he fell in beside her as she walked to church.

Perla wanted to snub him after learning about his wife. Then she'd gotten Imogene to fill her in on the real reason Sonny was there, and she felt sorry for him more than anything. He'd secretly married Hannah, the daughter of a man his father claimed had cheated him out of a fine horse. Sonny's parents were horrified when they found out, as were Hannah's parents. The adults, never having had common ground before, came together to separate their children. Hannah was sent to her aunt in Kentucky while Sonny was banished to Chuck and Imogene's. The hope was that they would forget each other and the marriage could be quietly put down.

Perla had almost asked Imogene what Sonny's real name was, yet she couldn't bring herself to do it. It was his to tell—or not.

"Guess you miss your wife," she said.

Sonny looked like a rabbit caught out in the open by a fox. He stumbled a step and then settled back into his usual saunter. "I shouldn't have told you about that."

"Why not?"

"You might not like me so much now."

Perla flipped her hair and tugged at one glove. She smiled sideways. "Maybe I never did like you all that much. Maybe I was only pretending."

Sonny stopped and turned toward her. Perla went past him a few steps, then looked back. Maybe she shouldn't tease him like that—she'd just wanted to lighten the mood.

"Perla, I don't think you'd ever pretend to like someone. Not even a little bit." He looked so serious. "You're the most honest person I've ever met." He ducked his head. "And I surely am grateful for your friendship."

Perla started walking again, and Sonny fell in beside her. She didn't speak for a moment, trying to get her thoughts in order.

"Thank you for saying that." She glanced at him and felt her cheeks grow hot. "I'm glad we're friends, too."

Sonny gave her a sad smile and reached out to squeeze her fingers. She felt something pure and good move between them—understanding, sympathy, maybe even love. Not the romantic kind, but the kind when two people find they understand each other better than they thought possible. When Sonny's hand slid away, Perla had to restrain herself from reaching after him. She wanted to feel like that always.

O F COURSE SHE CAN'T COME WITH US." Sadie shoved a
pair of shoes into the bottom of a suitcase and stacked
clothes on top. "She's still a very sick woman."

"I'm just saying I think it might be really good for her to get
out of the house. And this is probably the last chance for any
of us to see Delilah." Ella tried to sound reasonable.

Gran wasn't helping. She sat in her chair, nose stuck in the
air, as though it didn't matter a bit to her one way or the other.
But Ella knew differently. She couldn't say exactly how she
knew, but she did.

"Aunt Sadie, will you pray about it?" As soon as the words
left her mouth, Ella wondered where they'd come from. She
hadn't exactly kept up with her church raising since getting
out on her own.

Sadie stilled, and even Gran seemed surprised, her eyes flick-
ering. Sadie turned and considered Ella, hands on her hips.

"That's hardly the sort of request one can refuse," she said.
"Fine. I'll pray about it, but I'm not expecting God to change
my mind."

The following morning, Ella sat up front while Sadie drove, soft music on the radio playing in the background. Ella had been so sure prayer would win the day, but Sadie remained adamantly opposed to Gran coming with them. Maybe she was right. Gran did have a lot of healing still to do.

"Ella, do you have any idea how long Robert has been gone?" Sadie asked. "I've forgotten if I ever knew."

"Gran showed me some of Delilah's letters. He passed sometime in the early eighties, I think. Seems like they moved to South Carolina in 1966. Do you know why they moved?"

"I suppose there wasn't much need for a general store anymore. Business was thin, and I think they kept going as long as they did because Robert loved socializing with the old coots who sat around that stove drinking coffee every morning."

Sadie smiled. "That store was the very heartbeat of the community. Delilah kept something of a lending library going, but when the county opened a public library I don't suppose many came anymore. I heard the people who put that convenience store in offered them a pretty penny and they wisely accepted."

"Seems like it would be hard leaving everyone and everything you know to move all the way to South Carolina."

"Oh, they had family there. Robert's younger brother had five children and they'd grown up and had children of their own by then. I hear there are grandchildren now, which means Delilah is a great-great-aunt—something I imagine suits her well."

"Do you think Delilah minded not having children of her own?" Ella was beginning to wonder if she ever would herself.

Sadie grimaced and shifted lanes. "I know she did. She once told me she wanted children more than anything until she met Robert. Then she learned to want whatever God had in mind for her, since it was sure to be better than anything she could think of for herself." Sadie finished passing a truck pulling a trailer and eased back into the right lane. "She always adored children—they hosted sledding parties and sing-alongs, and I for one always knew the store as a refuge from whatever was troubling me. Delilah may not have had children of her own, but I think she found satisfaction all the same."

Ella shifted sideways in her seat so she could see her aunt better. "What about you? Do you mind not having children?"

Sadie laughed. "You know, I really don't mind. When I was a little thing, I assumed I'd have babies one day. It's just what girls thought about back then. I would get married, and children would naturally follow." Sadie gave her a playful smile. "Of course, that's before I knew how you got babies."

Ella giggled. "Did Gran tell you?"

"She did, and I thought she was joking. I grew up on a farm and it seemed people should have a method a little more sophisticated than did the bull in the pasture."

Ella got serious again. "Is that why you never married? Men are too . . . messy?"

"No, I was more than a little determined to marry when I was younger—nineteen to be exact. There was this fellow. He was tall and had dark hair that always fell into his eyes, and he was so quiet. Hardly spoke a word. I wasn't much to look at myself. 'Pleasantly plump' is something that's always applied, I'm afraid. And of course no one knew who my father really was . . ." Sadie hesitated, as though that fact still weighed heavy on her. Then she resumed her story. "Albert was so quiet and didn't seem to fuss about girls the way so many boys did. I thought I had a chance." Sadie laughed, but it sounded sad. "About all he ever did was work his father's farm and go to church. He didn't attend dances or socials or anything like that."

"So what happened?" Ella said. "Did you date him?"

"Noooo." Sadie dragged the word out. "It was really quite awful. In those days girls weren't nearly so forward as they are now, and I didn't know what to do to get his attention. I tried to sit where he could see me in church and about wore myself out keeping my shoulders back and holding my stomach in. I'd position myself in the churchyard so he'd have to pass by and maybe speak to me on his way out, but all he ever did was nod and tip that poor excuse for a hat he wore. And then one day I decided bold action was required."

"What in the world did you do?" Ella asked.

"I baked him a pie."

"That sounds pretty tame."

Sadie laughed. "In those days, the only time a woman fed a man not in her family was when someone died or was sick. Baking an apple pie and walking it over to an unmarried man was what you might call bold. Especially since I knew that his father—his mother had died—was in town on Wednesday afternoons. Papa would have stopped me if he'd known what I was up to. And then when I got there, I learned Albert had been courting his second cousin over in Evergreen for quite some time. The young lady and her mother were visiting on that precise afternoon. I was never more humiliated in my life. It was hard enough to be rejected by the one man I thought might have me, but for it to happen in front of a lovely young woman and her mother . . . oh, I cringe to this day.

"They were nice enough about it. I think the young lady felt sorry for me. But the town gossips got ahold of the story, and if there had been a man who would have married me before, there surely wasn't after. And you know what the worst of it was? No one thought I was a hussy—I guess I wasn't pretty enough for that—they only thought I was pitiful and desperate."

"I'm so sorry, Aunt Sadie," Ella said. "But surely you've met men since you left home. Haven't you been tempted to marry?"

"Yes, I've had a few gentlemen callers in my day—some nice ones who probably would have suited me quite well." An extra bounce came into her voice. "There might even be someone of interest now."

"But what about—" Ella hesitated—"the physical side of things? Haven't you ever . . . ?"

"I have not," said Sadie. "Oh, I've wondered about it, and I've certainly felt that urge, but my heart always said no. And now I wonder if that isn't just as well. Who knows what genetic deficiencies I might have passed on?" She took her eyes off the road a moment to look over at Ella. "Now, why all these questions? Is it Will and Laura's impending nuptials? Or is it yourself you're thinking about? Seems you have the attention of several young men these days."

"I guess. I'm not quite sure I *want* their attention. How do you know when you've found the right one?"

Sadie took a minute to answer. "You know, I've always felt you would marry one day, and when you did, it would be a love match for the ages. Can't say why, but the women in our family have always had a little bit of the second sight. Delilah always had a knack for knowing exactly what people wanted even if they didn't know themselves. Of course, you'll probably have to get out of your own way. We're usually our own biggest obstacles when it comes to getting where we need to go. Maybe you've been trying too hard."

Ella laughed. "Second sight? Oh man, let's hope that skipped my generation. Life is mysterious enough without special powers."

"Humph," said Sadie. "Maybe it's not the second sight, but there's bound to be something unusual about a woman in this family."

16

A FTER A NIGHT IN A HOTEL in Loris, South Carolina, Ella
was surprised at how excited she was to see her great-aunt
Delilah. How had she gone this long without meeting her? Ella
picked at the continental breakfast in the lobby of the hotel,
which was just as well since it was mostly all carbohydrates
with a bowlful of overripe bananas for the health-conscious.

Finally it was time to drive over to The Pines Health & Rehabilitation. Ella was afraid it would be one of those sad nursing
homes where the smell of disinfectant couldn't quite overcome
the odor of desperation. She was pleasantly surprised when
they pulled up in front of what looked like a plantation house
with white columns out front and wide verandas leading out to
paved paths through azalea and camellia beds. The camellias
were blooming and it all looked so very Southern. Ella almost
expected a woman to sweep out the front door in hoop skirts
and a broad-brimmed straw hat.

Instead, there was a woman in street clothes to greet them
from the front office and orderlies in scrubs moving among
the gray-haired residents with their wheelchairs and walkers.
And the place smelled like baby powder. Ella smiled, glad that
Delilah lived in such a pleasant environment.

Holly, the woman who'd greeted Ella and Aunt Sadie at the door, led them through the facility while pointing out features along the way. They passed the dining hall, a day room with half-finished puzzles and game tables, a courtyard with roses, and a chapel. As they approached Room 117, laughter bubbled out into the hall. Ella caught herself grinning—it was such a happy sound she couldn't help herself. Just then a stream of little girls in Brownie uniforms poured through the door, splitting and ebbing around them with giggles and chatter. A woman with brown hair in a ponytail, wearing a vest with a name badge and pins, was obviously trying to wrangle the group.

"Girls, line up a minute," she called over the din.

Little bodies formed two lines as though this were a regular request, although their obedience did little to quiet the hall.

"Phew. Sorry about that. We didn't mean to overwhelm y'all. Are you here to see Miss Delilah?"

"We are. She's not too worn out for visitors, is she?" Sadie stood up a little straighter.

"I've never seen her 'worn out,' and as best I can tell, visitors give her energy. It's as if the children fill her tank." She laughed. "Though goodness knows they empty mine." She turned a stern eye on a tussle in the middle of the far line. "Lovell, you leave Maddie alone." She returned her attention to their little group. "Lovell is Delilah's great-grandniece—she always gets a little sassy when we come over here."

Ella looked at Lovell with interest. A pretty child with light hair and sparkling blue eyes, she did appear to be a handful. Ella calculated her relation to the child and settled on cousins of the third or fourth order. The leader wished them a good visit and moved to the head of the lines to march her cackling crowd toward the front entrance. They left a happy feeling in their wake.

Ella had some idea that her great-aunt would be a wizened

old woman with snowy hair. She'd seen pictures of a young Delilah who looked sophisticated with her dark hair and beautiful clothes. She had the feeling Delilah would be a bit proper, the sort of woman who knew which fork or spoon to use no matter how many surrounded her dinner plate.

Then Ella saw her aunt and stifled a gasp. The woman in the rocking chair near a sunny window looked, well, her looks were contradictory. The hands folded in her lap over a brightly colored fleece blanket were knobby and veined. And her face was wrinkled, though not as much as Ella would have expected for a woman well into her nineties. But her hair. It was still as dark as it was in any of the photos Ella had seen, shiny and recently styled. It was thinner—she could see the scalp through a crown of hair—but otherwise it appeared much the same as it had in those photos from fifty years ago.

Delilah opened her arms wide. "Sadie—Holly told me you were coming, but I hardly believed it could be true. I'd say you look just the same, even though it's been . . . what, forty years? Oh, my dear, time will have its way with us."

Sadie laughed and leaned into Delilah's arms. "I seem to remember Robert saying it was better than the alternative."

"Yes indeed," Delilah said with a chuckle. "That man had an answer for everything."

Ella was surprised at the strength of Delilah's voice and how clear her mind appeared to be. They pulled chairs over and settled in for a chat. It was a small room, but comfortable with the bed in one corner of the living space, a bathroom, and even a kitchenette.

Ella was content to soak up the conversation as her aunts reminisced. It was fun to hear a new perspective on everything from her grandparents' romance to Sadie's growing-up years. She especially enjoyed a story about Sadie curing a child's earache with fermented grape juice.

"You weren't much more than five years old and you had more sense than the rest of us put together," Delilah laughed. "Of course, you made an awful mess and you caught me out with wine in the house."

Ella felt like she was part of a larger story than she had realized. Maybe she'd been so focused on the places that contained her history that she'd lost sight of the people who lived there. She decided she'd be more intentional about asking questions and unearthing stories about her family. It might even inspire some new quilt designs, like a group of women in juice-stained aprons laughing together. The image captured her imagination, and she almost missed it when Sadie finally asked Delilah the questions she'd come to ask.

"Delilah, do you know anything about my biological father?"

The older woman turned serious and tapped the arm of her chair. "You mean the man who . . . ?"

"Yes."

"Why do you want to know?" Delilah looked at her niece with clear, expectant eyes.

"Mother tried to tell me once, but I refused to listen. It felt like I was betraying Papa. But now that she's . . . sick, I'm afraid I may never know. If nothing else, I'd like to learn my medical history. Mother obviously has some issues—what if my father did, too?"

Delilah shrugged one shoulder. "Seems likely we'll all go to our graves not knowing a great deal."

Ella stifled a laugh. Delilah was sassy.

Sadie pursed her lips. "Yes, well, that may be true. Still, I'd like to find out if at all possible."

"And then what?" asked Delilah.

It was Sadie's turn to shrug. "Then I'll know," she said with a defiant tilt of her chin. "I'll be able to make more informed decisions about my health."

Delilah laughed. "Oh, you always were a stubborn little thing, and I shouldn't push you so. Especially since I don't have any notion who your father is."

Ella thought she could see Sadie getting smaller right before her eyes.

"I think my sister—your grandmother Charlotte—had some idea, but she never confided in me and I didn't try to find out. I always supposed that was Perla's business."

Sadie visibly stiffened. "Perhaps. But since I share this man's genetic material, I think it might be a little bit my business, too."

Delilah reached over and patted Sadie on the knee. "Then I hope you find out. And I pray it will be a blessing when you do."

Sadie relaxed. "Thank you."

Delilah smiled, and Ella realized she was wearing red lipstick that looked surprisingly good on a woman her age. "Now, I want to know more about my great-grandniece." She turned those sharp eyes on Ella. "Do you have a young man?"

Ella jiggled her knee, wishing Aunt Sadie were still the one on the spot. "Um, not really. There was someone for a while, but he . . . wasn't a good match." Suddenly she wanted to tell Delilah all about Mark—his dishonesty, his anger that bordered on violence, the time he'd left bruises on her arm. "I thought he was the one, but now I'm afraid . . ." She couldn't finish the sentence.

Delilah watched her with complete calm while Aunt Sadie looked alarmed. Ella was afraid she'd tell her mom everything.

Delilah wagged a gnarled finger at her. "It's a hard thing to see the dream you've put all your faith in disappear like the morning mist. You might even feel like it's your fault somehow." She squinted at Ella. "You might be afraid to try again."

Ella's mouth dropped open. "I . . . well, I don't want to get it so horribly wrong ever again."

A tear tracked Ella's cheek. Aunt Sadie leaned over to wrap a strong arm around her shoulders.

"My dear, getting things wrong is nothing more than one of the steps on the way to getting them right. All you've done is learn a valuable lesson that many a woman has paid a much dearer price for. You've simply eliminated an inferior candidate. Good for you." Delilah fiddled with the edge of the blanket over her legs, a half smile curving her red lips. "Now, if you find one that's not fickle or foolish, you snatch him up. Men are prone to develop an attachment to whatever's in front of them."

Ella then surprised herself by bringing up Seth. "There's another guy—Seth—who seems really great, but I don't know if he's even interested. And I think our pastor, who's really very nice, *is* interested." She paused. "And of course, I'm not getting any younger and I'd like to have children."

"A woman after my own heart," Delilah said. "I wanted children more than anything."

Ella's curiosity swelled. "But you didn't have any."

"Nary a one in the usual way. But God has sent me more children than I can count. That child whose ears Sadie cured was half raised by Robert and me. And when we moved here, there were all the nieces and nephews and now I have a Brownie troop to help wrangle." She leaned her head back against the chair. "Oh yes, God has surely blessed me with children."

"It's not really the same, though, is it?"

"No, it's probably better. Anything God gives you is sure to be better than what you thought you wanted in the first place." She leaned toward Ella. "What do you want?"

"I . . . I thought I wanted to get married and be an artist living on the farm, hanging out with my family and bringing attention to traditional crafts and their roots in the Appalachian Mountains." Ella flushed—that sounded a little egotistical, even to her own ears. "Now I guess I want to—" she paused, feeling tears threatening to surface again—"I want to help take care of Gran as long as she needs it. And if I do fall in love, I want it to be with the right man, for the right reason."

Delilah nodded. "Those are all good things. But I didn't hear anything about God in there." She laid a blue-veined hand on Ella's knee. "You get to the place where you want whatever the Lord wants and you'll find you have more than you ever dreamed. My years with Robert, that store, the children, the family He poured into my life . . . oh my. I could never have dreamt something that good."

Ella felt frustrated. She wasn't sure she understood what Delilah was saying, but it sounded lovely.

Delilah smiled as though she recognized Ella's struggle. "Have faith, my dear. God is nothing if not patient."

17

Y OU'RE ALL INVITED TO HUNT THE PRESERVE the first day of deer season." Keith extended the offer without any fanfare after church one Sunday in early November. "All the amenities aren't in place yet, but I'd like to give the hunting a trial run."

Will looked like he'd been offered a cherry pie and a day off work, and Seth said he'd be glad to hunt the Monday before Thanksgiving, but Dad grumbled.

"Need to hunt our own property. We know the lay of the land, and there's that ten-point I saw last week. This is the year to bag him."

"C'mon, Dad. We can hunt the farm later in the week." Will jostled his father's elbow. "That ol' granddaddy deer isn't going anywhere, and considering the price of a membership, this could be our last chance to hunt the land around Laurel Mountain."

And so, on the first day of deer season—practically a holiday in West Virginia—the men gathered at the farm before dawn to drive together to the hunting preserve. Ella didn't actually care who hunted where, but she liked that Seth was being included in the party. She was getting used to having him around, and there was no denying he looked good in his boots and hunting jacket.

While the men were off rounding up a year's worth of venison for the freezer, Ella decided to set up a quilting frame at Gran's house. Sadie had gone back to Ohio after their failed trip to SC, leaving Ella happily in charge of Gran's care. Her aunt planned to return over the long holiday break, and Ella figured if the frame was already in place, her aunt couldn't protest. Sadie had shown Ella a quilt top she found in all her digging through boxes, which Ella was itching to finish. She layered the backing, batting, and top together and pinned it all to the frame. It had been a long time since she'd done any traditional quilting, but she found herself looking forward to the work.

She pushed all the furniture in Gran's living room back against the walls so the frame would fit. Gran watched everything out of the corner of her eye. As if she felt wary of Ella's intent. On the second day of December, Ella settled in at the frame and picked up her needle. Gran stood in the doorway watching, arms crossed, kneading the arm that still wasn't quite right. She shifted over until she was directly in Ella's line of sight, then pointed at the quilt.

"Where?" Gran asked.

"Aunt Sadie found it in the attic. It's really quite lovely. I wonder that you never finished it."

Gran looked annoyed.

"Who said . . . finish this?"

Ella raised her eyebrows and continued making tiny, immaculate stitches. "No one. It's just something I wanted to do. I thought if you didn't have another purpose in mind, it could be Will and Laura's wedding quilt."

Gran puffed air out of her nose and furrowed her brow. She hobbled over to the frame and laid her good hand on the fabric. It was a crazy patch with velvet and satin mixed in among other plainer fabrics. Gran stroked a bit of burgundy velvet and closed her eyes.

Ella thought she knew how Gran felt. The brush of fabric under her fingers had long stirred her heart and soul, made her want to create something. She hoped Gran felt that way, too.

"Needle."

Ella reached into her sewing basket and pulled out a threaded needle. She handed it to Gran and then resumed stitching.

Gran sat and worked her jaw a moment. She raised her weak right hand and thrust the needle into the fabric. She closed her eyes and her lips moved. She reached under the quilt with her left hand, pulled the needle through, and then pushed it back up. After making a few stitches that were only a little uneven, she guided her right hand with her left. She appeared to be fully absorbed in the work, her focus on the needle as it slid in and out of the fabric. Ella just kept stitching.

⁂

Perla fought tears. She would not cry over sitting down at a quilt frame. After the second stroke she hadn't allowed herself to think about what she would and would not be able to do beyond getting out of bed and speaking. But now she admitted to herself that quilting was just one of the many tasks she had feared might be lost to her forever.

She examined her stitches with a critical eye. Pitiful. She didn't know if she'd ever be in a position to finish an entire quilt by herself again. She glanced at Ella, who seemed to be lost in devising intricate stitches. She'd gone from herringbones and chevrons to feathers. Perla wanted to lean over and admire her granddaughter's handiwork, but she chose not to disturb the peace of the moment. For now, they were simply two women working on a quilt. Never mind that Perla was practically a mute cripple. She resumed her own sewing, satisfying herself with a simple blanket stitch, knowing that she'd soon be too tired to continue.

It reminded her of that day, after she'd done the unthinkable. It was summer by then, early June. Imogene insisted they join some of the women from church in a frolic. They were making a quilt for Luann Samples, who was getting married later that month. Some suggested there was cause for hurry if Luann wanted her first child to be born on a date that allowed for common decency.

As hints were dropped and eyebrows raised, Perla grew warmer and warmer. They might be doing something nice for Luann, but Perla wondered if the poor girl would ever find peace sleeping under a quilt bathed in gossip and innuendo. She'd finally taken refuge on the porch where she fanned herself with a handkerchief, even though the day wasn't that warm.

Imogene came out to fetch her when it was time to eat. "What in the world are you doing out here?" She laid a hand across Perla's forehead. "You look flushed. You aren't taking a summer cold, are you?"

Perla ducked from beneath her aunt's hand. "I'm fine, just felt a little warm inside."

Imogene pursed her lips. "Is it your time of month, then? I know I used to feel all het up when it was my time."

That was when Perla felt the first fingers of panic trace her heart. She counted in her head, fumbling over days and failing to come out right.

She shook her head and tried a feeble laugh. "No, not for a while yet. Must be spring fever."

"Humph. I'd accuse you of being lovesick, but there's isn't anyone for you to lose your head or your heart over." She narrowed her eyes. "Least not that I know of."

Perla reached for the screen door and slipped inside, saying over her shoulder, "Now, isn't that the truth?"

The second week of December, Ella answered a summons from Keith to come out and look at the hunting lodge, which was nearly complete. She still felt somewhat skeptical about helping him, but since he didn't seem to have any designs on the church property she decided to give him a chance.

Ella drove over familiar roads for a few miles and then turned past a rustic sign in fancy lettering that read *Laurel Mountain Hunting Preserve*. She couldn't decide if she liked that Keith had used a local name or not. On the one hand it might show that he was honoring the place. On the other, it felt a little like he was taking what didn't belong to him. Ella decided to let the question of which was more accurate rest for now. Once she saw how open he was to her ideas, she'd have a better feel for the man and where he stood.

The lodge rose up from the top of a knoll, and Ella felt her heart lift in spite of herself. It was gorgeous. Made of native stone and massive logs, the peaked roof shot heavenward with a chimney puffing smoke to keep it from being too grand. Although it had a rustic lodge feel, it still managed to be elegant and sophisticated. Ella wanted to run her hands over the rough stones and smooth wood, textures that spoke to her.

She got out of her car, grateful for the mild weather, and walked toward the porch, which looked like it needed a grander name, though she didn't know what else to call it. A veranda maybe? Keith stepped out through the massive double doors and leaned against the railing that appeared to be woven of branches—random yet beautiful. It reminded Ella of the crazy quilt she and Gran were working on—chaotic yet contained.

"Glad you could make it." Keith looked as relaxed as Ella had ever seen him, as though he were finally in his natural surroundings. It occurred to her to wonder what her natural surroundings were.

"Glad to come," she said, trying not to gawk.

"What do you think?" He stood and made a sweeping motion to encompass the entire lodge.

"It's certainly grand."

Keith tilted his head as if considering her comment. "Yes, it is. But not too grand, I hope. I'm counting on you to make it . . . welcoming. Personal."

It warmed Ella to know Keith thought she could do that. She ran a hand over a silken log—it was just as delightful as she anticipated—rubbed to a sheen and sealed against the elements.

"Grand and yet warm," she said. "I think maybe it's the natural elements. It's hard to be too fancy when you're using West Virginia wood and stone."

Keith beamed. "Exactly."

"Ladder-back chairs with woven seats," Ella blurted. "Having some rocking chairs out here is a given, but ladder-back chairs, that's the sort of thing folks drag out onto the porch after dinner to catch the breeze. Make them sturdy so the men can tilt them back on two legs, because they will."

Keith laughed full and loud. "Yes, ma'am. Do we need tables?"

Ella blushed, but was too caught up in picturing furniture scattered across the flagstone floor to care if she was embarrassing herself. "Yes. A long farmhouse table down at that end for playing cards or having drinks and then some simple wooden side tables over here." She pointed, feeling lighter than she had since, well, maybe since she was a child still on the farm.

"Come on in the house," Keith said, opening one side of the double doors.

Ella tried not to gasp as they walked inside. The ceiling soared with a network of beams, and a massive stone fireplace dominated the far side of the room. There was a sort of check-in desk off to the right, but otherwise the room was nothing but space begging to be defined.

"My decorator is planning several seating groups," said Keith. "The main one around the fireplace, then one in that corner where the light is good for reading, and an area over there with a few tables for activities or socializing." He gestured with enthusiasm and seemed to almost bounce on his toes. "What I'm looking for from you is the details. Accessories, art, rugs, lamps—that sort of thing." He looked at her with expectancy, and Ella was surprised to realize she didn't want to disappoint him.

"Hooked rugs—probably in floral designs to soften all this wood and stone," she said, waving her hands toward the ceiling. "Put out books by West Virginia authors. Include displays of local crafts—Fenton glass, pottery, and woven throws over the backs of chairs."

Keith nodded and walked through the space as though picturing what she was describing. "Can you help me find all of that?"

"Sure." Ella smiled. Shopping with Keith's money would be a pleasure. She could find some wonderful things.

"What about art? For the walls?"

Ella took a deep breath. "That's where I'd like to help you on a more personal level. Wait here." She scurried out to the car and lifted the box layered with tissue from the backseat. She closed her eyes and whispered—was it a prayer? She'd only just started to feel inspired again and was nervous about sharing her work.

Keith stood inside, gazing at the fireplace mantel as though envisioning some grand piece of artwork hanging there. "What about mounting a deer with a really impressive rack and hanging it up there?"

Ella cringed. She'd never been a fan of mounted heads, although it would make sense since this was a hunting lodge.

"I've seen some lovely art incorporating things like feathers, horn, fur, and other elements. Maybe that could work in place of the usual mount."

Keith rubbed his chin and looked thoughtful.

"But what I'd like to suggest is this." Ella didn't look directly at Keith, folded back tissue paper and lifted out a piece she'd finished just the day before. She draped the oversized panel across the check-in desk and stepped back to admire it, still not looking at Keith.

In shades of autumn, the fabric featured a grouse taking flight, each feather a slightly different shade or texture of fabric. Gold thread had been worked in to create the illusion of light and movement along the bird's body. The eye was a jet button that had belonged to Gran. Ella kind of hated to part with that, but she'd felt a strong urge to bring the piece to the lodge today.

Silence stretched between them until finally Ella braved a glance in Keith's direction. He stood staring at her work, and Ella worried he was trying to find a way to refuse it without offending her. At last he cleared his throat and reached for the quilt, but then pulled back before touching it.

"Do you have others like this?"

"Not exactly, but this is what I do, so yes."

"I knew you were an artist, but I was imagining something more . . . traditional."

Ella laughed, relieved that he wasn't refusing her outright. "Gran's the one who specializes in traditional. Although there's a place for that, too. As a matter of fact"—she pointed at a high wall above the front entrance—"that spot would be perfect for an antique quilt."

"Done." Keith slapped his hands together. "Kristen will be here this weekend to get started on the furnishings, and I'd like the two of you to put your heads together." He stepped over and traced a finger along a gold-tipped feather. "My only requirement is that this goes above the mantel."

Ella felt a glow of pleasure. There were few things more gratifying than someone appreciating her art. She hadn't expected it of Keith when they first met, but maybe that was her own prejudice and no fault of his.

Keith looked up toward the front door and raised a hand. "Hey there, Seth. Ella and I are just finishing up. I'll be right with you."

Ella saw Seth standing there looking outdoorsy in field pants, flannel shirt, and a shooting vest. He also had a beautiful dog sitting patiently at his feet. Seth smiled, and the warmth in his eyes completed the all-around feeling of contentment Ella was enjoying. It occurred to her she felt more at home right here, right now, than she had felt at the farm since coming back to help with Gran. The thought made her feel guilty.

She replaced the hanging in its paper-lined box and turned back to Keith. "Saturday then? What time?"

"Come around late morning. I think you'll like Kristen. She's surprisingly unfussy for an interior decorator."

"Great. Should I take this with me or leave it here?" She indicated the box.

"Leave it if you don't mind. And I'll be paying you for this as well as the time you spend helping to get things in order."

He named a price for the quilt that Ella assumed included her time spent decorating, but he clarified that his offer was for the quilt only. He'd pay extra for everything else. Ella swallowed hard, thinking it was too much and trying to figure out how to ask for less. She'd never been in the position of asking for less.

"Worth every penny," Seth said.

Ella glanced at him and there was that warmth again. The dog wagged its tail as though it could feel the energy passing between them. She tugged at the hem of her shirt and smiled.

"Thanks for saying so." She stuck out her hand toward Keith. "It's a deal."

Keith shook her hand like he'd struck the deal of a lifetime. "Excellent. I'll see you Saturday." He turned to Seth. "We can head back to my office. I'm eager to get some dogs bred."

Seth nodded. "Be there in a minute. Just let me speak to Ella first." He smiled and hooked his thumbs in the pockets of his vest.

"Sure, sure. Don't take too long."

Ella thought she saw the older man wink but wasn't certain. Once Keith disappeared through a door in the back of the room, Seth turned his full attention to her.

"Seems like you and Keith are getting along okay."

"I guess maybe I like him better than I expected. I thought he might have ideas of his own about the décor—goofy stuff—but he's pretty much giving me carte blanche."

"He's smart." Seth rubbed the dog's ears. "So, I was wondering if I could take you out to dinner sometime."

Ella felt breathless at how direct he was. And she felt her heart take flight. Seth drew her in a way she hadn't experienced before. She wanted more of what he made her feel, but at the same time she was afraid to feel too much. She thought about what Delilah told her and stiffened her resolve.

"That sounds great."

"How about Saturday after your day with Kristen? You'll need a break after working all day, and if we wait too long, it'll be Christmas."

Ella's heart soared higher than the massive beams over their heads. "I'd like that."

"Good. Now Banjo and I have some business to talk over with Keith. He's hoping to breed some good hunting dogs, and Banjo here is one of the best."

Ella walked toward the door, stopping to caress Banjo's silky ears. The texture was heaven beneath her fingers, and the dog seemed to be equally delighted, moving closer and leaning into her leg.

"Banjo's a fool for pretty girls," Seth said.

Ella ducked her head and slipped out the door before he could see her blush.

18

ELLA THOROUGHLY ENJOYED spending Saturday with Kristen. Keith made the required introductions and then left them to their own devices. It turned out Kristen was a Texas girl with a personality as big as her home state. At first, Ella felt intimidated by her willowy grace, perfect hair, and the fact that she was a good fifteen years older, but she soon found herself very much at ease.

At the end of the afternoon, Kristen wrapped Ella in a hug that seemed to exceed her reach. "You sure you don't want to borrow my earrings?"

Ella had admired the dangly opal earrings soon after they met, and Kristen had immediately offered to lend them. Mid-afternoon, when Ella confessed she had a date that evening, Kristen removed the earrings and tried to hand them over.

"Seriously, wear these tonight. They've always brought me luck."

Ella laughed the offer away but had been touched by her new friend's impulsiveness. Not to mention the way she gushed over the quilt pieces Ella brought. Ella suspected she had a new friend for life.

After mapping the space, they agreed to meet the following

Tuesday to get a start on their shopping before everyone got distracted by Christmas. Ella drove home to her parents' house, her mind jumping back and forth between decorating ideas and her impending evening out. Seth was turning out to be more distracting than she anticipated. Goodness knows she hadn't felt this level of anxiety before lunch with Richard. Of course, feeling half sick and distracted wasn't necessarily a good thing.

After standing in front of her closet frozen for five minutes, Ella grabbed a pair of soft, brown corduroy trousers and pulled them on before she could change her mind. She donned a cream-colored sweater and added her favorite sterling silver chain with a tiny teacup suspended from it—a gift from her mother. Ella dabbed on a little eye makeup and some lip gloss, even though she knew she'd probably eat it off before they got to the restaurant. She gave her hair one last vigorous brushing and considered herself ready.

Unfortunately it was still ten minutes until she expected Seth, which was more than enough time to rethink her whole ensemble and put her hair into a ponytail. But no, Ella decided, she wasn't going to second-guess herself. She took her hair back down, and after making certain she was alone, flipped her head upside down and fluffed like crazy. She righted herself and was thinking the effect wasn't half bad when she heard voices.

She had planned to be waiting at the door when Seth arrived in order to avoid any small talk with her parents, but obviously he'd arrived early. She closed her eyes and said a silent prayer. Straightening her shoulders and tucking her hair behind one ear, she headed down the stairs where she found Seth sitting on the sofa, having a relaxed conversation with her parents.

And why shouldn't it be relaxed? Her parents were nice, easy to talk to, and they'd known Seth longer than she had. Apparently Will had brought him home several times, and Mom pretty much adopted everyone she fed more than once. The thought that he was familiar to her family was both comforting and unsettling at the same time. He looked up and smiled, his eyes crinkling in a way that made it impossible not to smile back.

"Hey," he said, "ready for a night out on the town?"

"Sure, looking forward to it." That wasn't exactly scintillating, but it got him up off the couch and helping her on with her coat.

"Good seeing you, Mr. and Mrs. Phillips," he said. "Don't worry, I'll have Ella home at a reasonable hour."

Ella could swear he winked, but she was too busy heading for the door and his truck to dwell on it. Seth hurried to catch up and then stepped around to the passenger side to open the door for Ella. *Nice touch*, she thought, sliding in. The truck was extra clean and even smelled good. Ella wondered if Banjo usually sat in her spot. If he did, Seth had managed to eradicate all traces of dog hair.

Seth drove to the local pizza parlor and asked Ella to wait so he could open her door. Once he'd taken her hand to help her out, he reached into the bed and pulled out what looked like a wicker picnic hamper. He ushered Ella inside and headed for a table in the farthest corner of the restaurant. Once there, he set the basket down and pulled a burgundy tablecloth off the top. He gave it a shake and draped it over the chipped faux wood tabletop. Then he pulled out a pair of candlesticks, napkins, china plates, goblets, silverware, and a bud vase with a red rose. Seth set the table while Joey, the owner, shook his head and smiled behind the counter. Table arranged, Seth held Ella's chair and seated her with a flourish. He sat opposite with a smug look on his face.

Ella couldn't hold it in any longer. She laughed, and soon Seth and Joey joined in. Another couple came in and looked confused. Joey bustled out from behind the counter and seated them as far from Seth and Ella as possible. Then he came to their table.

He lowered his voice. "You want I should close the place? Saturdays are good for business, but this looks like a good show."

"No, but thanks for offering," Seth said. "What point is there in doing something that'll make everyone talk if no one sees?" This time he definitely winked at Ella. "Now, how do you like your pizza?"

They started with salads and agreed on toppings for their pizza, each sipping a glass of the house Chianti. Ella was beginning to think this was quite possibly the best date she'd ever been on.

There were only a few other customers as the evening wore on and only one knew Seth well enough to speak. She was a mother of teenagers rushing in to pick up a pizza after soccer practice, and she did a double take when she saw the couple with their fancy table setting. She waved like she wasn't quite sure she should, and Seth stood to say hello and ask how her mother was doing after her recent gallbladder surgery.

"Fine," the woman said. "Thanks for asking." She peered around Seth to see the table and Ella. "Is that Ella Phillips over there?"

"Yes, ma'am. I'm taking her out for a night on the town, and we opted to dress Joey's up a bit." Seth gave her a winning smile.

"Oh, well, you have a nice evening," she said, backing out the door with her pizza box balanced on one hand.

As the door closed behind her, Joey came around the corner. "Enough," he said. "I ain't got no more pickups and it's almost nine o'clock. We're closed." He flipped the dead bolt and turned the *Open* sign around. "Now, I got some cannoli in the back with your name on it. You sit tight and I'll bring 'em out. On the house." He nodded as if this was an important and final decision.

He appeared a moment later with two crockery plates, each with a perfect cannoli in the center dusted with plenty of powdered sugar. "Now, just for you," he said, waving a woman out from the kitchen. She carried a little tray with four glasses containing a deep red liquid. "Vin Santo," Joey proclaimed, lifting a glass while the woman passed the tray around. "For the lovers. Salut." He drained his glass as the woman beside him sipped from hers and smiled. Ella felt her cheeks flame. "Now we leave you. Take your time." Joey shooed the woman—probably his mother—back into the kitchen.

"I guess I picked the right place after all," Seth said, looking amused. "Who knew Joey was such a romantic?"

Ella still couldn't get over the fact Joey used the term *lovers* to describe them. Is that what they were? She hardly thought so, but then again the idea sent a thrill through her that was not altogether unpleasant. She looked at Seth and tried to think of something to say, feeling a flutter of panic in her belly.

"I guess we should pack all of this stuff up," she said. Was that surprise in Seth's eyes?

"Yeah, I guess so. Joey's been a good sport, but we don't want to take advantage of him. Although . . . I do want to polish off this cannoli before we go."

He grinned, and Ella felt the pressure building behind her breastbone release. She laughed. "We mustn't disappoint Joey the Romantic."

They ate and then packed up everything. As Seth drove back to her parents' house, Ella glanced at the dashboard clock and was astonished to find it was almost ten already. She found she didn't want the evening to end, but couldn't think of a way to stretch it out. She couldn't invite him in to watch the ten o'clock news with her dad, and a moonlit walk might be too much, too soon. Ella guessed she would have to let this one go. As the headlights bounced across the front of the farmhouse, Ella blurted, "I had a great time, I wish . . ." And then she ran out of steam.

Seth stopped the car on the dirt drive and switched off the headlights so that moonlight filled the interior. "What do you wish?" he asked.

"Oh, I don't know," Ella said. "I really like talking with you and spending time with you, but I've messed up relationships before and I'm not sure I know how to do them right."

"Maybe the thing is not to look too far ahead," Seth said, turning to face her more fully. He looked thoughtful. "When I can't get a handle on the big picture, I just try to do the next thing in front of me. And then the next." Seth smiled and there was that warmth in his eyes. Ella could see it even in the dim moonlight. "I tend to think the Spirit will lead us if we let Him."

Ella was a little overwhelmed by the depth of what she was feeling, but what Seth said made sense. She'd come home, at least in part, to get away from a life that hadn't turned out the way she'd hoped. But maybe it wasn't about trying to fix anything. Maybe what she needed to do was start from right here, right now. Maybe she needed to learn to take life as it came instead of trying to plan it out so that everyone would be happy.

Ella leaned across the gulf between them that couldn't have been more than a foot and kissed Seth ever so softly on the mouth. Seth seemed to gather his wits and leaned into the kiss even as she was pulling away. She smiled, ducking her chin. "I had a wonderful evening. Thank you."

Seth cleared his throat and took a deep breath. "So did I. Do you think—would you want to do it again sometime? Not the pizza part necessarily, but . . ." He laughed and raked a hand through his hair. "What I mean to say is, would you like to see me again? Soon?"

Ella laughed, feeling like champagne was bubbling through her veins. "Yes. Soon sounds good."

He jumped out to come around and open her door. Then he escorted her onto the porch and reached around her to grasp the doorknob. Ella stood, almost encircled by his body and arm. She felt him lean in—this time he'd kiss her—when there was a rattling sound as Dad tugged the door open. Seth jerked back and gave her what almost amounted to a bow. Dad stood in the open door, grinning.

"Thanks for getting her back at a decent hour, Seth."

Seth nodded. "Don't want to jeopardize any future dates, sir."

Dad laughed. "Call me Henry. Come on in, Daughter. It's cold out here on the porch."

Ella smiled and gave Seth a little shrug before ducking inside the warm house. She listened intently for the sound of his truck door slamming and then the rumble of the motor as he drove away. She sighed and flopped down on the sofa, where Dad had clearly been settled in for the nightly news. The Christmas tree twinkled in the corner, and she thought she saw a couple of new packages stacked there.

"Have a good time?" Dad asked.

"Yeah," Ella said, "it was . . . special."

"Oh-ho, that sounds promising." Dad muted the TV.

"Promising." Ella tilted her head. "Maybe. I don't know. I thought Mark was 'promising' and I got that wrong."

"Ah, doubt and uncertainty, the hallmarks of any worthwhile romance." He sat next to Ella and wrapped an arm around her shoulders. "When I met your mother, I wasn't fit for any woman. I was so angry over your grandpa dying, and poor Margaret got to see me at my worst. And yet there was a spark. I guess for both of us. She was just what I needed to set my heart to rights, and I think maybe I was just what she needed to see how priceless she is.

"Once upon a time I thought I'd be a great musician and your mother would follow me from town to town while I played my fiddle. But her heart was always here, on this farm. I think she needed a family, a foundation that her own family never offered her, and it turns out that's what I needed, too. I see some of that in Seth, I think. He likes you, but he also likes what you represent." He snugged Ella against his side.

"I happen to think any man would be an idiot not to fall head over heels for you, but then again, being a man, I know quite a few of us are idiots."

Ella giggled and rested her head on his shoulder.

"Don't worry, favorite daughter. When you find the right one, your heart will let you know. And if it doesn't, ask me."

Ella smiled and found that she didn't wish it could be like old times with her dad. She wanted this time to be exactly like it was. New and shiny and perfect.

19

CHRISTMAS ARRIVED before Ella was quite ready for it. Late that morning everyone gathered around the big tree in the family room to exchange gifts. Ella looked around the room, counting faces and loving how each one—including Laura—fit in her heart.

Dad fished packages out one by one, handing them to each recipient, who had to finish opening the package before he'd move on. Ella had found this process torturous when she was a child, but now it felt like tradition and she reveled in it.

After collecting a book about Appalachian quilts from Aunt Sadie, and a cashmere sweater from her parents, Ella accepted her third package. She turned it over and over, looking for a tag.

"That one came special delivery," Mom said with a mysterious look.

Ella giggled. As if she still believed in Santa Claus. The package was classic Tiffany blue with silky white ribbon. She was astonished that her parents would even think to get her something from Tiffany. Then again, maybe it was just a ploy and she'd find a candy necklace inside. She unwound the ribbon and lifted the lid to find . . . an absolutely lovely cuff bracelet in sterling silver. The piece was made up of a lacy filigree of leaves that left Ella speechless. She looked around the room.

"Who? Is this from you guys? This is too much." She lifted the cuff out and held it, afraid to actually wear it.

"No, it's not from anyone here." Mom had that coy look again. "Someone who thinks you're very special asked me to tuck it under the tree."

It hit Ella like snow down the back of her neck. "Mark. This is from Mark." She stuck it back in the box and replaced the lid, her face stony. "I can't accept it. I'll send it back as soon as possible."

Silence reigned as Mom's features worked, and everyone else seemed intent on finding something other than Ella and her blue box to look at.

"It's just a bracelet," Mom finally said. "A token of esteem from a respectable young man who would like another chance."

"How do you know that?" Ella demanded. "How do you know anything about him? Can't you trust that I know what I'm doing when I say I'm not interested in him?"

Mom crossed her arms and looked at the tree. "Henry, hadn't you better keep the gifts coming?"

Dad cleared his throat and handed a package to Will. "Son, did I ever mention that giving gifts to women is one of the most dangerous activities a man can undertake?"

No one moved for a moment, but then Will cracked a smile. Sadie let go a very unladylike snort.

Mom huffed, then smiled. "I'm sorry, sweetheart. I only want what's best for you."

Ella sighed and put the box on the floor under her chair. "I know, Mom, but you'll have to trust me on this one."

"Ella, your mother knows you'll never find a man with even half the talent and charm she found in me." Dad scooped up his fiddle, played a few rousing bars, and shoved a package toward

Mom with his foot. "See? It'll take a dozen silver bracelets to beat that."

They all laughed and resumed opening gifts. But Ella could feel the bracelet like a time bomb ticking away under her chair. And she couldn't help wondering what it would take to properly defuse it.

Ella skipped church the Sunday after Christmas. The holidays had been hectic, and since starting work on the crazy quilt with Gran, she'd been having the most marvelous ideas for art quilts. She craved a morning alone to sketch out some pieces and be away from her family for a bit. So while everyone else went off to church, she camped out at the kitchen table at Gran's house, where the late December sunshine streamed over her paper and colored pencils. She became so absorbed, she hardly noticed the passage of time.

When Gran's mantel clock—which sat on a side table rather than a mantel—struck noon, Ella felt like she'd been jolted back into the real world. She stretched and rubbed her eyes, admiring the drawings she'd completed. Two were exactly the way she wanted them, while the third still needed work. She debated skipping Sunday dinner with the family. Aunt Sadie would bring her something when she and Gran came home. She looked at the drawing again and decided it might do her good to step away and come back with fresh eyes.

Ella slipped on her jacket and walked to her parents' house. "How was the service?" she asked, easing into the friendly whirl of activity.

Sudden silence met Ella's question. Her parents looked uncomfortable. Only Gran would meet her eyes.

"T-t-tell her," Gran said.

"Tell me what?" asked Ella.

Dad cleared his throat. "Looks like there's a pretty strong movement to sell the church property to Keith Randolph. I didn't really think it would happen, but it seems quite a few members are convinced it's a good idea."

"What? Sell the church? But . . . but it's our church." Ella wasn't sure what she wanted to say as questions swirled through her brain.

"Yes, but as Steve Simmons pointed out, the church is dying. I guess there was some hope Richard could come in and revive it, but we haven't really gained any ground since he came." Dad pulled a chair out from the table and sat, stretching his legs and folding his hands across his belly. Ella had the distinct impression he'd already resigned himself to the inevitable.

"Ella, I know you're sentimental about the church, but it's only a building." Aunt Sadie helped Mom transfer hot dishes to the table. "It could be a good thing. If you build somewhere else with better road access, the congregation might have a chance to grow."

"But we'd be losing the church our ancestors built," Ella protested. She glanced at Dad, stunned that he wasn't more upset. "Right, Dad?"

He shrugged, so Ella turned her attention to Gran. "What do you think?"

Her grandmother sat at the table, the fingers of her left hand tracing the place setting in front of her as though memorizing the silverware. "Luke . . . warm."

Ella's mouth dropped open. "Are you saying the church members don't care enough, don't have faith enough to keep the church going?"

Gran sighed. "No passion."

Ella sputtered, at a loss for what to do or say. She braced her hands on the counter and took a deep breath. "I want to save the church."

Dad glanced up at her. "Do you now? You know some folks are so upset by the way Keith's come in and taken over, they don't even want to go up there anymore. It's not just about the church. Emotions are getting pretty heated. Even if we keep the building, it's going to take a lot of work to maintain peace between our little country church and that big, expensive preserve next door."

"Fine. I think it's worth saving."

Gran smiled her crooked smile that had become so very dear to Ella. "Why?"

Ella cocked her head. "Why is the church worth saving?" It seemed so obvious. "Because it's the church our family's been going to for a century. Because it's an important part of the history of Wise. Because all of you got married there. Will's getting married there. Shoot, I'd like to get married there. How can you even ask that question?"

Gran nodded. "God?"

"Well, of course we serve God—it's the purpose of the church."

The rest of the family watched Ella and her grandmother as though they were speaking some foreign language. Ella knew she sometimes understood Gran better than they did, but anyone could see what she was saying now—suggesting that the church had outlived its usefulness. She'd rarely been angry at Gran, but at the moment she felt the need to direct anger somewhere.

She took another deep breath and tried not to glare at her grandmother, who might still be recovering from a stroke but who struck Ella as being just as opinionated and sassy as ever. Gran shook her head once and opened her hands as if releasing a balloon into the sky.

Ella opened her mouth to continue her argument when Mom jumped in.

"Enough of this talk." She set a platter of leftover Christmas ham in the middle of the table. "The sale is far from certain, and we aren't going to change anything by talking about it now. Let's have a nice meal and see what happens."

Dad scooted his chair in and nodded at Ella to take her seat. She did, but found that her appetite had disappeared.

❧

Perla dug into the ham, mashed potatoes, and green beans. She still struggled with her right hand, yet if she moved slowly and focused, she could feed herself well enough. While she hated this crippled feeling, she honestly didn't miss cooking. It had been such a mixed blessing to her over the years. She was glad to let someone else take over, if only for the time being. If she really wanted to, she felt certain she could learn her way around the kitchen again—given time.

She smiled to herself. The conversation had more or less died once Margaret decreed an end to the talk about the sale of the church. She tended to think this dose of reality and controversy was exactly what the members of Laurel Mountain Church needed. They'd been slumbering for far too long. And Ella had, perhaps, never been truly awake. She only wanted to fight for the church because it was familiar—known. What she needed was to get to know God a whole lot better, then He'd be her rock instead of some rickety old building with gaps in the windows.

"What does Richard have to say about all this?"

Perla sensed Margaret's silent disapproval of Ella's question.

"I know you said no more talk, Mom, but I'm curious."

Henry's fork clicked against his plate. "I'd say he'll be satisfied to go along with the majority. He hasn't been here long enough to be invested in the property, and it would probably be a good thing for him to lead the church into a new building and a new life."

"Is anyone else in favor of keeping the church?" Ella asked.

Margaret sighed even as Henry spoke again. "Mavis Sanders

and a few of her friends seem pretty keen on it. I thought she might whack Steve over the head with her cane this morning."

Perla could hear the amusement in her son's voice.

"And Keith definitely wants to buy—"

"Enough." Margaret slapped her napkin onto the table, cutting Ella off. "Perla, would you like some dessert?"

"Yes, p-p-please."

This time the sigh came from Ella's end of the table. "I think I'll pass, Mom. I'm going to run over and talk to Will. I, uh, need to ask him about the wedding."

Perla smiled to herself again. Her granddaughter was beginning to come alive and that was a very good thing.

⚜

Ella knew her brother had been at church and would likely know more than her parents did about this ridiculous plan to sell their very history off to the highest bidder. Gran's comments popped into her mind, but she banished them. Of course the church was worth saving, and it was silly to even suggest it wasn't fulfilling its purpose. What else was a church for?

Bursting through Will's front door, Ella didn't consider the possibility that he might not be alone. The house was small—she could see the dining area beyond the living room—and there sat Will deep in conversation with Seth and Keith. She could see their vehicles parked out back of the house now that she was inside.

"Oh." She skidded to a stop. "I didn't know you had company."

Will waved her in. "No problem. We were just discussing land-management practices. Don't tell Gran we were doing business on a Sunday."

Ella's frustration shot up. This wasn't how she wanted to confront the issue of saving the church, but now that she saw

Keith, the anger she'd pushed down earlier returned full force. "You mean the kind of land management that practically rips people's land away from them?"

Keith stood and stuck his hands in his pockets, looking like a little boy who'd been caught playing in the mud in his Sunday clothes. "Guess you heard the church is looking to sell. I want you to know I didn't ask for the land—they came to me. I'll give them a fair price. More than fair. I've kind of grown . . . fond of your little congregation." He rocked back on his heels. "I might even be in a position to help with the founding of a new church. Seems to me like something worth investing in."

Ella felt like she'd swallowed her tongue. They talked like it was all a done deal. Her eyes darted to Seth, who watched her intently. "What about you? Are you in favor of this?" She didn't know why she asked Seth. He was less invested in Laurel Mountain than any of them.

Seth looked down as he smoothed his hands over the table in front of him. "I don't really have a dog in this fight." He looked back up and seemed to consider her. "Unless . . ."

"Unless what?" Ella demanded.

"No, I guess there's no unless. I'm just here to look out for the land and the wildlife."

Ella felt tears pool and fought them back. No one was on her side. No one cared like she did. Maybe not even Dad or Gran. Certainly not Seth who she'd thought really liked her. The church was nothing more than wood and glass to them. And maybe she didn't much matter to them, either. Apparently fretting over what everyone else thought didn't mean they'd do the same for her.

Keith lifted a hand as if to reach out to her. Ella sniffed and turned back toward the door. "Well then, I guess we don't have anything to discuss after all. You boys have a nice afternoon."

She slammed the door on her way out.

⚜

Perla heard someone sling the door open so that it cracked against the wall. She flinched and looked to Sadie on the far side of the quilt frame. They'd been sewing since coming home from dinner, and Perla had been trying to figure out how to take a break without making Sadie think she was still frail. Never mind that she was; if she tried hard enough to hide the truth she might fool the others. She might even fool herself.

"Mother, why don't you go lie down? I have a feeling that might be Ella expressing her frustration over the church property."

Perla nodded and gave her best imitation of a bright smile, but rather than lie down, she simply moved to her favorite armchair and let her head rest against its high back. She wanted to hear what Ella had to say. Sadie clucked at her but didn't say anything more.

"No one cares that some big, fancy corporation is coming in and changing things. Or if they do care, they're not doing anything about it. And some people"—Ella's brow lowered as she crossed her arms—"are consorting with the enemy."

Sadie clucked again, and Perla was glad it was directed at someone else for a change. "You're getting awfully worked up about something you can't change."

"Can't I?" Ella's chin went up, her eyes flashing fire. "Maybe I'll have to see about taking legal action."

Perla felt her eyebrows go up, one not as high as the other. This was a new twist.

"I feel confident a big, fancy corporation as you call it has been very careful to follow the letter of the law," Sadie said. "And at any rate, it's not likely you'd find a lawyer in Wise who'd even look at the situation."

Ella paced, then turned and planted her hands on her hips.

"It just so happens I know a lawyer back in Craggy Mount. He worked for a chief judge of the Virginia Court of Appeals. I'd say he might have some connections. He'd know what strings to pull."

Perla thought Ella looked a bit pale as she dropped into a chair at the quilt frame and fiddled with a pair of scissors.

"Are you talking about Mark? Your old boyfriend? I thought you wanted to be rid of him."

Ella blew out a breath. "I'm not talking about dating him. I'm talking about getting some legal advice. I need to return that bracelet anyway."

Sadie snorted. "Seems to me a piece of jewelry would be the lesser of those two evils."

Ella shot her aunt an annoyed look. "I haven't said I'd definitely call him. I'm just thinking through my options."

She looked at Gran as though asking for her opinion. And oh, did Perla have an opinion. No building, no bit of property was worth playing with fire. She focused, trying to think how she could get a few words out to get her meaning across. Then Ella looked away and shook her head.

"Gran, you look worn out. Maybe you'd better lie down."

Perla wanted to roll her eyes, but instead she nodded and let Ella help her up so she could make her way to her room. She gave Ella an it'll-be-all-right look that she would surely understand and eased her bedroom door shut behind her. Sadie was already turning away and gesturing for Ella to move back into the kitchen, probably to sit at the table. That's where so many of life's problems were hashed out.

Perla leaned against her door, summoning the strength to remove her shoes and lie down. She slid into a wooden chair next to the door and bent forward to ease off her left shoe—it was always easier to do. As she straightened, she realized she could still hear the voices of her daughter and granddaughter and paused to see if she could make out what it was they were saying.

"The church is the least of our problems." Sadie sounded angry. Perla furrowed her brow. What did she mean by that?

"I hardly think it's the *least*," Ella said. "That church is part of your past, too."

"Yes, but I'm far more concerned about my future. My mother—your grandmother—is not getting any better. It's been months and she can still barely complete a sentence, much less a thought." Perla heard a pause and a heavy exhalation. "I simply cannot take the spring semester off. It would be the end of my career. There's no way around it, Mother will have to go to a rehabilitation center."

"You can't." Now Ella sounded upset, and Perla was right there with her. "I'll take care of Gran. I can stay as long as I need to and I'm really good with her. Mom and Dad will help too, I'm sure of it."

"It's already been decided. Your father and I will take her tomorrow."

Perla heard Ella begin to speak, but Sadie plowed ahead in what was probably meant to be a whisper but rose along with her emotion. "The doctors said most of the recovery would come in the first few months. After that it's an uphill battle. It's been four months and her language ability hasn't improved since those initial gains. I'm beginning to doubt she'll ever recover sufficiently to carry on a normal conversation. This is for her own good, and if she does work hard she can certainly come home again. That should provide incentive for her."

"But she'll hate it." Ella sounded defeated.

"I'm not pleased with the situation, but I've learned you don't always get what you want in this life. Mother's ability to communicate is severely compromised, and Henry and I believe this is her best hope."

Ella spoke again, but Perla didn't listen anymore. She pressed her hands to her ears and stumbled to her bed to fall into it, right shoe still on her foot. They didn't think she'd get better. The fear she'd been fighting reared up and overwhelmed her. It was hopeless. She'd known it all along, but now she had confirmation. She would never be able to tell her story.

20

E LLA SAT ALONE AT THE QUILT FRAME at her grandmother's house, trying not to worry. Mom was supposed to be over soon to help. Ella threaded several needles, prepping for her mother to begin as soon as she arrived. But no amount of busy-work could distract her from one simple fact: Gran was going downhill.

Sighing, Ella resumed her work. She'd been so sure Gran was getting better before they moved her to the nursing home. And no matter what they called it, that's what it was. Now it seemed Sadie's prophecy would be fulfilled. Gran wasn't getting better. She spent more and more time in bed and attempted to speak less and less. Ella had tried to understand what Gran was feeling, but it was as though she'd pulled a curtain inside her mind. And Ella was afraid she couldn't push it aside anymore.

Ella looked at the old-fashioned phone where it sat, receiver in the cradle, on an end table. She lifted the receiver, spun Aunt Sadie's number on the dial, and waited. Her aunt answered on the third ring.

"Hello?"

"Hey Aunt Sadie, thought you might like an update on Gran. I'm kind of worried about her."

Sadie exhaled long and slow. "She's just being obstinate. Mother has a stubborn streak as wide as the Blue Ridge Mountains. Now, perhaps you would be interested in hearing how the search for my father is going."

Ella tried not to roll her eyes, but since there was no one to see, she went ahead and did so. After several minutes of listening to Sadie, she cleared her throat.

"Why don't you just ask Gran? She tried to tell you once; she'd probably be glad to give you information about your father."

Sadie huffed. "I'll not go begging for the truth now. And I'm not sure she could tell me even if she wanted to. It's entirely possible her mind is slipping along with her voice and dexterity."

Ella cringed. She didn't think so, yet she couldn't explain Gran's deterioration beyond her sadness at being away from home. Every time she saw her grandmother, Ella reminded her that she could go home as soon as she achieved certain milestones. Speaking a complete sentence, walking across the room unaided—things like that. But Gran just turned away.

Ella finally got off the phone with Sadie as her mother breezed through the kitchen door. She kissed Ella on the crown of her head and settled in a chair opposite her.

"Who was that?"

"Just updating Aunt Sadie about Gran."

Mom nodded, plucked a threaded needle from the pincushion, and set to work. While Ella continued to fashion her fanciest stitches, hoping Gran would approve when she came home and saw the work, Mom's technique was purely practical.

"Do you think we'll have this done in time for the wedding?" Mom reached behind the glasses perched on her nose to rub her eyes.

"I think so." Ella turned toward the window, letting her gaze lose focus. "It's going to be a lovely wedding. Not too big, not too fancy. Laura's making her own bouquet, assuming the lilacs bloom on time, and we picked out bridesmaids dresses last week. They're actually pretty, kind of a peach color. And Laura's dress is just gorgeous." She sighed, wondering if she'd ever get to wear a wedding dress.

Mom didn't comment, just gave her a sympathetic look that made Ella feel, for once, that maybe someone understood her.

The following Tuesday, Ella sat staring out the kitchen window, a wild array of tweeds and wools scattered around her. Sylvia had challenged her to create a rustic art quilt inspired by the traditional log cabin patch, but she kept getting lost in the bleak February landscape outside. The sky raced with clouds, alternately sunny and overcast, creating a mad pattern of light and dark across the fields and forest. If only she could capture that, as it so perfectly described how she felt these days.

It was a relief when the phone rang, distracting her from gloomy thoughts.

"I have a clue," Sadie crowed without preamble. "I hauled several boxes of papers from Henry's attic home with me and I finally found something. It's a letter Mother wrote to her own mother during the summer of 1948—around the time I must have been conceived."

Ella idly sifted through her fabrics, trying to work up interest. Why couldn't Sadie ask about Gran before launching into her news? "What does it say?" She'd try not to rain on Aunt Sadie's parade.

"It would seem Mother spent the spring and much of the summer helping an aunt and uncle on her father's side. Chuck and Imogene had a farm over at Brook Hill. Chuck broke his leg, and it sounds like poor Imogene was susceptible to migraines. Of course, they probably didn't have any notion about something like that back then. Poor woman."

Ella felt a spark of sympathy. Then she wondered why her grandmother had never mentioned Chuck and Imogene. It sounded like quite the adventure, helping family members run a farm for a summer. "I don't think Gran's ever mentioned them."

"Exactly. Which makes me think that's where it happened."

Ella felt uneasy. Like she was reading someone else's diary or poking around in their medicine cabinet. Maybe there was a reason Gran never talked about that summer. She stood and paced. "How about I ask Gran when I visit tomorrow. Maybe it'll give her a spark to talk about old times."

"No. I plan to track down this aunt and uncle and find out what they know about that summer and whether or not Mother had a beau." Ella heard a quiver in her aunt's voice. "This is the first solid lead I've had. Let's not trouble Mother with it until I know more. I'm pretty sure Imogene was my grandfather's sister, which makes her maiden name Long. I should be able to track her down with that."

Ella sighed. "Okay. How can I help?"

"Poke around in Mother's things—see if you can find any other correspondence with Imogene."

Ella made some noncommittal noises and finally hung up. She had no intention of digging around in Gran's personal papers. She stared at the phone. Sadie never did ask how Gran was doing.

⁂

Two days later, Ella picked up her buzzing cell where it lay on the crazy quilt while she worked. It was Aunt Sadie, who sounded breathless.

"I think I've found Imogene."

Ella looked up from the quilt, feeling as though she were waking from a deep sleep. She sometimes got like that when she was absorbed in her work. She realized the room had dimmed, the sun nearly gone. It was time for supper and she hadn't done a thing about it.

"Great, but you probably want to hear how Gran's doing before you tell me your news." Ella was a little surprised at her own boldness.

"Oh. Well. Certainly. How is she?"

Ella stood and stretched her back. "I think her dexterity is improving, but her speech continues to give her trouble. It's like she's given up on some level. It worries me."

"If she's given up, that's proof the main problem is a lack of will on her part. Honestly, I think it's stubbornness more than anything."

"Maybe," said Ella. "But I still think coming home would encourage her. We can have therapists come in and I'll work with her every day. Seems like it's worth a shot."

There was silence on the other end of the line, and Ella thought maybe Aunt Sadie was really considering her suggestion. Then she realized she could hear Sadie pecking at her keyboard.

"Mother's better off where she is. Now let me tell you what I've found." More tapping. "Yes, this is almost certainly a census record for my father's family including my great-aunt. The names are right, the location is right, and the ages are right. Now all I have to do is find the surname of the man she married. But first let's see how old she'd be now."

There was another pause and Ella was tempted to hang up. She could pretend she'd lost her cell signal.

"Right. She would have been thirty-four years old in the summer of 1948. So if she's still alive, that would make her . . . ninety-four now." Sadie paused. "It's entirely possible that she's still alive. The women in this family seem to live to a ripe old age."

Ella opened the fridge and pulled out a container of her

mom's chili to warm up for dinner. Maybe she'd even make fresh corn bread to go with it and bring some to Gran. Surely she could tempt her poor appetite with corn bread and butter.

"It's also entirely possible that she's dead," Ella said, grabbing buttermilk and an egg.

"Either way, I intend to find out. Even if she's gone, she might have left behind letters or papers or something to point us in the right direction."

Ella didn't state the obvious, but instead oiled a cast-iron skillet and stuck it in the oven to heat. She'd add a dab of sugar to the corn bread, the way Gran liked it.

"I'm in the middle of making supper. Thought I'd make some corn bread and take it to Gran this evening."

"I'm sure she'll enjoy that. I'm going to see what more I can find online. I'll need to research more of Imogene's life, find out Chuck's full name, if they had children, if they ever moved—that sort of thing."

"What if you can't find any more?" Ella measured her dry ingredients while trying to juggle her cell. Really, would it be wrong to just hang up?

"We'll cross that bridge if we come to it. I'll let you go now."

Ella said goodbye thinking that asking Gran would be the easiest route to take, but then she'd been stubborn herself on more than one occasion. She guessed it was Aunt Sadie's turn now.

Perla knew she was sulking, but couldn't bring herself to stop. She supposed Hillside Acres was nice as such places went, and the people were kind, but she was too horrified at being there to be appreciative. There were so many . . . old people. And most of them were in much worse shape than she was. Perla kept to her room and her thoughts, preferring to revisit old memories rather than face up to the physical challenges of the present. If it weren't for Ella, she might give up completely.

The aroma of fresh corn bread teased Perla as soon as Ella walked through the door. And the sight of it with fresh butter melting into the nooks and crannies, well, it almost convinced her to take a deep breath and resume the fight. She broke off a piece of the bread and popped it in her mouth the second Ella placed it on the despicable little table that extended over her bed. She wouldn't eat the whole thing. She didn't want to get Ella's hopes up by eating well. After all, she was determined to suffer.

She reached for another bite, remembering how Imogene always made the best corn bread. At least she did when she was feeling well. Perla placed the warm buttery piece in her mouth and thought about the day Uncle Chuck got his cast off. He was tender-footing around the house and yard, eager to get back to work, but hesitant with his leg still unsteady.

"Lordy if I don't feel like a newborn colt," he said, rubbing his thigh. "Reckon it'll come right?"

Perla wasn't sure who he was asking, but since Imogene just sat with her hand over her eyes, she opted to answer, "Doctor says it will. Don't suppose he'd tell you a story, would he?"

"Reckon not. Doc Albright has always done right by us." He cast a worried look at his wife. "Although I shore do wish he could do something for Imogene's sick headaches."

Imogene shook her head and waved her husband off. "It's not too bad today. Might be that powder he give me is helping."

Perla looked at her aunt more closely, noticed the way her eyes pinched and her neck strained. Maybe she wasn't just making a to-do. Maybe she did have troubles greater than any of them knew. Perla's hand fell against her abdomen as though of its own will. Secrets. They all carried secrets. She glanced at Sonny where he leaned against the porch post. He was a married man, and she supposed no one else around these parts knew it except them. She kind of wished she didn't know herself. Might be nice to drift along in a fool's paradise imagining they might have a future together.

Imogene roused herself. "Perla, guess you'll be able to head on home soon. You too, Sonny. If I know that husband of mine, he won't take but a day or two to get back to his old self."

Perla stiffened. She hadn't thought about having to go home. If what she suspected was true, she wouldn't be welcome there. Her father . . . well, it didn't bear thinking about.

Sonny, on the other hand, brightened at the mention of going home. "Well now, I don't want to leave you'uns shorthanded. Although it seems to me I might have some business to attend to back home."

Perla glanced at him, and the look he gave her was so tender she thought she might burst into tears. She knew his business back home and it broke her heart. Which was her own fault. She never should have let her heart get involved.

"Guess I'd better make some supper to go with that corn bread you baked," Perla said. She stood and moved toward the door.

Sonny caught her hand as she passed him. "Arthur." He spoke so softly she didn't think the other two could hear. "My given name's Arthur."

She squeezed his hand and fled to the kitchen before she made a bigger fool of herself than she already had.

21

"I MOGENE BENNETT."

Although Aunt Sadie had come home to visit Gran, she was also using the time away from work to ramp up her research. She clapped her hands above the keyboard where she sat at the kitchen table and stared into the backlit screen. "Imogene Long married Chuck Bennett in 1932 and they lived in Swain's Gap until 1938 when they moved to Brook Hill. That's what was throwing me off."

Ella paused in her window washing, something she almost never bothered to do in her own home. But she knew Gran did it every few months and so here she was with crumpled newspapers dirtying her hands and vinegar burning her nose, hoping Gran might be home soon to appreciate it.

"Does she still live there?" Ella asked.

"That's the next step," Sadie said. "I'll follow the census records as far as they go and hope there's some other record if she moved." She tapped her mouth with an index finger. "I'm going to the library after I visit Mother. They should have access to West Virginia records that might not be online."

"I'll come with you and stay with Gran while you do your research. You can pick me up on the way back home."

"Excellent. I'm sure Mother will like that."

Ella tidied up her mess and grabbed her sewing bag with the quilt hanging she was working on for the hunting lodge. She was less excited about the job now that she feared the church might sell out to Keith. Still, she needed to honor her word. Keith couldn't help it if the members of Laurel Mountain were wanting to sell the church building.

She should probably stay and try to finish Will and Laura's quilt. The wedding was just over two months away and she was doing her best not to mind that she wasn't the one getting married. Of course, she had more important things to worry about. Between Gran's health and the threat to the church, romance was pretty low on her priority list at the moment.

At the nursing home, Sadie bustled around Gran's room— moving things, tidying books and magazines, and chattering on about work and the upcoming wedding. Ella felt certain that Gran would much prefer they just sit with her and maybe share a few bits of news that really mattered. Brimming over with nervous energy, Sadie finally excused herself, saying she had errands to run and would be back in an hour or so. Her leaving allowed a sense of peace to settle over the room.

Gran waved her good hand at an armchair, and Ella helped her from the bed into the chair. She knew Gran preferred to be up, but suspected she'd stayed in bed because she knew Sadie was coming. There was still a strong undercurrent between the two of them, which Ella had no idea how to ease.

Gran's chair was positioned to take advantage of the March sunlight that seemed to shine right through her pale skin, illuminating blue veins beneath. She exhaled deeply and placed a reverent hand on the quilt piece Ella had pulled out and draped across her lap while Aunt Sadie was flitting around. She'd used both fly and herringbone stitches and was now in the process of adding beads for embellishment. Ella could feel Gran's approval of the piece and it made the job more palatable.

A knock at the door startled Ella. She looked up to see Pastor Richard standing there. He visibly brightened when he saw her. "I'm so glad you're here," he said, then flushed. "I haven't made a pastoral call on Perla in a few weeks. Thought it was high time."

Ella smiled, feeling flattered by his pleasure, though she wasn't sure she should. "Come on in. You've picked a good day. Gran and I are doing some quilting."

Richard strode into the room, and Ella found herself considering him afresh. She'd been distracted by Seth for a while, but now that he seemed to not care about selling off the church property, she found him somehow less attractive. And watching Richard pull a chair over to sit beside Gran and talk to her reminded her of what she'd admired in the preacher when she first met him.

Richard took Gran's hand. "We've missed seeing you at church." He glanced at Ella with a smile. "And not only because your lovely granddaughter has been staying away, as well."

That earned Ella a stern look from Gran.

Richard continued, "I wanted to check on you and see if there's anything I can do to help, to get you back into church and involved in the community."

Gran's smile faded and she pulled her hand free, tucking it under the afghan Ella had spread over her legs. She gave a little shake of her head and angled her body away from Richard as though to look out the window. Richard turned to Ella, a confused expression creasing his face.

"Thank you so much for asking, Richard, but Gran's doing so much better already. She'll be out and about again before we know it." Ella pasted on a smile to make up for Gran's deepening frown. "Tell us what's been happening at church."

She meant the comment to be light, to steer the conversation away from Gran, but of course something really was happening at church. Richard plowed a hand through his hair and leaned back in the chair.

"I'm afraid this business of selling the property to Keith Randolph is putting a great deal of strain on the congregation."

Ella leaned in. No one in her family had mentioned anything lately, and she'd hoped the talk had died down. "How so?"

"Those who want to sell and those who want to stay aren't exactly getting along and I'm having a hard time mediating." He tilted his head like a small boy trying to figure out how to climb a tree. "It seems to me this ought to be a primarily practical decision. We ought to weigh the value of the property against the offer, consider the feasibility of building elsewhere, look at how the land will be managed and even preserved, consider how best we can serve God, and then come to a conclusion."

Ella was torn between incredulity and laughter. And she thought *she* was naïve.

"Look to the past." The words rang out clear and true from Gran. Ella looked at her, but Gran continued to stare out the window as if she weren't aware of the conversation.

"Right," Ella agreed. "You aren't taking into consideration the history of the church and the people who attend there. Most of us are descendants of the founders. It's more than a building and plot of land worth so many dollars." She shifted her sewing in her lap. "And then there's the fact that the hunting preserve is, well, fancy. Most folks in Wise are pretty plain, and the Laurel Mountain Hunting Preserve tends to make them feel alienated—maybe even inferior." She glanced at her work. "No matter how much Keith invests in including local crafts and artwork."

Richard nodded and crossed his legs like he was settling in for a long chat. "I can see that, but then I think about, say, the Israelites. They were pretty attached to their lives in Egypt even as slaves. God didn't give them much room for sentimentality when He uprooted them and sent them into the desert. But His ultimate plan was better than anything they could imagine."

Ella started to make a smart comment about how all the older Israelites died before reaching the Promised Land, leaving their children to benefit, but it sounded petty even inside her own head. Instead she smiled and said, "We're a long way from the Israelites."

"Sure, but all those stories—all that history—is there to influence us, to teach us how to live in relationship with God. There were plenty of others who had to give up earthly things. David had to live in caves while he was fleeing from Saul. When Ruth's husband died, she uprooted her life and moved to her mother-in-law's country." He was talking with his hands, his eyes lit as though he'd landed on a favorite topic. "When Jesus sent out the seventy-two to spread the gospel, He said, 'The harvest is plentiful, but the workers are few. Go! I am sending you out like lambs among wolves. Do not take a purse or bag or sandals.'"

Ella felt her frustration with Gran and now Richard knotting her stomach. "Yes, yes, and somewhere in the Gospels He says we shouldn't store up treasures on earth." She wished she could quote chapter and verse. "But that doesn't mean we should throw our treasures away, either."

Richard dropped his foot to the floor and leaned toward her. "Oh, but it does. That's exactly what it means. There isn't any treasure this side of heaven."

Ella wanted to stalk from the room. Richard was just being obstinate and refusing to see her point. But she glanced at Gran and saw a look of . . . pleasure. Was Gran enjoying their exchange? She gritted her teeth.

"You might have a point, but I still think we should be sensitive to how some members of the congregation feel about the church."

"Absolutely. And you know, I'm beginning to think it's my role, as pastor, to help them let go of their attachment to earthly things and focus more on the real work of the church." He sprang from his chair and took both of Ella's hands in his. "Thank you so much. I know now what I need to preach this coming Sunday. You've really helped me clarify a few things in my own mind." He squeezed her hands and released them. "Now I'm off to rewrite my sermon." He turned to Gran, gave a courtly bow, and grinned at Ella before dashing for the door.

He skidded to a stop and whirled around. "Hey, seems like your mother mentioned you have a birthday coming up," he said to Ella.

"Oh, well, yes. I guess we won't have a big celebration or anything." She darted a look at Gran. "Maybe some cake—cake is always good."

"How about I take you to dinner next Wednesday to cel-ebrate?"

"I, uh, sure. That'd be nice."

"Great," he said with a big grin. Then he was gone.

Ella stared at the door in stunned silence. What had she done? She turned back to Gran just in time to see a smirk before she shifted in her chair and looked out the window again. Well, if nothing else, she'd managed to entertain her grandmother.

"Think maybe you'll feel up to going to church this Sunday?" she asked.

Gran pressed her lips together and shrugged, then gave a nod. That, at least, was something.

Ella settled into her usual spot in the third pew next to Gran. They had to bring her in a wheelchair and fashion a ramp at the second entrance, but here she was and that was a triumph in Ella's mind. She looked around noticing that while church attendance still hadn't picked up, Keith and Seth were both here. And Keith had a young woman with him. A pretty woman who looked almost elfin with her short dark hair, green eyes, and pale skin with the most adorable sprinkling of freckles across her pert little nose.

Seth seemed to take notice of the new attendee, as well. Ella tried to steer her attention back to the sermon rather than stewing over a new face attracting a great deal of attention.

After church, Richard got caught up in conversation with Keith and the young woman. Ella determined not to butt in no matter how curious she was, but Richard motioned her over.

"Ella," he said, "come meet Keith's daughter, Tara."

Ella plastered a smile on her face as she shook hands with Tara. Up close, she was even more appealing. Ella caught herself before she reached up to touch her own nose, which she'd always thought turned up too much on the end. Tara smiled and glanced up through long, luscious eyelashes that probably didn't even need mascara. As a matter of fact, Ella suspected the other woman wasn't wearing any makeup at all.

"Nice to meet you," Tara said, her voice as delicate as she was.

"Oh, and you too." Ella's voice sounded too loud against Tara's softness. "Isn't Richard a great pastor?" she said, laying a hand on his arm in a way that felt awkward to her and probably looked awkward to everyone else.

"He's wonderful," breathed Tara. "His sermon was practically poetry. I've been asking him about the imagery he used."

Ella had found the imagery of earthly treasures heavy-handed and obvious. She'd also found the sermon annoying in the way it kept harping on eternity and the ephemeral nature of this world. Richard had actually used that word. *Ephemeral.* Who talked like that?

Richard looked to be blushing. Ella squinted at him, and he flushed deeper with an unconvincing laugh. "I'll see you on

Wednesday," he said. Tara smiled and nodded before heading out the door.

Then it clicked in Ella's brain. Wednesday was when they were going to dinner.

"Wednesday? We have plans for Wednesday, don't we?"

Richard smacked himself in the forehead. "I've been planning to start a Bible study on Wednesday evenings ever since I got here, and when Tara asked if there was anything going on that she could participate in, I figured it would be the perfect time." He smiled like a cat inviting her to leave the birdcage open. "Of course I'm counting on you being there, too. We could go to dinner on Friday."

Ella didn't realize Dad was at her elbow until he spoke. "Richard, why don't you come celebrate Ella's birthday with the whole family on Friday. Will's bringing Laura and I'll be bringing Mom home for the evening—it'll be a regular party."

"Perfect." Richard smiled. "I'll bring flowers."

Ella ramped her own smile back up—she could feel it slipping. "Yep. Sure. That sounds good."

And the next thing Ella knew, she didn't have a date, but she did have a birthday party. Not only were Richard and Laura coming, but Aunt Sadie invited Keith and Tara while Will asked Seth. Funny—no one asked how she wanted to celebrate her birthday.

Ella stewed all the way home over the church property, Richard's fickle nature, and the way everyone assumed she'd go along with what they wanted. So what if she usually did. It didn't make them any less inconsiderate. Back at the house, she headed for her room and grabbed her laptop. Quickly, before she could change her mind, she rattled off a quick email and hit send. As soon as it was gone, she felt something hard form in her gut.

She told herself she was just being wise. And Mark would know if there was anything she could do to legally stop the sale of the church property. It wasn't like she was suggesting they get back together—this was purely business. Mark hadn't been in touch with her since she sent his bracelet back to him. It was March now. Obviously he'd moved on.

Closing her laptop, Ella stretched her neck. Mark probably wouldn't even respond. He wasn't the sort of person to do favors unless he could get something out of it. Yup. Sending him an email was nothing more than an outlet for her frustration. No harm done.

E LLA AND AUNT SADIE went to Bible study, although Ella
wondered if her time wouldn't be better spent sitting with
Gran. Especially once they entered the church and found that
they were the only ones there other than Tara and Mavis Sanders. Mavis greeted them by suggesting that she was getting too
old to play the piano and someone else had better learn to play
if they wanted music.

"I play," said Tara.

Of course she does, thought Ella. Probably sings like an
angel, too.

Mavis eyed the dark-haired beauty. "I don't know you."

"I'm Keith Randolph's daughter. I'm studying creative writing at Wesleyan over in Buckhannon, but I'd be happy to play
whenever I'm in town."

"Humph. I can't see as that would be necessary." Mavis
thumped her cane and turned her attention to Sadie.

As Richard was about to open the study with prayer, a door
swung open followed by Seth's entrance into the room. He
glanced around with what Ella would call a wild look.

"Where's Will? He talked me into coming. Said there'd be
a crowd."

Richard gestured toward a chair. "We haven't seen Will, but maybe he'll join us. We were about to open in prayer."

"But I wasn't . . . I didn't mean . . . ah, whatever." Seth slumped into a chair and looked at Ella as if his being there were her fault.

She felt her eyes go wide in defense, then squeezed them shut as Richard prayed. This was already one of the strangest Bible studies she'd ever attended.

Richard said they would be covering the first two chapters of the book of Acts. Ella followed along, discussing how Jesus was with the disciples for forty days before being taken up into heaven, and how Matthias was chosen to replace Judas.

"Is there anything in this first chapter that jumps out for any of you?" Richard looked around the small group. They looked back at him blankly.

Finally, Seth ran a hand through his hair. "Seems like the big deal here is that mention Jesus made of baptism with the Holy Spirit."

Ella scanned her Bible. There it was: *"Do not leave Jerusalem, but wait for the gift my Father promised, which you have heard me speak about. For John baptized with water, but in a few days you will be baptized with the Holy Spirit."*

"That's the part that speaks to me, as well," Richard said with approval. "Let's follow it on into chapter two." He stood and held his Bible up. "'When the day of Pentecost came, they were all together in one place. Suddenly a sound like the blowing of a violent wind came from heaven and filled the whole house where they were sitting. They saw what seemed to be tongues of fire that separated and came to rest on each of them. All of them were filled with the Holy Spirit and began to speak in other tongues as the Spirit enabled them.'"

Tara shivered and clasped her hands. "So dramatic. I can see it so clearly—the wind whipping their clothes, flames dancing in the air—and just like that they could speak other languages."

Seth snorted. "Wish I'd had a little of that when I took Spanish in high school." He flushed and looked at the others. "Not to be disrespectful."

Richard laughed. "Not at all. It truly is wonderful to contemplate. But of all the gifts the Holy Spirit could bring, why do you suppose it was speaking other languages?"

"Communication," Sadie said. "Words and language are the lifeblood of communication. The disciples needed the ability to share the gospel far and wide. A most apt gift at the time."

Richard nodded. "And what about now? What's an apt gift for this time? I haven't met anyone who could suddenly speak another language, but I have met Spirit-filled people with a variety of gifts. How does the Spirit work today?"

Answers varied from preaching and teaching to acts of service and kindness. Ella offered a few comments, but mostly she was thinking about how often she understood Gran—and other people too—without needing words. Her English teacher back in high school said she had a gift for communication, for understanding. And yet she didn't understand her own life, her own purpose.

Ella realized Richard had moved on with the rest of chapter two. She tuned in just in time to hear, "'Repent and be baptized, every one of you, in the name of Jesus Christ for the forgiveness of your sins. And you will receive the gift of the Holy Spirit. The promise is for you and your children and for all who are far off—for all whom the Lord our God will call.'"

Ella left that evening no longer sorry Richard had stood her up for a Bible study. Instead she thought about God's gifts and His promises and how they were for her just as much as anyone else.

❦

Ella woke on the morning of her twenty-ninth birthday with the sinking feeling that her old dream of living the artist's life on the family farm somehow wasn't good enough anymore. Thirty was right around the corner and here she was using her grandmother's illness as a convenient excuse to hide out from an old boyfriend. She wandered downstairs where the smell of bacon suggested there might be consolation in breakfast if nothing else.

"Happy birthday," her mother crowed. "Are you hungry?"

"Absolutely." Ella smiled in spite of herself. "You know bacon always lures me to the table." She sat as her mother put a plate in front of her loaded with bacon, fried eggs, hash browns, and a biscuit. Ella hoped calories didn't count on your birthday.

"Any plans for today other than this evening's get-together?" Dad asked.

"I kind of wanted to hang out with you guys," Ella said. "What do you have planned?"

"I need to get out and check on that cow of Will's that's about ready to calve. I was going to wait for Will, but you'll do in a pinch." He winked.

"That's just the sort of thing I'd like to do on my birthday," Ella said, swiping up the last of her egg yolk with a bite of biscuit.

Ella grabbed one of her brother's castoff flannel shirts to wear over her turtleneck. She pulled on thick socks and found a pair of her mother's old rubber boots—it could be mucky out in the pasture now that the snow had mostly melted. By midmorning she was ready and headed to the barn, where Dad was tending to a few chores before they walked the fields.

Ella stepped into the dim interior of the barn. She'd spent many a happy hour here, especially on rainy afternoons when the metal roof offered a music all its own. Dad rounded the corner.

"Ready to go, Elly Belly?" he asked, using a pet name she hadn't heard in years. She laughed and patted her full belly, thinking it fit on this particular morning.

They headed for the Rexroad Place, named after a family who had owned the property a good hundred years earlier. Names tended to stick in the mountains. The morning was fresh and clear. Ella filled her lungs and felt a sense of satisfaction. Maybe getting older wasn't so bad so long as she could do it like this—striding across the hills beside her father. *Maybe I need to marry a farmer*, Ella thought. Although she well knew farm life was more about hard work than fresh morning strolls across early spring pastures.

After about fifteen minutes they saw the first of the small herd of Hereford cattle. The bull was in another field with last year's steers. This time of year, the cows stayed in the "nursery"—a gentle pasture without too much brush. Several cows had already calved, and Ella laughed to see the youngsters kicking up their heels with the sheer joy of being alive.

Dad counted cattle. There were only a dozen or so, and he quickly noticed a heifer was missing. "It's her first pregnancy and she's close," he said. "As a matter of fact, she's the one I wanted to check on. Time to beat the bushes."

Ella knew what that meant. The two headed off in opposite directions, walking the edges of the pasture. They peered behind trees and poked through brambles. After about ten minutes, Ella thought she caught a glimpse of red hide behind a rock near a low spot in the field. She crept closer and saw the heifer lying down and apparently in distress. She hollered for her dad, who hurried over.

"Ah, there she is," he said. "And under way, I'd say. Come help me check her."

Dad quickly established that the delivery was moving along fine. They gave the cow some room and watched as the calf slid into the world.

"It's a bull. And a fine stout fellow," Dad said with the sort of pride you might expect him to feel at the birth of one of his own children. Ella had to confess she felt a certain pride and wonder, too. The mother lumbered to her feet and licked the little guy who seemed determined to stand. He finally got upright and stumbled toward his mother to push at her teats.

"How in the world does he know to do that so soon?" Ella wondered. "You'd think it would take him a minute to figure things out."

"Instinct." Dad smiled. "He's gonna be just fine and so is his mother."

Ella watched a moment longer. "Would you call that a miracle?"

Dad looked thoughtful. "Well, sure. I think that's a good name for it. Even if you know the science behind conception and birth, when it comes right down to it, the whole thing is pure miracle." He put his arm around her shoulders. "Just like you're my miracle. The day you were born . . ." He swiped at his eyes and cleared his throat. "At one point in my life I didn't think I'd ever be a father—didn't think I wanted to—and then your mother came along and it turns out a family is exactly what I needed."

"Why didn't you want children?"

Dad squeezed her tighter. "Thought it would hurt too much. What if something happened to one of you? When your grandpa died I gave up caring about people for a while. It took your mother and your aunt Mayfair to teach me how to love again." He kissed her temple. "A lesson well worth learning."

That afternoon, Ella went with her dad to bring Gran to the house for the party. Gran grumbled, but Ella chose to see her monosyllabic complaints as a positive sign. At least she was speaking. They helped Gran into the farmhouse, which was a flurry of activity with Laura helping Mom in the kitchen and Will blowing up blue-and-white balloons in the family room.

"I didn't get balloons for my birthday," he grumped. Then he elbowed her.

Ella gave her brother a playful shove back and took a balloon the color of an October sky and tied it to her wrist. This might be fun after all. She walked into the kitchen, balloon bobbing along with her. Her mother sent her a distracted smile.

"I don't know where we're going to put everyone. We may just have to take plates and eat on our laps."

"I don't think anyone will mind." Ella eyed the crisp fried chicken her mother loaded on a platter. "I'd be content to eat your chicken sitting on the floor."

Mom smiled, paused, and gave Ella a quick hug. "I'm so glad you're here for your birthday. We've spent too many of them apart over the years."

Ella swallowed an unexpected lump in her throat. "I know."

Sounds of more guests arriving drew her back into the family room. She realized she was still wearing Will's ratty old shirt and struggled to take it off, but got tangled with her balloon.

"Let me help."

Ella knew instantly that it was Seth by the way a shiver shot up her spine. She froze at his touch, then gave herself permission to enjoy the feel of his fingers tickling her wrist as he unfastened the balloon and helped her shrug out of the worn shirt. He reached up to resettle her turtleneck where the fold of the collar had flipped up. Their eyes met, and for just a moment Ella thought he might give her a celebratory kiss. Instead, his lips curved and he said, "Happy birthday."

Ella smiled and reclaimed her balloon. Why did she feel like he'd said so much more?

"There's the birthday girl," Richard said, tugging her attention away from Seth.

Without even pausing to remove his coat, he swept Ella into

a hug and presented her with a bouquet of pink-and-white carnations. "They looked feminine," he said.

"And so they do." Ella had never been fond of carnations, but it was the thought that counted. "Thank you so much."

"Did you enjoy Bible study the other night?" He moved closer, forcing Seth to take a step back. "Reading about Pentecost always gives me a thrill. The idea of the Holy Spirit descending in such a tangible way—wonderful."

Ella opened her mouth, but Seth spoke before she could.

"Do you believe in miracles?" he asked Richard.

Ella's eyebrows jumped and she looked toward Richard.

"Of course I do."

Seth stuffed his hands in his pockets and rocked back on his heels. "Like the disciples suddenly speaking in different languages?"

"Well, sure, the Bible tells us it happened." Richard looked smug. Ella didn't think it was a good look for him.

"Has anything like that ever happened to you?" Seth's expression was open and clear, like he was asking if Richard preferred vanilla or chocolate ice cream.

Richard crossed his arms. "Perhaps not on that scale," he said with a tight smile. "It was a very special time in the life of the church. I guess you could say God was kick-starting the process."

"So you're saying that couldn't happen to us."

"I'd say it's improbable."

"Sounds like your faith might not be all it could be."

Richard's gray eyes turned steely. He moved his jaw from side to side and then seemed to make a decision. "Ella, have you had a good birthday thus far?"

Ella started. She thought they'd forgotten about her. She kind of wanted the discussion to continue, to hear what Richard thought about his own faith, but she also sensed the situation was getting unfriendly. She smiled and opened her mouth to play along with the change in conversation when the door opened again.

"Looks like the rest of the crowd is arriving." Richard nodded toward Keith and Tara, who were entering with a dusting of snow on their shoulders.

Ella glanced out the window. It was indeed snowing, which wasn't unheard of in March in the mountains. She knew she should go greet the new arrivals, but she felt drawn to the soft flakes falling beyond the crystal panes of glass. Another car pulled up to the house, causing Ella to glance over her shoulder. Who were they missing?

She turned back in time to see someone lifting an elaborate bouquet of peach-and-pink flowers out of the passenger seat of a shiny new SUV. Ella froze. How did Mark end up here?

She whirled toward the door and watched him enter. Snowflakes glistened in his dark curls. Mom hurried to the door and took his coat. She darted a look at Ella, her smile too bright.

"We're so glad you were able to make it, Mark. What a lovely surprise for Ella's birthday."

His eyes flickered and he looked at Ella. He stepped closer and presented her with the bouquet that was, honestly, breathtaking. She could identify two kinds of roses, wax white, eucalyptus, and Hypericum. There were several other blooms she didn't know offhand, though she felt certain they were out of season and expensive.

He smirked. "Surprised?"

"I . . . yes, I am. When you didn't reply to my email, I thought—"

"I called intending to speak to you, but got your mother. She mentioned this little—" he looked around at the group and the simple food Mom was setting out—"party, so I thought I'd come give you my counsel in person." He smirked again. "She seemed pleased with the idea."

"I suppose she would be," Ella said.

"And what about you?" Mark reached over and tucked her hair behind her ear. Ella tried not to jerk away.

"Mark, this is awkward," she hissed. "I thought when I returned the bracelet I made it clear—"

"Are you thinking this is some sort of pursuit? Don't flatter yourself. I'm just doing a favor for an old friend and her lovely family."

Mark drifted away and struck up a conversation with Keith. Ella watched him, flowers still clutched in her arms. She saw Richard staring at the flowers and noticed that Seth had disappeared—probably with Will. Everyone else seemed oblivious to her discomfort.

Gran shuffled her walker up next to Ella. She worked her mouth and finally said, "Snow."

Ella blinked, then looked back out the window. It was snowing harder now, like God was laying down batting before beginning the final work on a quilt. Ella watched for a moment and sighed.

"It's lovely, Gran. So peaceful."

Her grandmother spoke then, like she'd never had a moment's trouble. "'Peace I leave with you; my peace I give you. I do not give to you as the world gives. Do not let your hearts be troubled and do not be afraid.'"

Ella glanced at Gran whose mouth was curved in a soft smile. Had she spoken? Ella looked back out the window as dusk swallowed the snow and transformed the glass into a mirror reflecting the group of people behind them.

"Yes," she whispered. "God's own peace sounds good."

23

ELLA LAY IN BED THAT NIGHT, wishing she'd never sent that email to Mark. It was all the opening he'd needed to get a foot back inside the door. Now Mom was singing his praises once again, and she was afraid Seth and Richard were thinking she was playing the field. And then there was his so-called legal advice.

Ella punched her pillow and replayed what he'd said. As guests were leaving, Mark cornered her in the bedroom where she was retrieving jackets.

"So you want to put a stop to this business of Keith's," he'd said.

Ella had noticed him deep in conversation with the developer. She felt a moment's hope that Mark really had come through for her. And she softened toward him just a smidge.

"I do."

"I doubt there's much you can do up front," Mark said. "He seems to have everything well in hand—he's experienced and professional."

Ella let her shoulders sag. She'd just been through a somewhat torturous birthday party and wasn't even going to get any good advice out of it.

"However . . ." Mark stepped closer, and Ella felt a zing up her spine—an unpleasant sort of feeling. She forced herself not to move away. "If someone were to be involved in an accident on the property—preferably a hunting accident—life could get very complicated for Mr. Randolph. If it happened before he's finished with construction and has all his insurances in place, all the better. A big enough lawsuit might convince Keith this project isn't worth pursuing."

Ella did step back this time, grabbing another coat to add to the two already in her arms. She held them like a shield. "An accident. That would be horrible. I'm glad you let me know there's nothing I can do *legally*."

Mark shrugged one shoulder, grabbed his own coat, and looked at Ella like she was his favorite dessert. "Think hard about what I've said. Accidents happen all the time, and not only at hunting clubs." He moved toward the door. "Family farms can be incredibly dangerous."

Ella stood, frozen to the spot. Will stuck his head through the doorway. "What's the holdup with the outerwear? We need to get going." He plucked his jacket from Ella's arms, gave her a confused look, then hurried back out. Ella tried to swallow past her dry tongue and followed him back into the whirl of departing guests.

⚜

The following week, Ella went to her parents' house to gather up some castoff clothing. She'd been meaning to do it for a while and somehow Mark's parting words made her want to check in. Not that she'd taken what he said seriously.

Since Aunt Sadie had gone back to Ohio and left her free rein of Gran's house, her creative juices were flowing again. She had an idea for a series of quilt pieces she would call Appalachian Blessings. She'd use scraps from clothing that had once belonged to family members and friends, people who were the most important blessings in her life. Ella knew Mom had a secret sentimental streak. She hoped that would extend to things like Dad's old flannel shirts and maybe a few things of her own.

When Ella asked about castoff clothing or other fabric, her mother pinked. "There might be a few things packed away in that cedar chest in my closet. No reason to save most of it, but there you have it."

Ella grinned. "I was counting on that."

She practically skipped into her parents' room and burrowed into the closet to drag out the chest. The smell was lovely— laundry soap, lavender, and cedar. It smelled like Mom. She flipped up the lid and dug into the treasure trove just as Dad wandered in.

"You've discovered your mother's secret. Has she sworn you to never tell?"

"No, I think she might be kind of glad I'm relieving her of having to do something with all this."

Ella felt for the bottom of the chest, thinking any childhood items would be buried down there. But instead of fabric, her fingers brushed something hard. She pulled out a metal box with a bit of rust on it. It was an old Whitman's candy tin with an Art Nouveau design.

"This is pretty." Ella tilted it toward her father.

"Well now, I haven't seen that in a long time." Dad stretched out his hand.

"Love letters?" Ella teased, but she doubted it. The box was too heavy for that and it clanked as she handed it over. Maybe it was old coins or an antique pocket watch. Ella itched to know.

Dad smiled. "Love letters of a sort."

He flipped up the lid and peered inside. His expression softened, and his eyes glistened. Whatever it was, Ella thought, Dad was getting emotional about it. He reached inside and lifted out . . . a rock.

Ella laughed. "A rock? Mom saved a rock?"

"No, I did." The rock he held was almost white, smooth, with a touch of sparkle. "Found this one in a creek on an icy morning after I'd been up to no good."

He handed the stone to Ella. It felt weighty, cool, and fit perfectly in the curve of her palm. Dad pulled out another stone, this one rough and squared off—probably quartz. "And I found this one the day my gun misfired and your aunt Mayfair . . ." He trailed off.

"Aunt Mayfair what?" Ella liked to hear stories about her aunt, who had gone to the South American mission field before Ella was born. She'd only met her once but loved her instantly, the way everyone seemed to.

"It wasn't long after your grandfather died when I was still pretty torn up about it and Mayfair was a real comfort to me. That's the year I got to know both her and your mother." Now his eyes twinkled. "And fell in love against my own better judgment."

He dumped the rest of the box out on the bed where he sat. There were maybe a dozen stones in all. Dad picked through them, rubbing each one as though conjuring the memories they sparked. Ella felt like he'd traveled miles and miles or maybe years and years in the moments he sat there looking at the scattering of rocks.

"But why did you save these?"

Dad cleared his throat. "As a reminder."

"A reminder of what?"

"Of God's love for me. Of my own father's love for me. Of the gift your mother's love brought into my life." His voice sounded raspy. He cleared his throat a second time. "And this one"—he held up a small round stone—"is the one I found the day you were born and brought a new love into my life." He patted the bed beside him. Ella went to him and leaned into his embrace.

"I'm so glad you found these. I've been feeling like something's missing and couldn't put my finger on it. Now I think I know what's been bothering me." He pillowed his cheek on the top of Ella's head and pressed a stone into her hand. "I'd forgotten how much God loves me and how all I have to do is love Him back. I hope you learn that lesson sooner and more thoroughly than your old hardheaded dad did."

⊱⚜⊰

"We're having a congregational meeting after church this Sunday." Mom fussed over a basket of food she wanted Ella to take to Gran.

"What for?"

"To vote on whether or not to accept Keith's offer to buy the church property."

"That isn't really going to happen, is it? Just because a few people who talk too loud think it's a good idea doesn't mean it is."

"I'm not sure it's such a terrible idea." Mom tucked a dish towel over the top of the basket.

"Mom, how can you say that?"

"The reality is that attendance has been down for a while now. Giving is down. The building is so much trouble to keep up. It might be worth looking into starting over somewhere else."

"What does Dad think?"

Dad appeared around the corner. "I think it would be nice to take some of the bits and pieces from the old church—the pulpit, the offering plates and communion things, maybe some of the furniture." He brightened. "We could even take the pews."

Ella felt betrayed. She'd just had such a lovely moment with her dad and now he'd turned traitor.

"Don't you care that it's our heritage?"

Dad tossed one of his stones up and caught it. "Guess I've realized our past can't be contained by the walls of a church. Maybe it's time to share our faith with more than the handful of folks who trek up Laurel Mountain each week."

Ella grabbed the basket her mother placed on the counter and stomped out the door. She knew she was being rude, but she wanted Mom and Dad to see how displeased she was. Three days. She had three days to save the church. This called for drastic measures.

⚜

Ella was both surprised and relieved to find that Seth's address was listed in the phone book. It felt so old school, looking up Seth Markley in the white pages, but it sure was better than asking her overly curious brother for the address. She hopped in the car and headed out to Raccoon Ridge.

Seth lived in a cabin that had probably been around since the 1800s. The squared-off logs were stained a dark red, a stark contrast to the pale chinking in between them. Ella walked up onto the porch with its swing and pots of winter cabbage mixed with pansies. She wouldn't have thought of Seth as the domestic type, but then what did she know?

Taking a deep breath, Ella knocked on the screen door. Nothing. She knocked again. All remained quiet. Ella wasn't ready to give up quite so easily. She walked around the cabin to see if there was a back door. She heard a metallic clang as she rounded the last corner and there was Seth, bent over fencing attached to a chicken coop or some such. Banjo lay in the grass nearby, soaking up the sun. Seth cursed under his breath, and Ella smiled. He'd probably rather no one heard that.

"Chicken wire giving you some trouble?"

Seth froze and slowly turned. He straightened and looked Ella up and down without smiling. "As a matter of fact it is. Weasel or maybe a ferret's been getting the eggs. Won't be long before it kills a chicken. Best to nip these things in the bud."

Ella felt uncertain of her plan for the first time since leaving the house. "Sorry to hear that. I . . . uh, I was hoping you might help me out."

Seth gave her an appraising look. "Come sit on the porch and you can tell me about it."

He took off a pair of leather gloves and stuffed them in the back pocket of his jeans. Ella realized that his shirt was open almost to the waist with the warmth of the early spring sun and his labor. She looked away as he began buttoning it.

"The congregation is voting on selling the church property this Sunday," she said, looking up at the treetops as they walked to the front of the cabin.

"So I hear. I'll probably be there. Although I don't have a vote, not being a member."

"That's right. You once said you don't have a dog in this fight or something like that." She risked a look back at him. Why was it that she could often tell exactly what Gran was thinking, but Seth was an utter mystery?

"Right," he echoed.

Ella felt a little braver for no good reason. "So maybe you'd back my dog."

Seth laughed as he stepped onto the porch, flopped in a chair, and propped one booted foot on the railing. "Tell me about this dog of yours."

Twenty minutes later, Ella was on her way to Mavis Sanders's house with Seth in the passenger seat. He'd rolled his shirtsleeves up and had his right arm resting on the edge of the open window. All the air whipping around was a bit more than Ella liked, but she wasn't about to suggest he roll the window up.

"You figure Mavis is the place to start?"

Ella returned her focus to the road in front of her. "She's been the strongest advocate for saving the church."

"But that means she's already on your side. Don't you need to be working on the naysayers?"

"Maybe. I'm hoping Mavis can give us ammunition." She liked the sound of "us."

Mavis must have been watching through the window as they pulled up, because she was on the top step, waving them into the house before they could even get out of the car.

"Get on in here," she called. "You here about the church?"

"We are," Ella said. "I'm hoping we'll vote to keep it."

They sat in a family room that looked like it was straight from a 1955 issue of *Good Housekeeping* magazine. The carpet was a vibrant blue, the furniture a mix of Naugahyde and a strange nubby fabric that made Ella feel itchy just looking at it. She perched on a chair that might have been plastic made to look like wood.

"You know how I'll vote, and I can count on five others who won't be in favor of selling, plus you. That leaves seven I'm sure want to leave and another ten or so I don't know about." She stabbed her cane in Ella's direction. "And some of them are kin of yourn." She resettled the cane. "The real problem is that Steve Simmons has been out beating the bushes for members who haven't been to church in a decade or two but who'll vote in favor of selling."

"Don't they have to be active members?" Ella asked.

Mavis waved a dismissive hand. "That's probably how it's supposed to work, but they haven't purged the rolls in a month of Sundays."

"Do you know who he's enlisted?"

Mavis rattled off several names, some Ella knew well and some she didn't. She jotted them down, nodding her head as she did. "Thanks so much. I'm going to do all I can to keep the church right where it is."

Mavis grunted. "What's the feller for?" She poked her cane at Seth.

"He can explain about the hunting preserve to anyone who thinks that'll be a detriment to staying where we are. It might even be a good thing. Right, Seth?"

Seth looked uneasy, but he nodded his head. "Sure. Could be."

Mavis got a gleam in her eye. "Ah," she said. "Well, good luck to ya. I sure hope you change folks' minds, but I'm not holding my breath."

They headed back out to the car and climbed in.

"Are you up for this?" Ella asked. "I plan to go change the minds of four of the people she named this very afternoon."

Seth looked at her for a moment without speaking. His warm eyes seemed to search the very depths of her soul. "This means a lot to you, doesn't it?"

"It does," she whispered.

He reached over and tucked a piece of hair behind her ear. She tried not to react, but couldn't keep her eyes from widening or her breath from catching. It was a far different feeling than what she'd experienced the last time Mark touched her.

"All right then. Let's tilt at some windmills."

Ella grinned and put the car in gear.

24

B<small>Y</small> S<small>UNDAY MORNING</small>, Ella felt like she had a fifty-fifty chance of winning this battle. Seth had actually been a big help, and she was pretty sure at least one family would stay away, another would come and vote in favor of keeping the church, and the others were anybody's guess. She whispered a prayer as she entered the church behind Dad, pushing Gran in her wheelchair.

The service seemed to take forever. The only part Ella paid attention to was yet another sermon from Richard about storing up treasures in heaven—he'd apparently decided to do a series on the subject. His words left her feeling gloomy. He made some excellent points about not putting too much stock in what you had on earth, but looking ahead to eternity instead. But surely the church wasn't earthly treasure; it was the house of God. This was different, wasn't it? Ella toyed with Gran's ring on her right hand. It was valuable to her because it was a gift from her grandfather to her grandmother, not because it was gold studded with a diamond. Didn't that make it the right sort of treasure? Ella felt less certain than she once had.

She admired the arched windows with their etched glass, the mellow wood floors, the coal stove that was rarely used anymore, and the high ceiling with the pendant lights hanging at intervals. How could anyone not love this place? She glanced at Gran, who looked peaceful and poised. She still couldn't say more than a word or two, but she'd made her desire to be there for the vote abundantly clear. For the first time, Ella wondered how Gran would vote.

Finally, Richard offered up the closing prayer and invited members to stay for the congregational meeting. No one got up to leave, not even the handful who weren't members, like Seth and Keith Randolph. Ella looked around at the biggest crowd she'd seen in the building maybe ever. If only they'd come sooner. Still, this might be the impetus they needed to renew their faith. She tried to get comfortable on the hard pew, determined to remain optimistic.

"Let's open in prayer," Richard said.

Thankfully the prayer was short. Richard called Steve Simmons to the pulpit. "Steve, I believe you're the one who's going to present the proposal to sell the church property."

Steve stood, blew his nose, made his way to the pulpit, cleared his throat three times, and finally launched into a droning list of reasons why it would benefit Laurel Mountain Church to sell the property. He recommended relocating to a lot two blocks off Main Street in Wise that was currently available for a song through his cousin's brother-in-law's uncle. He resumed his seat amid much head nodding and a few agreeable murmurs. Ella watched those she thought were swing votes, but didn't trust her interpretation of their expressions.

Richard stepped forward again. "And now I believe Mavis Sanders is going to offer a recommendation to remain here at the current location."

Mavis sprang to her feet more quickly than you'd expect a woman who needed a cane. "Ella Phillips is going to make our case," she said and plopped back down.

Ella choked, coughed, and swiped at her suddenly watering eyes. She looked around as though for an escape but only found expectant faces. Dad nodded and winked. Gran grinned like she'd gotten exactly what she wanted for Christmas, and Seth tilted his head toward the pulpit.

Ella wiped sweaty palms on the rough fabric of her skirt and stood. Were her legs shaking? She made her way to the front and looked out at people she'd known most of her life. She took a deep breath, inhaling on a prayer. She could do this.

"Laurel Mountain Church has been standing for more than a hundred and fifty years. My family has been attending here for seven generations, and those of us who aren't sitting in the pews are out there in the cemetery." She laughed lightly, but her audience barely cracked a smile.

"I know there are challenges with this building." She waved a hand to encompass the water-stained ceiling, rattling windows, and cobwebby corners. "But there are memories here we can't just pack up and move to a new building. Mavis's great-great-grandfather built this pulpit"—she caressed the wood—"and my own grandfather Casewell made the collection plates. Our ancestors saw the need for a church in this community and they built it from the ground up. Their children and their grand-children were baptized, married, and buried in this place." Ella felt like she was gaining ground. She spoke with more animation.

"There's still a need for a church in this community. The answer isn't to sell the property and sacrifice our heritage; it's to stay right where we are and build on the foundation our fore-fathers laid." Ella wondered if using the word *forefathers* was a bit much, but she kept going regardless. "Those who want to sell the church think it's better to start over from scratch rather than continue building on what we have right here." Ella ran out of steam. "So, I hope you'll vote to keep the property"—she caught Keith's eye—"and continue to make our new neighbors feel welcome."

Ella made her way back to the pew and sat near Gran, who reached for her hand and gave it a squeeze. She risked a look at Seth, and his warm smile made her feel like they'd already won.

Richard asked for any other comments, and after a few church members added their pros and cons to the discussion, it was time for the vote. Members were given a slip of paper with the words SELL and DON'T SELL printed on them. They were asked to circle their preference and drop the slips in the very collection plates Casewell crafted. Ella dropped hers in and helped Gran make a mark on her paper, holding her breath until Gran indicated that she didn't want to sell. Ella inhaled deeply, feeling like this might turn out all right after all.

Richard, Dad, Steve, Mavis, and two others took the slips up front to tally them. Maybe it was just Ella, but the tension seemed to swell and thin the air in the sanctuary. Gran kept patting her hand, which felt annoying after a bit. Finally everyone resumed their seats as Richard moved back to the pulpit. He took a deep breath and lifted a slip of paper.

"Well, folks, it was really close, but we do have a majority." He looked out over the congregation. "And the majority is in favor of . . . selling."

❦

Ella couldn't breathe. Then she gasped and started to jump to her feet, but Gran kept a firm hold on her hand. Ella registered surprise that Gran was that strong.

"All right," Gran whispered. "All right."

Tears sprang to Ella's eyes as she watched Steve shake hands and accept what had to be congratulations. She saw Mavis disappear out the door and felt like she'd let the older woman down. Richard approached her, and she rose to her feet, not sure what to feel.

"I know you're disappointed," Richard said, "but I hope you might find consolation in the fact that God uses everything for good and He'll use this, too."

Ella stared at Richard as though he were speaking a foreign language. "Good?"

"Absolutely. This could be His plan. Maybe it's time to let go of the past and try something new."

Ella felt Gran lay a hand on her elbow. Ella could feel comfort radiating from her even without words.

"Of course, it may take some time to adjust to the idea," Richard said, taking a step back. "I think I'll go speak to Henry about next steps. Selling the property will require a great deal of paper work."

Ella stared at the space where Richard had stood. Maybe she was in shock. She just couldn't believe that the members would let the church go.

"You won't have to move the cemetery."

Ella whirled to find Keith standing just behind her in the aisle. "What?"

"We can put a nice fence around the cemetery and leave it right where it is. Won't matter a bit to the hunters or the preserve. The church property is a little over ten acres and the cemetery is less than two, so it should be fine." He had such a sincere look. "Of course, you won't be able to add to it."

"Right." Ella wanted to be appreciative, but was having a hard time getting through the haze of . . . well, grief. "Thank you for that."

Keith nodded and moved to join his daughter, who was chatting and laughing with Richard.

Ella suddenly wanted to go home more than anything. "Are you ready, Gran?"

Gran gave a nod, and Dad began pushing her out to the car, Ella dragging her broken heart along behind them.

⁂

Perla could feel the disappointment coming off her granddaughter in waves as they started the drive back to that awful nursing home.

"I was so sure we would win." Ella spoke as though to herself.

"Win?" Perla echoed.

"You know what I mean—keep the church. And I can't believe Richard would try to tell me it's a good thing. And I used to think I liked him."

Perla dredged up the word she wanted. "Fickle."

Ella's voice rose a notch. "It's obvious he doesn't care about our history and heritage. He just wants more people to come to church."

"Hmmm."

The quiet didn't last long. "What do you mean, 'hmmm'?"

"Church . . . business."

"What? Getting more people to come? But he can do that at Laurel Mountain. If the church wasn't growing, we just needed to do something different. Maybe Richard isn't the best pastor for us. Maybe we need someone local who can appreciate our heritage and understand us better."

Perla concentrated until she'd pinned down several words and then chose the one she liked best. "Invitation?"

"What?"

"Who . . . invited?"

Ella huffed. "I went house to house with Seth talking about the importance of the church in the community. I did more than anyone else to save it."

Perla breathed a prayer and kept her tongue, which was certainly easier now than it used to be. Henry was also remaining admirably silent. He'd gotten smarter over the years.

"I just . . . I don't know, Gran." Ella reached for the door handle as they pulled to a stop at Hillside Acres. "I'll think about what you said."

Perla smiled. Considering how little she'd spoken, she felt optimistic that Ella was hearing from someone much wiser than her grandmother.

Ella didn't understand why they had to practice the wedding ceremony. How hard could it be? The family entered, followed by the bridesmaids and groomsmen, then came the bride down the aisle, there was some music, some words, and voilà, Will and Laura would be married. They'd almost certainly be the last couple to get married at Laurel Mountain Church. Maybe that thought was what soured Ella as they fussed over each person's entrance. Their steps had to be timed to the music, making sure everyone arrived up front when the song ended and the bridal march began. And the infuriating step . . . pause. Step . . . pause.

As the best man, Dad escorted Laura's sister Helen while Seth accompanied Ella up the aisle. At first, all of Ella's energy had gone toward maintaining just the right degree of irritated silence so everyone would know how upset she was about the sale of the church. But as soon as Ella linked her arm through Seth's, she forgot about her frustration. That hair-raising tingle happened every single time she touched the man. It would have been frustrating if it weren't so delicious. And she'd gotten over being mad at him since he'd helped her fight for the church.

On their fifth trip up the aisle, Ella got the giggles. She was tempted to touch, release, touch, release just to see if the jolt would happen each time. She tried to compose herself, but Seth got tickled too. Then Dad smiled, and Ella did a little skip to match her steps to Seth's and Helen started laughing. Finally, even Will and Laura recognized that they'd walked up the aisle one time too many, and all of them had a good laugh before deciding the rehearsal was over and moving on to dinner. The restaurant they'd chosen had a buffet featuring prime rib on Friday nights.

Richard left early, saying he needed to get ready for Sunday's sermon as well as the wedding. Ella spent a good part of the evening chatting with Seth and found that the more she was around him, the more she liked him. If only he weren't going to be part of destroying Laurel Mountain Church. Of course, Keith was paying her to help decorate the lodge, which made her feel like she was in cahoots with him herself. She and Kristen had finished all their shopping back in March and would begin arranging everything the week after the wedding. Ella tried hard not to look forward to it.

On her way back from the bathroom, Ella stopped to watch her family interacting with Laura's. They all seemed so happy, so pleased by the wedding. And Gran sat in the middle of it all. She and Aunt Sadie, who'd come in for the wedding, arrived late and planned to leave early, although it looked like Sadie was having a good time talking to Laura's uncle Gilbert. Maybe Ella should offer to take Gran home.

She started toward Gran, but then pulled back, stumped by a sudden thought. Where was home? Was it with her grandmother? Her parents' house where she'd grown up? Could it be the apartment back in Craggy Mount where she thought less and less of returning? Ella's heart told her home was where her family had lived for generations, even if they were about to lose the church. Home was the place where her roots had taken hold, and even if she tried, even if she wanted to, she could never pull them up. She squared her shoulders. Maybe it was time to take Richard's sermon to heart and consider exactly where her treasure lay.

25

"A COVERED-DISH RECEPTION? Who does that?" Sadie stood in the kitchen, hands on hips, asking the question of no one in particular.

Ella stood at the window, watching for Laura and her sister Helen, who planned to get ready for the wedding at Gran's. They'd have a light lunch and then it would be time to do hair and makeup and who knew what else in preparation for the afternoon ceremony.

"I think it's kind of creative. Let's everyone feel like they're involved and saves money on catering. I'm not saying I'd do it, but it works for Will." Ella leaned her forehead against the cool glass of the window. "And they are springing for a proper wedding cake, which in my opinion is what really matters."

"Yes, well, I'm not taking a dish. Making lunch for all you girls will have to suffice for my contribution." Sadie pulled chicken salad out of the fridge and started slicing croissants. "And your mother shouldn't feel obligated, either. She's bringing over fruit and dessert."

Ella saw her mother pull up to the house. "I doubt she feels obligated—Mom likes feeding people."

"Humph. Feeding that brother of mine for the past thirty years should satisfy any woman's urge to cook."

Mom breezed in, setting a bowl of fresh fruit and a plate of frosted sugar cookies shaped like wedding bells on the counter. "Helen and Laura are maybe five minutes behind me." She rubbed her hands together. "This is going to be such a fine day. I don't think I've been this excited since the day Henry and I finally got married."

"Smartest thing he ever did," Sadie said, giving Mom a rare hug.

"Where's Perla?" Mom looked around hopefully,

Ella sighed. "She's in the living room. She threatened to stay at Hillside Acres, but I don't think she could resist all the hubbub." She leaned through the open doorway. "Could you, Gran?"

Gran gave her a pinched look to indicate her disapproval, but Ella just grinned at her. "I'm calling your bluff, Gran. You're glad we're all here and you can't wait for Will and Laura to get married."

Gran waved her off, but she was smiling that crooked smile of hers.

Just then, Laura and Helen spilled into the kitchen in an avalanche of laughter. Even Aunt Sadie couldn't resist the joy percolating through the room. Soon they were seated in the living room, plates of food on their laps and crystal punch cups on the coffee table.

Helen had dropped a flowered tote at the door as she came in. As soon as they finished eating, she retrieved it and laid various beauty implements out on the kitchen table.

"Before I decided to become a teacher, I toyed with the idea of going to beauty school," she said. "Always had a knack for doing hair and makeup and I can't wait to get my hands on you, Ella."

Ella tried not to look worried. She wasn't exactly adventurous when it came to her beauty routine, and she wasn't altogether certain she wanted to take a chance on whatever Helen had in mind.

"I'm okay, you focus on Laura. I can just do my usual thing."

Laura settled into a chair and let Helen begin work. "Ella, trust me when I tell you not to settle for your 'usual thing.' Helen is amazing, and you'll want to let her work her magic."

Since it was the bride making the suggestion, Ella decided to give in. How bad could it be? It wasn't like she saw lots of pink blush and blue eyeshadow. Plus, watching Laura's transformation from pretty girl to gorgeous bride gave her confidence. This might even be good.

Finally they all trooped into the bedrooms and bathroom to look in any available mirror. Ella thought Laura was breathtaking, and Helen looked sleek and stylish with her hair perfectly straight. She stepped in front of the mirror and had to do a double take.

Her hair fell in glossy sheets, swishing softly around her face, which was . . . well, frankly, Ella had never looked this good. Apparently she had a thing or two to learn about applying makeup. Her eyes looked huge and dewy with perfectly arched eyebrows. Her cheeks were rosy and her lips, slightly parted in shock, were a luscious peach. Laura and Helen were trying not to roll on the bed laughing at her.

"I look . . ." Ella was at a loss. Laura wrapped an arm around her shoulders. "Yes. You do!" she said.

"Wait till Pastor Richard gets a look at you," Laura giggled. "He'll forget the words to the ceremony. And Seth—those two may end up having a duel out in the road."

Ella waved them away and pulled dresses from hanging bags. "Oh, hush. This is your day and I can't hold a candle to you. You look like something out of a fairy tale."

"I know," Laura said. "Helen is the best."

Dressing took up the last bit of time before they headed for the church. Gran opted out of attending, making it clear being part of the afternoon's festivities had worn her out. Ella suspected she could manage the ceremony if she put her mind to it, but didn't argue. Aunt Sadie would take her back to Hillside Acres on her way to church.

Mom rode with Ella while Laura's mother drove the bride and Helen in her minivan with sliding side doors that allowed Laura to sidle inside in her layers of gown. There was no place to dress at the church, and they planned to arrive after the guests were inside to avoid being seen before the ceremony. Of course, that plan didn't work out at all. Almost everyone was milling around outside, half trying to look nonchalant, and the other half not even pretending they were doing anything other than waiting to see the bridal party. Ella got out and shooed everyone indoors.

As the last guest shuffled through the door to find a seat, Richard approached Ella. He did look the teensiest bit awed by her beauty. Or she might be imagining things.

"Hi," he said. "You look amazing." Okay, maybe he was impressed.

"Thanks." He looked like he might say something more, but Seth came out and moved to Ella's side. The two men looked at each other for a long moment before Richard said he guessed he'd better take his place up front.

Seth watched him go before turning his attention to Ella. "You look . . . different."

"Helen did my hair and makeup." Ella couldn't read his expression.

"It's nice, but I think I like it better when it's just . . . you."

Ella felt a flush rise. Was that a compliment or was he saying she had on too much makeup? She decided to take it as a compliment, but the way he was looking at her left her feeling unsettled and a little off-balance.

After the ceremony, they all went out to the side yard for the reception. Most of the cars had been parked in a rarely used lower lot so there'd be plenty of room. Thankfully it was a warm, sunny day with a hint of a breeze to stir the flower petals. Tables and chairs were scattered across the spring green grass, with white cloths weighted down by clips made from chandelier crystals. More tables had been arranged on the concrete pad in front of the church. As soon as the first guest stepped out of the sanctuary, dishes and coolers and baskets began to reveal the most amazing feast Ella had ever seen.

She saw Mavis directing her grandson to unload several trays of fried chicken. Others brought out every kind of food, including a whole ham studded with pineapple slices and maraschino cherries, succulent slices of roast beef, every imaginable kind of casserole with rich, brown crusts and layers of cheese, towering congealed salads, breads ranging from biscuits to airy fresh-baked loaves, plus pitchers of iced tea, lemonade, and if Ella wasn't mistaken, buttermilk. And there was a gorgeous crystal punch bowl with a circle of ice that had flowers and mint leaves frozen inside. Someone had even set folks to turning the handles on ice cream churns. Ella was pretty sure she'd never had wedding cake with ice cream, but why not?

"Too bad Norman Rockwell is dead," she said to Dad, who stood next to her. But she wasn't sure he heard—his eyes were glued to a white van pulling up to the church.

"I think that's them," he said.

Ella watched as band members spilled out, setting up equipment and a wooden dance floor under a spreading oak. Dad pitched in and apparently knew the fiddle and banjo players. He looked like a kid whose best friends had showed up to play. After they were set up, Dad jogged to the car and pulled out his fiddle with a massive grin. He played off and on all afternoon, even dedicating a mournful ballad to his father.

Mavis sidled up to Ella and motioned for her grandson to step over. "This is Simon. He's my oldest grandson, come to spend the weekend with me."

Simon stuck out a hand and offered a shy smile.

"He's going to West Virginia University to study . . . what is it?"

"Sociology," Simon offered. "I find the behavior of the human species keenly interesting."

Mavis looked at him with a mixture of affection and pity. "Can't think what he'll do with a degree like that, but he's smart as a whip and it's high time someone in the family did something other than farm or work an assembly line."

Ella tried to make small talk with Simon, but it was clear he preferred fading into the background to watch everyone else. She was relieved when she could step away to watch Laura and Will open their gifts with laughter and exclamations of joy. She was thinking about getting another chicken leg when a hush fell. She looked up to see Laura holding a card with a look of astonishment on her face.

"What is it?" someone called out.

Will plucked the card from her hands and whistled.

"Is it a joke?" asked Laura.

"Looks like the real deal to me. Who sent it?"

Laura's eyes flicked to meet Ella's. "Mark Arrington."

Ella stiffened and stepped closer. "What did he send?"

Will shook his head. "You sure can pick 'em, little sister. It's two passes for tandem BASE jumps off the New River Gorge Bridge on Bridge Day this year. Do you have any idea how much those cost? And there's only maybe a dozen spots." He waggled his eyebrows at his bride. "You up for it?"

"No!" Ella cried out. Then she flushed and added, "I mean,

that sounds kind of dangerous. You just got married. Seems silly to take a risk like that."

Laura laughed. "This is the craziest wedding present ever, but it's also the most memorable." She hooked her arm through Will's. "I'm not saying I'll do it, but you do have until October to persuade me."

Will kissed her and whispered in her ear. They went back to the last few gifts including the crazy quilt, finally finished thanks to all the Phillips women. Laura hugged Ella, who was still fighting the urge to steal and burn the jump passes. She was probably being silly. Mark was just showing off. He wasn't really trying to hurt her family. Nonetheless, Ella felt as if some of her joy in the day had been stolen.

Next, the newlyweds cut the cake and exchanged dainty bites. Slices were passed around, along with scoops of vanilla ice cream for those who wanted it. Ella took a slice and sat on the steps to the church. The white frosting and flowers hid moist yellow cake with tangy lemon filling. Trying to put all thoughts of Mark out of her mind, she was thinking it tasted the way daffodils looked when Richard stepped up beside her and gave her something like a bow.

"May I have this dance?" he asked.

The band was playing a ballad, and Ella let Richard lead her onto the dance floor. They must have looked like children at a cotillion with their backs straight, arms stiff, and a distinct gap between them. Ella realized how wooden she was and giggled, relaxing a little. She didn't exactly melt into Richard's arms, but she did crack a smile and tried to stop acting like she had a fence post up her spine.

"This is my first covered-dish reception," Richard said.

"I think this is everyone's first," Ella laughed. "Leave it to Will to get the whole community to cater his wedding."

"They do look happy," Richard said, nodding toward Will

and Laura, dancing as though they would fall over without holding on to each other. Will touched his forehead to Laura's and then kissed her, quick and soft.

"I don't think they'll be staying much longer," Richard said as though to himself. He glanced at Ella, and his cheeks turned ruddy. Although Ella had been thinking more and more about Seth in a romantic way, she still found Richard appealing—not to mention confusing at the moment. She pushed back a notch, hoping it seemed natural as they moved to the music.

"They've cut the cake, so as far as I'm concerned we're done with them," she said. "They're going to Abingdon, Virginia, for their honeymoon, but I think they're spending tonight at Will's." Now Ella found herself blushing and wishing desperately for some other topic of conversation. Richard came to the rescue.

"So, how's Perla? I haven't had a chance to spend much time with her, considering the demands of Easter and then this wedding."

"She's . . . still making up her mind."

"What do you mean?"

Ella wished she hadn't spoken so honestly. "I think she has to make up her mind to really fight to get better, and for some reason she's not there yet."

"If there's anything I can do to help, let me know," Richard said.

Ella smiled and then the song came to an end. She started to move away when Richard grabbed her hand.

"Hey, will I see you in church tomorrow?" he asked.

"Sure."

"Maybe we could meet and talk at some point. We could get together Sunday afternoon . . ." He trailed off.

"Let's see what tomorrow brings," Ella said. "I'll let you know after church."

As she walked away, she noticed Seth bringing her mom a

slice of cake, then laughing and talking with her dad while he took a break from playing. Ella felt a stab of something like . . . jealousy. Seth hadn't even asked her to dance. He was too busy waiting on her parents and making jokes with Will. And he hadn't been all that impressed with her new look. For a moment she wondered if what Seth liked most about her was her family.

⚜

Will and Laura announced they were leaving not long after six that evening. The guests formed a double row from the cake table to the waiting car and threw birdseed at the bride and groom as they paraded down a gauntlet of people who loved them. When they reached the end, Laura stopped to throw her bouquet of lilacs over her shoulder. Ella had the feeling Laura was throwing the flowers at her, but Dad leaned out to get a better look at the departing couple and the bouquet nearly hit him in the face. He caught it and stood there with a befuddled look. Mom whacked him on the arm and pointed to Ella.

The party quickly broke up as the band packed their gear, ladies collected casserole dishes, and children were rounded up and herded into cars. Dad drove Mom and Aunt Sadie home so that Ella could take the bouquet to Gran at the nursing home.

Ella slipped into Gran's room and found her asleep in the armchair. She touched her forearm and squeezed. Her grandmother stirred and rubbed her eyes. She looked at Ella, and a tenderness stole over her expression. "T-tired."

"I know. I'll tell you all about the wedding tomorrow. Right now we should get you in bed." Ella helped Gran to her feet. "I brought you the bouquet and put it in a vase on your nightstand."

Gran closed her eyes and smiled. "Lilies."

Ella knew she meant lilacs and chose not to correct her. Sometimes the word Gran meant to say wasn't the one that came out. She was just glad Aunt Sadie hadn't heard. It would only confirm her notion that Gran wasn't going to get better.

⟨⟨⟨⟩⟩⟩

Back at the house, Aunt Sadie had already showered and changed into her nightclothes. She settled into Gran's chair with a gusty sigh of relief. "I should know better than to wear high-heeled shoes at my age."

Ella, changed into yoga pants and a T-shirt, settled on the sofa and drew an old quilt around her. "You looked wonderful."

Sadie waved a hand as though batting the compliment away. "I looked presentable, and after all it's the bride's appearance everyone should be focused on." She picked up a book from the end table and ran a hand over its cover. *Anna Karenina*. Ella had never made it all the way through that one.

"I found records for Imogene all the way up to Chuck's death in 1992. The fact that I can't find a record of her in the Social Security Death Index makes me think she's still alive."

Ella felt nonplussed. She'd almost forgotten about Sadie's quest. "Really?"

Sadie nodded. "After Chuck died, Imogene moved to Wetzel County. I've been anxious to check the tax records for the county. But they aren't online, and I haven't had time to get back to the library with all the wedding preparations."

"So you think this could be it?"

"I do. I'll find out on Monday." She rubbed at the spot where a price tag had once been stuck to the thick paperback in her hand. "Will you come with me if I find her?"

"To visit Imogene Bennett?"

Sadie looked her in the eye. "Yes. I confess the thought that I might be close to learning the truth has left me feeling . . . out of sorts."

Ella felt a stab of compassion for her aunt. Sadie could be

216

abrasive at times, but the depth of her vulnerability at the moment moved Ella.

"Of course I will. She's family, right? I love meeting family."

Sadie looked as if she'd been given some sort of reprieve. "Good. I'm going to turn in and read now." She held up the book.

Ella picked up her own novel, but couldn't seem to follow the story. She rose and pushed the curtains aside to peer out the window at the cold stars glittering in the soot-black sky. Stars usually looked warmer in the spring, but they had a January glint tonight. Ella thought about how those oblivious stars would go on shining for years, for centuries, heck for millennia for all she knew. Cold, uncaring stars.

And then Ella surprised herself by praying. She prayed that God would bless Will and Laura. That He would restore her grandmother's health. That He would lead Ella into the life He'd planned specifically for her. That He would forgive them all for letting the church slip away. That Sadie's quest would be a blessing and not bring pain to anyone. And then she waited, thinking if God was really listening it would be the perfect moment for Him to speak or give her a sign. But there was no voice from heaven, no angel descending, not even a whisper. Finally, Ella gave up and prayed that God would do whatever He thought best. Ella felt something like peace begin to creep over her. She opened her eyes to see that the stars had come closer and were winking at her warmly.

That's when the car with flashing lights pulled into the driveway.

26

SADIE AND ELLA SAT IN THE LIVING ROOM, blinking against the overhead light. They almost never turned that light on, preferring instead to use table lamps. The bright glare felt harsh and unfriendly.

"We're checking with all the church members who were in the vicinity this evening," said the uniformed deputy. He was young and seemed to be trying to grow a mustache that wouldn't take. Sadie kept rubbing her upper lip, and Ella had to resist the urge to pull her aunt's arm down.

"Looks like the fire started around the time the wedding reception was winding down, so there are quite a few suspects." He flushed. "Not that we automatically think it was someone from the church, but it's our understanding some folks were upset about this hunting lodge going in and might have felt that was justification for doing some damage." He smiled, but even his smile appeared textbook. "Routine investigation. Now, if you can give me an accounting of where each of you went when you left the church."

Aunt Sadie explained that her brother brought her home and dropped her off. The deputy flipped through his little notebook.

"Yup. Here we go. That matches the statement I took from

Henry and Margaret Phillips next door." He turned red again. "Oops. I'm not supposed to tell you that." He tucked his chin and pushed his shoulders back. "Suffice it to say, I can corroborate your story." He looked at Ella. "What about you?"

"I took the bridal bouquet to my grandmother at her nursing home."

He frowned. "Did any of the staff there see you?"

"I . . . I suppose so. I didn't talk to anyone in particular, but they might have seen me come in."

He scribbled in his notebook. "I'll check on that first thing tomorrow."

Ella felt a twinge of fear. Surely they wouldn't think she'd had anything to do with a fire at the new hunting preserve. "Was there much damage?"

"No, I think they got to it pretty quick. Probably an amateur who didn't really know what he was doing." He snapped his fingers and made a face. "I gotta quit telling stuff. This is my first real investigation." He laughed. "Don't worry. I doubt the sheriff would send me out to interview anyone he really suspected."

He slapped his notebook closed and stood, resting a hand on his gun. Ella tried to feel reassured, but the mere fact that someone had set fire to Laurel Mountain Hunting Preserve was deeply unsettling.

⚜

Perla awoke feeling . . . hopeful. She considered rolling over and refusing to do anything about it. The last thing she wanted to feel at the moment was hope. She wanted to prove her daughter right by failing to recover. By taking her secrets to the grave. By leaving Sadie to sort out her life on her own.

But doggone it, all the life those girls brought into the house with their wedding preparations stirred something inside her and made her miss being at home. She'd been so busy blaming Sadie for sticking her in Hillside Acres, she hadn't considered that maybe she could do something about it.

All she'd been thinking about lately was where she'd gone wrong in loving Sonny—Arthur. But Will and Laura's wedding reminded her of how she'd gone right in loving Casewell. She'd fallen in love the first time all on her own. The second time she'd come to realize she needed God's blessing before she chose to love anyone. And oh how God had blessed them.

It had been more than thirty years since that terrible morning when Casewell didn't wake up. She still grieved him, but time had softened the pain and sharpened the knowledge that with God all was well. She thought about the Scripture the pastor shared at Casewell's funeral. It was from First Thessalonians, if she remembered right. *"Do not grieve like the rest of mankind, who have no hope."*

She sat up and swung her feet over the side of the bed. She'd been refusing to do therapy with that chirpy young man who tried to cajole her into exercising, but she'd continued doing what she could on her own when no one was watching. She guessed hope, when it came from God, was harder to give up than she expected.

Sunshine slanted through the window, and she could see birds on the feeders out in the courtyard. Oh, how the birds sang the day she married Casewell. Sadie—the very embodiment of her mistake—was beside herself with excitement that day. She wore a ruffled dress, and her curls bounced free of the ribbons Delilah wove in to contain them.

When Perla arrived at the church in her soon-to-be-mother-in-law's dress, she thought her heart might fly right out of her chest. Casewell was so tall and handsome. Though he'd worn a beard for many years, he was clean-shaven on their wedding day, and Perla feared for a moment that he'd change his mind.

But then he smiled at her and held out a hand for Sadie to come to him and Perla knew without a doubt that God had ordained the day.

Then when the whole town came out to celebrate their union—and brought enough food to feed everyone twice—she knew God had forgiven her and she could start over fresh. She hoped Arthur had found the same sort of peace. She knew he'd gone back home and claimed his wife in spite of the opposition of their families, but she had no notion what happened after that. She made it a point never to seek him out in any way.

Of course, she could give Sadie the name of her father. Then Sadie could look Arthur Morgan up even more easily than she had Imogene Bennett. Perla suspected Sadie didn't want her to know what she was up to, but Ella had filled her in.

Perla opened the drawer in her bedside table and rummaged for a pencil and a scrap of paper. Surely she could scratch out the name if she focused. But then she paused and considered. Maybe it was better this way. Maybe it was good for Sadie to do this on her own.

She remembered the child who used to chase birds and laughed softly. It had been the oddest thing. Around the time she was six, Sadie started chasing every wild bird she encountered. Crows, turkeys, robins—they were all fair game. She would run after them as hard as she could, not slowing down until the birds disappeared into a tree or the sky. Returning with her little chest heaving, she'd shake her head as though it had been so close.

Perla finally asked her why she chased birds.

"I want one," Sadie said.

And that was that. Sadie wanted a wild bird and she pursued what she wanted with every fiber of her being. Perla dropped the pencil back in the drawer. She'd let Sadie chase her bird and maybe, this time, she'd catch it.

꧁꧂

After spending the night on Gran's sofa, Ella tried to behave as though she wasn't dying to know more about the fire at the hunting preserve, but finally gave in and practically jogged over to the farmhouse and entered through her parents' back door. If nothing else, Mom would give her breakfast.

"Mom, Dad, what's the news this morning?" She almost skidded to a stop as she rounded the corner to the kitchen and found her parents relaxing at the table with Seth. They were all sipping coffee, and Seth had a plate with the remains of toast and eggs on it.

Dad reached out and welcomed Ella with a side hug. "Guess you're likely meaning that poor excuse for a fire over at the hunting lodge. Seth and I were just laughing at how most of the folks we know are off the hook because they would have done a better job."

Seth smiled as if laughing and having breakfast at the Phillips farm were a regular occurrence.

"So they still don't know who did it?" She narrowed her eyes at Seth, who widened his in return.

"If they do, they sure haven't told me. Probably some kids trying to cause a ruckus."

"Well, it worked," Mom said, taking Seth's plate and rinsing it in the sink. She looked intently at Ella. "And I imagine there are more than kids who would be happy to see that lodge come to harm."

"It wouldn't hurt my feelings if it burnt to the ground," Ella said. Seth's eyebrows lifted. "But I'd never have the nerve to attempt arson. If anything, I'd try to find legal grounds to keep that place out of Wise." She winced inwardly even as she spoke. Little good that would do.

"I'd better get going." Seth stood and swallowed the last of his coffee. "Thanks for breakfast."

"You know you're welcome anytime," Mom said.

Seth smiled, settled his ball cap in place, and headed for the door.

Ella spun after him. "I'll see you out.

Once they were on the back porch, she turned to face Seth. "I didn't expect to find you here this morning."

He shrugged. "Your mom invited me. I think she'd be happy to feed me every morning, but I can't let her do that." He looked back toward the door. "Much as I'd like it."

"Don't you have a family of your own?" Ella snapped. As soon as she heard her own words, she wished she could snatch them back. "I mean, I know you have a family. Why are you so attached to mine?"

Seth flicked the bill of his cap, raising it a notch so that his face wasn't in shadow. "You know, Ella, I'm not sure you realize how lucky you are to know who your parents, grandparents, great-grandparents, and so on are. Me? I have no idea. Guess I kind of like hanging out with folks whose roots run deep. Especially when they're ready to treat me like one of their own." He resettled the cap and stepped down off the porch. "I'm headed over to the preserve to see if I can help Keith fix what damage has been done." He glanced at her over his shoulder. "Even if some folks wish the damage had been a whole lot worse."

Ella watched him drive away, feeling as though someone had tied a knot in the middle of her chest. She'd been trying to convince herself that maybe Richard would be good husband material, but the agony she felt at the moment made her realize her heart was committed elsewhere.

27

On Monday, Aunt Sadie returned from her library trip practically jumping up and down. Ella, accustomed to her aunt being more sedate, couldn't help but get caught up in her excitement.

"I found her," Sadie sang. "She's living in a nursing home in Fairhope near New Martinsville. I called and the staff said she's welcome to have visitors." Sadie sank into a kitchen chair, a look of astonishment on her face. "She's alive, and we can go see her."

"Well then, let's go," Ella said, suddenly eager herself.

Sadie clutched at Ella's hand. "This could be it, Ella. The information I've hardly even allowed myself to consider."

"I know." Ella sat and held Sadie's hand. "Are you sure you want to know?"

Sadie pulled away, folding her hands in her lap and staring at them. "I . . . yes. Casewell Phillips is my father, but I cannot deny that I have a strong desire to know who is responsible for bringing me into this world. And in all honesty, concern over my long-term health is only a small part of why I want to find him."

"Then we'll go and see what we can learn."

Sadie gave Ella a grateful look. "Can you come with me

tomorrow? I'm due back at work on Thursday so we don't have much time."

"Then we'll go tomorrow."

They drove through spring showers all the way to Fairhope. Sadie drove while Ella drowsed to the rhythm of the windshield wipers. She woke as Sadie entered town, stopping at one of maybe three stoplights.

"It should be just ahead on the left." Sadie drummed her fingers on the steering wheel.

Ella rubbed her eyes and sat up straighter. "Have you thought about what you'll say?"

"Constantly. I think the best approach will be to simply ask her about that summer. If we get Imogene to reminisce, she may share details we wouldn't think to ask about. Once we hear what she has to say, we can consider follow-up questions."

Ella hid a smile. She wasn't sure when this interview had changed to something they were both pursuing, but she decided not to mention Aunt Sadie's excessive use of the word *we*.

"Sounds like a good plan," she said as Sadie turned in at Shady Creek Home.

They parked and approached the building. Sadie tugged at the front door, but it wouldn't budge. Ella pointed at a small sign indicating they should ring the bell, which they did. A woman who sounded entirely too perky responded via an intercom and buzzed them in.

Sadie swept up to the front desk. "We're here to see Imogene Bennett. I'm her grandniece."

"Oh, how lovely." The petite woman with gray-blond hair clapped her hands. "She doesn't get nearly enough visitors. You'll find her in Room 228, down that hall on the left." She pointed and beamed at them as though they'd won a prize.

"Very good." Sadie turned and strode down the hall with Ella trailing after her.

When they came to Room 228, the door stood half open. Sadie hesitated, peering inside. Ella looked over her shoulder and saw a white-haired woman sitting in a wheelchair in a pool of sunlight. She had an afghan tucked over her legs and seemed to be looking intently at a picture on the wall in front of her.

Sadie knocked. "Hello? Imogene Bennett?"

The woman didn't move. Sadie pushed the door all the way open and stepped inside. "Mrs. Bennett? We're members of your family. We've come to visit."

The woman spun slowly around and looked at them as if deciding whether they were friend or foe. "Family?"

Ella stepped around Aunt Sadie and knelt at Imogene's feet. "Yes, ma'am. But you've never met us before."

Imogene reached out a hand and touched Ella's hair. She furrowed her brow and closed her eyes for a moment. Then they sprang open. "Perla Long. I'm surprised at you showing your face around here after what you done. Although I see you've colored your hair as a disguise." Her features softened. "Still, it's good to see you."

"It's good to see you, too," Ella said. "How are those headaches?"

Imogene smiled and raised one hand, which she moved back and forth as she sang.

> "In the sweet by and by,
> we shall meet on that beautiful shore,
> in the sweet by and by . . ."

Ella joined in, "'We shall meet on that beautiful shore.'" She nodded her head. "Yes, the headaches will be gone for good when you get to heaven."

Sadie, clearly losing patience, pushed forward and leaned over, bracing her hands on her knees so she could look Imogene in the eye. "Imogene, I'm your grandniece Sadie Phillips. I've come to ask you about the summer Mother spent with you in 1948."

Imogene pulled her head back like a turtle. "I don't know you."

"No, we've never met. But you remember Perla Long—she's my mother. I was hoping you could tell me about that summer when Uncle Chuck broke his leg."

Sadie was talking too loud, but Ella didn't know how to tell her she didn't have to yell without upsetting her. She had a feeling Sadie hadn't fully grasped the situation. For such a smart woman, she was being pretty dense at the moment.

"Aunt Sadie, I think—"

Ella was cut off by Imogene, who broke into song again.

> "Precious father, loving mother,
> fly across the lonely years.
> And old home scenes of my childhood,
> in fond memory appear."

Imogene waved her hands at them as though she wanted them to join in. Ella complied on the chorus.

> "Precious memories, how they linger,
> how they ever flood my soul.
> In the stillness of the midnight,
> precious sacred scenes unfold."

Imogene smiled and cupped Ella's cheek in her hand. Ella smiled back, finding herself liking her great-great-aunt Imogene.

"What is she doing?" Sadie's whisper was loud enough for the nurses in the hall to hear.

"Aunt Sadie, let's step outside a moment." Ella squeezed Imogene's hand. "We'll be right back."

Imogene just smiled and hummed.

In the hallway Ella was tempted to laugh, but decided Aunt Sadie might not see the humor. "I'm guessing Imogene has dementia or Alzheimer's or something like that."

Sadie's mouth gaped open. "What? You think? You mean she's not lucid?"

A nurse, or maybe she was an orderly, stepped over. "Are you visiting Miss Imogene?"

"We are." Sadie drew herself up ramrod straight.

"Oh, I'm so glad. She doesn't seem to have much family, and even if she doesn't recognize you, it's good for her to have stimulation." She smiled, showing deep dimples. "Of course, she'll put up with anyone who'll sing with her."

Sadie cleared her throat. "Can you give us her, well, her status?"

"You mean health-wise? I guess she's healthy as a horse. It's just her . . . you know." The woman tapped the side of her head. "But she's sweet as can be. Not mean like some of them get. And she surely does love to sing."

The woman smiled and headed down the hall.

Sadie's shoulders slumped. "Do you mean to tell me we've come all this way and she's not even able to communicate?"

Ella shrugged. "She was communicating with us—just not in the usual way."

"What do you mean?"

"I think she chooses songs based on what she wants to say. Of course, we've only heard two, but that's how it felt to me."

Sadie rubbed her eyes with both hands. "This is not what I expected."

Ella laughed as she turned back to Room 228. "What ever is?"

They stayed in Imogene's room singing old-time hymns for more than an hour. Ella thought it was kind of fun, dredging up all those songs she didn't realize she knew. But she had a feeling Aunt Sadie wasn't having as good a time.

Sadie finally stood and tugged the hem of her shirt over her hips. "Well. It's time for us to go."

Imogene gave her a blank look.

"It's been a pleasure meeting you, Aunt Imogene. I'm only sorry you weren't able to tell us about the summer Mother spent with you." She let her normally perfect posture slump. "I was so certain you'd be able to tell us if she had a beau or someone special, but I suppose that was foolish of me."

Imogene perked up. "Mother?"

"Yes, my mother. Perla Long Phillips. She stayed with you the summer of 1948 when she became pregnant with me."

Imogene nodded and tapped her fingers on the arms of her wheelchair. She hummed and then sang,

"Blessed Book, precious Book,
on thy dear old tear stained leaves I love to look;
thou art sweeter day by day, as I walk the narrow way,
that leads at last to that bright home above."

Sadie blew out a gust of air. "Yes, well, thank you. Ella, shall we go?"

"You go ahead, Aunt Sadie. I'll catch up in a sec."

Sadie rolled her eyes and shook her head. "Don't be long."

Ella waited for her aunt to disappear, then leaned over to look into Imogene's eyes. "Where's the Bible?"

Imogene grinned and darted a look at the bureau to her right. Ella stood and opened the top drawer. There were photographs, a box of costume jewelry, some scarves, and a Bible.

"Ah-ha. May I?"

"He'll understand and say well done . . ."

Ella giggled and flipped through the Bible. There were several postcards, some pressed flowers, a ribbon, and near the back, in Revelation of all places, a letter. Ella pulled it out and slipped a crackly sheet of paper from the yellowed envelope.

Dear Perla, it began. She flipped it over and saw the words *Love always, Arthur.*

Ella looked at Imogene. "Can I ask someone to make a copy of this?"

Imogene blinked rapidly, and her eyes widened. "Take it," she said. She took a deep breath and sang,

> "Are you weary? Are you heavy hearted?
> Tell it to Jesus, tell it to Jesus."

Her voice faded away. She stared at the letter in Ella's hand. A tear welled and spilled down her cheek. "Tell it to Jesus."

Ella hugged the old woman. "He already knows," she whispered.

ELLA TUCKED THE LETTER into her bag and hurried after Aunt Sadie. The same woman who let them in buzzed them back out. There were signs on either side of the door warning them not to let any of the residents leave without the proper permissions. Ella looked back as they stepped into the fresh air and sunshine of the parking lot. At least Gran didn't have to be in a place like this.

Sadie stopped and braced a hand against her car, hanging her head. "I suppose it was foolish of me to think we'd find anything. Maybe you're right. Maybe we should go ahead and ask Mother."

Ella's hand hesitated over her bag. "Why don't you want to ask her?"

"Because she tried to tell me once and I refused to listen. If I'm honest I guess it's mostly pride that's stood in my way. Asking her now is like admitting she was right to try to tell me. I don't know if you've noticed, but I have a stubborn streak."

Ella stifled a laugh.

Sadie unlocked the door, opening it to let out the heat building inside. "And I suppose I hoped I wouldn't have to ask her." She made eye contact with Ella across the roof of the car. "I wanted her to try harder to tell me."

Ella opened her door and felt the whoosh of warm air. "Maybe you won't have to ask her, and she won't have to tell you."

Sadie slid behind the steering wheel and started the car, fiddling with the air-conditioning. "You asking her for me isn't much different. Even if you do understand her better than I do."

Ella laughed. "Maybe understanding skips a generation. I don't get Mom half the time, either. But what I'm talking about is this." She held up the yellowed envelope.

"What's that?"

"I had a notion Imogene was trying to tell us something with all that singing. When I hung back, she sort of led me to check her Bible. This letter was tucked in between the pages."

Sadie reached for it, but her hand shook and she dropped it back to the steering wheel. "What does it say?"

"That's the thing." Ella ran a finger lightly over the address on the outside. "I haven't read it yet, but it's to Gran from someone named Arthur Morgan and the date is October 26, 1948. That would be when Gran was pregnant with you, wouldn't it?"

Sadie looked stricken. "It would." Her eyes darted to Ella's. "Are you saying Arthur Morgan is my father?"

"I'm saying I don't know, but Imogene failed to pass this letter on to Gran and has kept it for the past sixty years. I'm guessing it has something important to say, but I'm wondering if it's right for us to read it before Gran." She laid the envelope on the dashboard. "It's addressed to her and I know I'd want to read it first if it were mine."

Sadie clenched her jaw. Ella imagined she could hear the sound of teeth grinding.

"I hate to say so," Sadie said, "but I'm afraid you are correct. I don't suppose we could . . . no. You're right." She put the car in gear and backed out of the parking space. "Which means we ought to hightail it on home."

Ella smiled. She never expected Aunt Sadie to use a word like *hightail*.

⁂

Perla was listening to one of those preachers on the radio when Sadie and Ella crept into her room as though trying to sneak up on her. As soon as they walked in, Perla could tell Sadie was in a dither about something. She looked a question at Ella.

Her granddaughter pulled a stool over to Perla's chair and took her hand—her weak right hand—in her own. "We had a lovely visit with Imogene. She's in good health, although it turns out she has dementia."

Ah-ha. It sounded like they'd failed to learn anything. Perla felt like gloating. Her story was still hers to tell or not to tell. Sadie had tried to go around her and failed. As soon as the thought passed through her mind, she regretted it. She was sorry Imogene wasn't well and she really did want Sadie to know about her father.

Sadie settled on the end of the bed, as far as she could get from everyone else in the room. Perla could tell something was afoot.

"Secrets?" That wasn't the word she wanted, but Ella seemed to understand.

"Actually," Sadie said, "we have a letter."

Perla wrinkled her brow. A letter? She'd certainly never written anything about her situation. And she'd left the farm before Imogene knew. Her parents had been so determined to hide her condition, tucking her away at home and keeping everyone away. Could her mother have written a letter?

"It's a letter to you, Gran." Ella gripped her hand more tightly. "It's from someone named Arthur Morgan."

Perla felt her world slip sideways. It wasn't unlike the moment when she'd had the second stroke and she was frightened

233

it might be happening again. But Ella's touch proved to be the anchor she needed. Slowly the world righted itself again.

"Sonny." She hadn't meant to speak the name aloud and was surprised at how clear it came out.

Ella wrinkled her brow. "No, Arthur. At any rate, we thought you should read it first." Ella stroked Perla's wrist. "Although we're awfully curious, as you can imagine."

Perla hung her head and held on to Ella for dear life. He'd found her. Six decades gone and here he was, a presence in this room where three generations of women sat holding their collective breath.

"Read," she said.

Sadie sighed and passed Ella a yellowed envelope. Ella laid it in Perla's lap.

"Even I understand you this time, Mother." Sadie crossed her arms over her chest. "You want to read it. Well, go ahead."

"N-n-no. Read." Perla struggled to find the word she wanted. "Aloud."

Sadie's mouth flew open and she started to speak, but Ella held up a hand. "Yes, ma'am. I'll read it to us all."

Dear Perla,

How can I ever express this unbelievable combination of joy and sorrow? I've come home and claimed my Hannah, my wife. Over the protest of both our families, as you can guess, but we're determined. I stood up to my own father first and then to Hannah's. It was quite a week, I can tell you! But we are together and will make a go of marriage no matter what anyone says about it.

My only regret is you. I've decided never to tell Hannah our secret, although I think it might relieve me to expose the guilt I feel. Still, it's my cross to bear. I only hope you don't feel the same pain and regret. I never should have taken what you offered. I was afraid I had taken it against your will, but your reassurances left me to think you only meant to offer me what love and comfort you could. And I was greedy enough to take it.

I will treasure our time together forever and pray daily that God will forgive our indiscretion. I fear he may not forgive me, as I was more to blame, but I will keep asking for as long as I feel I should. I also pray that you suffer no lasting damage. Men, I think, recover more easily from these sorts of things. I only hope you will find the kind of happiness Hannah and I have now. It is my dearest wish for you.

Tell Imogene I said hello and tell Chuck I said he's probably wishing he could break the other leg to get some good help again. Ha, ha.

Your friend, Arthur

❧

Ella let the paper flutter to her lap and looked around the room. Silent tears streaked Gran's face. Sadie was leaning forward in order to hear better, to catch each word as it fell from Ella's lips.

"Arthur Morgan is my father. And he was married to someone else when he . . ." Sadie leapt to her feet as though a spring had been released. "Who is he? Who was he?"

Ella stood too. "Aunt Sadie, I think we're all a little overwhelmed by this." She glanced down. "Especially Gran. Maybe we should let her rest awhile before we start asking questions."

Sadie inhaled deeply and looked at the ceiling. "Yes. Yes, you're right. I'll go for a walk and think it over. May I see the letter?"

Ella handed it over. Sadie walked out into the hall to a window and stood there reading and rereading. Ella guessed that was as far as her walk would take her.

"Gran, I'm betting you'd like to lie down right about now."

Gran nodded. She had yet to make a move to dry her tears. Ella helped her into bed, propped pillows behind her back, and tucked an afghan over her legs. "We'll talk later. Oh, Imogene let me take this, too." Ella pulled a small black-and-white photograph out of her pocket. "It says 'Arthur, June 1948' on the back, so I guessed . . ."

Gran held out a shaking hand. Ella gave her the photo of a lanky young man, a shock of hair falling in his eyes. He was sitting on the wooden steps of a porch, arms propped on his knees, looking into the camera like he might be mad about something. Fierce, Ella thought. He looked fierce. Maybe because he was trying to get home to his Hannah. If that was it, she hoped a man might look like that about her one day. Although, looking into Gran's eyes, she also wished he would have felt just as fierce about protecting her.

29

PERLA MEANT TO SLEEP. She meant to sink into oblivion and maybe dream of that time when she was still innocent. When she still thought she had the power to change Arthur's life without impacting her own. But sleep would not come. She held the photo of him against her heart. She'd stopped loving him a long time ago, had even learned to stop regretting him. After all, she'd been forgiven and was gifted with a beautiful daughter. A daughter who even now sat out in the hall reading a letter written by her father.

That was what troubled her. She and Sadie were at an impasse, had been for years, and Perla had let it happen. She should have insisted her daughter learn who her father was. Or better yet, dug deep to find out why Sadie didn't want to know. Was she ashamed? Did she feel like she would be betraying Casewell? Whatever the reason, Perla realized there had to be some pain buried there and she'd never attempt to exorcise it. She'd eventually convinced herself that she was protecting Sadie by never burdening her daughter with the fact that her mother had been with a married man. But now she doubted the wisdom of that. Sadie was a mature and accomplished woman. Surely they could have come to an understanding.

Perla thought of her own father. He'd always been gruff, but she thought he'd loved her. At least he had until she shamed him by getting pregnant. After that, it felt as though he stopped—like flipping a switch. Maybe that was the root of what was troubling her now. Casewell had been such a loving father to Sadie, and Perla didn't want to expose her daughter to someone who might bruise her heart. What if she decided to go looking for Arthur and he hurt her—denied her? She felt certain he'd never known about his daughter. Finding out now could cause unimaginable consequences.

She stared at the ceiling, folded her hands together, and parted her lips. "Not my—" she took a breath—"call."

She'd raised Sadie to know the best earthly father the world had to offer and more importantly to know her heavenly Father, perfect in every way. If she wanted to go find Arthur Morgan, well, that was up to her. Perla had done her best to equip her daughter with an education, good sense, and love. The rest was up to her. And God.

Perla swung her legs over the side of the bed and pushed herself to standing with her strong left arm. She took a moment to compose herself, grasped the hated walker, and shuffled in her stocking feet to the door. Sadie and Ella sat on a bench at the end of the hall, not speaking. Sadie looked up, and Perla saw something harden in her daughter's eyes. It almost froze her to the spot, but then she called on the Holy Spirit and pushed forward. Approaching her daughter, Perla held out the photo.

Sadie took it, furrowing her brow. "What's this?"

Perla pointed to the back of the photo.

Sadie flipped it over, read the spidery writing, then looked up to meet Perla's eyes. "Is this him?"

Perla nodded.

"Did you love him?"

Perla nodded again.

"As much as you loved . . ." Sadie's voice broke. "As much as you loved Papa?"

"No," Perla choked out. "And I love—" she swallowed convulsively, trying to make her muscles and mind cooperate—"you . . . more."

Sadie stood, pushed the walker aside, and drew Perla into her arms, tears dampening her mother's shoulder. "I wish we could really and truly talk about this. I wish we'd done it a long time ago. I've just been so . . . so angry that I was never really Papa's child."

Perla stepped back a little so she could look into her daughter's beautiful eyes. "So sorry." She worked her mouth, closed her eyes to draw up the words she wanted, the sounds she needed to make. "Will talk."

Sadie barked a laugh through her sobbing. "We will? You've always been stubborn, Mother, so if you say so I have to think you'll find a way."

Perla nodded once emphatically and drew Sadie back into a hug, regretting the weakness in her right arm. She had some work to do, and with God's help she'd get it done this side of heaven.

"Are you ready to read, Gran?"

Gran smiled, and Ella thought the right side of her mouth lifted a bit higher than it had even a week ago. Maybe she was being too optimistic, but she felt encouraged. They were settled in the living room of the little gray house once again. After several weeks of hard work and the start of summer break at Aunt Sadie's school, they'd finally brought Gran home.

"*Goodnight Moon*," Gran said, holding up her favorite book.

"Okay, but I think we might need to upgrade soon. Maybe we can try *Uncle Wiggily* or *The Wind in the Willows*."

Gran shook her head and closed her eyes. Ella waited, knowing this was how Gran formulated what she wanted to say, as though seeing the words in her mind made it possible to speak them.

"*The Velvet . . . Velveteen Rabbit.*"

Ella clapped her hands. "Yes, I'll get a copy this afternoon."

Gran held up a hand and Ella waited again. "In . . . attic. Sadie's copy in the attic."

"Even better," Ella said as she settled on the sofa to listen to her grandmother read the simple book open in her lap.

As she listened, Ella considered how the atmosphere in their family had changed. Aunt Sadie seemed like a whole new woman since their visit with Imogene. Or maybe it was since Gran gave her that picture of Arthur Morgan. It was almost as if Gran passed him on to his daughter, giving up whatever claim she'd held since 1948. It seemed to have been freeing for them both.

The day after Gran read Arthur's letter, she asked for a speech pathologist—something she'd refused until then. When the pathologist wasn't working with Gran, Ella was. In just a week's time she'd gotten to the point where she could speak in short sentences and rarely used the wrong word in place of the one she wanted. And soon they would step up to *The Velveteen Rabbit*.

Ella was thankful for Gran's renewed zeal and for Aunt Sadie's softening. It almost felt like everything was right with the world again.

Except for the church. And the small matter of her own faith and what truly mattered to her. She was beginning to understand that there was more to believing than going to church and praying before a meal.

Ella realized Gran had stopped reading. She blinked her eyes and looked down to see what page they were on.

"You're almost to the end. Just a little further."

"What are you . . . thinking?"

Ella scrambled a moment. "I was just thinking about how great it is that you and Aunt Sadie are getting along better."

"Piffle."

Ella giggled. "What did you say?"

"Don't believe . . . you. You're thinking . . . something—" Gran rolled her hand in the air, waving the right word in for a landing—"deep. Serious."

"I suppose I was." Ella shifted, turning more fully to face her grandmother. "Gran, even before I came home when you first got sick, I had this dream about moving back to the farm and living the artist's life. But I always imagined there would be a husband in that picture and I didn't do very well on that front with Mark. I love being here to help you, and it's good to be back on the farm, but I'm not sure what I'm supposed to be doing with my life. Is this enough?"

"Be content," Gran said. She closed the book and patted the cover. "Content."

For once, Ella didn't know what Gran was getting at. "What do you mean?"

"Trying . . . too hard." Gran closed her eyes, though Ella could see them moving beneath the lids as if reading something written inside. "Please God, not men."

Now Ella thought she knew what Gran meant, but she resisted. Happiness—or contentment—wasn't that simple. She loved Gran and was grateful to see her continuing to improve, but maybe her mind still wasn't at full capacity yet.

She patted her grandmother's hand. "Yes, you're right. Now I'm going up into the attic to see if I can dig up that copy of *The Velveteen Rabbit*."

Gran sighed and looked at Ella in a way that clearly let her know she was off the hook for now, but Gran wasn't finished with this conversation.

Aunt Sadie insisted on cooking supper. She said she'd been craving cassoulet, so Ella left her to it and pulled down the attic steps. The landscape up there was a bit daunting. The small attic was packed full of dusty boxes and black plastic bags with few hints as to what was inside. As Ella turned back the flaps on the first box, she wished for a hospital mask. The dust was going to play havoc with her sinuses.

She sneezed violently as she shifted a box of old linens to get at the container beneath it.

"Bless you."

Ella jumped, nearly hitting her head on a rafter. Whirling around, she saw a head poking up through the attic access in the floor. "Seth?"

He stepped up another rung so she could see his chest and shoulders in addition to his face. The single light bulb cast deep shadows, making him look spooky.

"I was next door talking to your dad about the fire at the preserve. Seems they found the culprit." He shrugged. "Thought I'd pop over and give you the scoop, too."

Ella felt her pulse quicken. She'd almost forgotten about the fire—assumed it would go unsolved. "Who did it?"

He took another step up and sat on the edge of the opening, his feet hanging down. "Looked like the sheriff had Mavis Sanders dead to rights."

Ella felt a jolt. She'd wondered about Mavis, but decided the older woman, cantankerous as she was, wouldn't stoop so low. Ella guessed maybe the cane was nothing more than an act.

Seth continued, "But turns out it was her grandson."

"What?" Ella moved closer and knelt down across from Seth. Did he mean Simon? That kid she'd met at the wedding?

"Apparently Mavis slipped over to the lodge during the wedding, thinking she'd burn it down, but Simon followed her and talked her into letting him do it. He said he tried to set a fire that wouldn't amount to anything. He figured that was how he could get his grandmother out of there with the least fuss, but it took better than he anticipated." Seth laughed softly. "Poor kid fessed up as soon as he heard his grandmother might be blamed."

"Will he be punished?"

Seth ruffled his hair where his hat had dented it. "I think there'll have to be something—at least a fine—but Keith says he doesn't plan to press charges."

"Poor Mavis. That church is her heart." Ella stood and dusted off her hands. "I'm just glad it didn't turn out any worse."

Seth looked at her intently. "Are you? I was pretty sure it wouldn't hurt your feelings if a tornado hit the lodge."

"Maybe I did feel that way for a while. But now that Gran's back home and she and Sadie are getting along so much better, I guess you could say my priorities have shifted. I'm sad about losing the church, but it's not as important as I once thought it was."

Seth smiled and stood. "Sounds about right to me. Now, what are you doing up here in all this heat and dust?"

"Gran's been reading children's books to improve her speech. She wants to try *The Velveteen Rabbit* and there's supposed to be a copy up here that belonged to Aunt Sadie."

"That's a great book," Seth said, reaching for a stack of boxes behind him. "Okay if I help look?"

Ella glanced at him over her shoulder. "Sure. If you want."

He flipped open a box and coughed. "This looks like clothes."

"There's a black marker around here somewhere. If you don't mind, write *Clothes* on the outside so we'll know next time. I might want to go through these later and pull scraps for future quilt pieces."

They worked in silence for a few minutes. Although it was a comfortable June day outside, the attic was warm, and Ella worried Seth might notice the sweat stains on her T-shirt.

"Hey, how about I work my way to that little window in the back and see if it'll open?" Seth didn't move but had his hands on his hips, as if considering the gauntlet between where he stood and the window.

"If you can, that would be wonderful. I can't take much more of this heat. Might have to leave it until the cool of the morning."

"Hang on." Seth pushed, shoved, and clambered over a chest to reach the window. When he popped it open, Ella felt a rush of air. She wanted to raise her arms for better circulation, but opted to maintain her dignity.

"Hey, there's a bookcase back here."

"Does it have children's books in it?"

"I think so." Seth disappeared as he crouched down.

Ella climbed back into the space in front of the window. It was a good ten degrees cooler here. She breathed a sigh of relief and crouched down next to Seth, who was pulling books off the shelf.

"Here it is," he said, blowing dust off the book and then wiping it on his jeans. He handed it to Ella.

"Excellent. Now we can escape this hothouse."

Ella took a step backward, right into a bag of who knew what, and fell in a heap on the floor. Seth was over her in a heartbeat, helping her to her feet and running his hands over her wrists and arms.

"Are you hurt? It looked like your elbow got the worst of it."

Ella felt so many emotions at once, she thought she might burst. Her elbow did indeed hurt, but she was also embarrassed. And the way Seth was touching her made her feel light-headed and shivery in spite of the heat. She took a breath and put her hands over his to still them.

"I'm fine. I'm thinking I'll have a bruise or two, but mostly it's my ego that's wounded." She tried a shaky laugh.

"Good." Seth's voice was deep and comforting.

Ella looked into his eyes and what had been a pleasant tingly feeling turned into full-fledged palpitations and shortness of breath. The way he was looking at her made her doubts about which member of the Phillips family he liked best seem silly. She touched the tip of her tongue to her lips, suddenly realizing how dry they were. Was he leaning in? Might he . . . ?

"Hey, what's that?"

Ella felt like someone had changed the channel in the middle of her favorite show.

"What?"

Seth released her and bent down to look at the bag she'd tripped over. "This looks like it could be one of your art pieces." He opened the torn bag to reveal a quilt.

"It's not one of mine. At least I don't think it is. Although this part looks kind of familiar." Ella rubbed the fabric between her fingers. Why did it seem so familiar? "Let's get it downstairs where we can spread it out."

"Your wish is my command," Seth said with a mock salute.

He hauled the bag to the opening in the floor and wrestled it through. Ella tucked the book under her arm and followed.

They took the bag outside where the dust wouldn't matter, extracted what appeared to be a full-sized quilt, and carried it back inside to spread out in the house. Sadie and Gran were working through some of Gran's voice exercises, waiting for the cassoulet to finish baking. It smelled wonderful, and Ella felt her stomach grumble. Maybe they'd ask Seth to stay and eat with them. But first she wanted to figure out what it was about the quilt that seemed so familiar.

Gran peered over her reading glasses, then removed them and smiled. "What . . . have you . . . found?"

"Ella tripped over it on her way to get the book you wanted," Seth said.

"Yes," Ella said. "I left the book on the table, but there's something about this quilt that seems really familiar. Is it one of yours, Gran?"

"It's yours."

"I don't think so. I mean, there's something familiar about it, but I don't remember making it."

Gran leaned forward and pointed at the center pieces.

Reaching down, Ella touched a quilt piece and wrinkled her brow. What was it about the texture of this particular fabric? Then she gasped, realizing what Gran meant when she said this was her quilt—hers alone. The pattern was made up of oval after oval of hexagon pieces that gave the outer edge a scalloped effect, which included an amazing variety of fabrics in a rainbow of colors. At the center was a block Ella remembered sewing when she was eight or so. One of her first attempts that she'd assumed was long gone. As she looked more closely, Ella realized she knew most of these bits of fabric.

There was the pink stripe from her first party dress, a full skirt with cap sleeves that Ella once wore with white stockings and shiny black shoes. She twirled herself sick in that dress. There were also scraps of dark-green velvet from a holiday dress she'd worn the year she recited "'Twas the Night Before Christmas" at school. Soft flannel from one of her nightgowns, plaid from a school shirt, denim from a pair of pants, corduroy from a jumper—she could go on and on. Each carefully trimmed and stitched bit of fabric brought back some memory from Ella's childhood. She touched them and held the soft, worn fabric to her cheek.

Smiling, Ella turned glowing eyes on her grandmother. "When did you do this?"

"Added . . . every . . . every year."

Ella examined the outer rings and saw scraps of fabric from her own quilt projects. "How did you get these pieces?"

"Your Margaret." She shook her head and started over. "Your mother helped." She sighed. "Your . . . wedding quilt."

Ella caught Seth watching her and blushed. "I'm sorry I spoiled the surprise."

"I'm glad," Gran said. "It's good."

"Yes," Sadie agreed, tears in her eyes. "This time I understand you, Mother. It is good."

30

"THIS TABLE WAS A BRILLIANT IDEA," Kristen said, propping her feet on its long farmhouse top. "Keith told me it was one of the first things you suggested."

Ella slouched in one of the chairs, not ladder-backed as she'd originally suggested but bent-twig chairs of willow and hickory. She had to admit they were more comfortable, much better for sliding down in at the end of a long day.

"The table would be even more perfect with a big pitcher of fresh lemonade and slices of Mom's pound cake."

Kristen groaned. "Don't tease me like that. I'm starving, but I'm too pooped to even think about where we're going to get dinner."

Keith pushed the door open and stepped out onto the porch. "The place looks absolutely perfect, ladies."

Ella started to push to her feet when Keith held up his hand. "No, no, stay right there. I'm pretty sure you moved every stick of furniture at least three times and all the other odds and ends six." He waggled his eyebrows. "Now I have a treat for you."

He disappeared inside and then popped back out with a woven hamper in his arms. He carried it to the table and set it down with a thud. Flipping off the lid, he lifted items out. There was sparkling water, beads of condensation sliding down the cool glass. Then wedges of cheese, grapes, strawberries, a baguette, salami, and chocolate chip cookies as big as Ella's hand.

He arranged it all in front of them, presented them each with a small plate and a napkin, and finally walked over to the railing to pluck a rose from a bush planted just a month earlier. "Ladies, you are worth your weight in gold." He handed the rose to Kristen with a flourish. "Now, I leave you to your repast. Enjoy." He gave a little bow and went back inside, probably to his office in the farthest corner.

Ella and Kristen exchanged looks.

"You'd think he'd be married," Ella said.

"He has been. I don't think the problem is getting a wife; I think it's keeping one." Kristen sighed. "I've worked with Keith long enough to know he'd be a real catch if he'd ever stop focusing on work long enough to get caught."

Ella plucked a grape and popped it into her mouth, thinking Kristen looked awfully wistful as she broke off a piece of the baguette.

❧

It was the end of June by the time the legalities were completed for the sale of the church property. The hunting preserve had been open on a limited basis through the spring turkey season. Ella supposed it was just as well they'd be moved out before the hunters arrived in full force. A final service before the church closed was scheduled for the first Sunday of July. Ella was still sad to see the property go, but after a long talk with her grandmother, prayer, and some time spent reading her Bible, she had come to see that she might have been overly invested in a building. Maybe the congregation did need a new start. And maybe she did, too.

On the day of the final service, Ella looked around wondering where all these people had been hiding. In spite of her recently found peace, she couldn't help thinking that if only they'd come sooner, things might have turned out differently.

It was a lovely service with an abbreviated sermon and testimonials from members whose families had been attending there for generations. Dad spoke on behalf of the Phillips family, and Gran got teary when he talked about Grandpa Casewell's funeral, the day he married Mom, and Ella and Will's baptisms. It was hard, but as the service neared its end, Ella realized she did feel a certain closure.

They sang "The Old Rugged Cross" and then Richard asked if there was anyone else who wanted to speak before they closed. Much to Ella's surprise, Keith Randolph stood and made his way to the front.

He stood, head bowed for a moment. Then he looked out over the congregation and smiled—but it was a sad smile. "I have an announcement. I'm not buying the church."

Gasps and murmurs rippled through the sanctuary. Steve shot to his feet. "But everything's been finalized. You can't back out now. We have a verbal agreement on the new property in town."

Keith waved Steve back down. "I'm not buying the church, but I am making a donation equal to the purchase price. It's up to you whether you invest it in this building or move downtown."

He started back down the aisle. Ella jumped up and grabbed his arm as he approached. "Wait."

Keith stopped and hugged Ella. Surprised, she returned the hug before extricating herself. "But why?"

"Those stories, these people." Keith looked around with glistening eyes. "Your family and people like Seth there have shown me more Christian love than I've seen in a lifetime. You welcomed me in although I was an outsider. You fed me. You clothed me in the kind of grace I didn't know still existed in this world." He reached out and laid a hand on Gran's shoulder. "I have faith in this church. Seems like a good place to make an investment, even if my attorney disagrees."

The room burst into chatter as people moved forward to shake Keith's hand, to hug each other, and to talk excitedly about what the money might mean to them. Ella felt alone in the midst of the celebration. Keith mentioned his attorney not approving of the move. Who, exactly, was his attorney?

A sharp whistle echoed over their heads. As one body they turned to see Seth, Will, and Richard standing up front, waving everyone back into the pews.

"Sit down, sit down, and let's sort this out," Seth hollered.

He nodded at Richard, who braced his hands on the pulpit and smiled. "God surely does provide, doesn't He? This is exciting news, and we don't need to be in any hurry to make a decision. Let's digest this information and then we'll form a committee and figure out the best course of action. Input from you all will be most welcome."

Will leaned in. "And all you folks who came out to say goodbye to Laurel Mountain Church might want to consider saying hello on a more regular basis."

Soft laughter eased through the room. To Ella it sounded like God's own sigh of satisfaction. Although she still had every intention of asking Keith about that attorney he mentioned.

⁂

After church that Sunday, Ella invited her entire family back to Gran's house for dinner. She knew it would be crowded, but she felt like having a party. Everyone piled into the tight space and soon managed to make it feel more cozy than crowded. As the smell of roasting chicken with rosemary filled the room, the group settled into the ease that Ella wished they could always enjoy. Dad and Will drifted into the living room deep in conversation about how the cows bred late that year and how many calves they would have come spring, while Laura and Mom insisted on helping in the kitchen. Aunt Sadie and Gran took their ease at the table.

There wasn't much to help with, so the women propped hips against counters and talked about food and their husbands and plans for the future. Ella wished she'd done this sooner, but then again maybe her timing was just right. Funny how things worked out when you listened to your heart and trusted your instincts.

Soon everyone crowded around the table, and after Dad said grace he carved the first of two perfectly browned chickens sitting on one of Ella's mother's best china platters.

"Mom, are you sure you don't mind handing off your china?" Ella asked. "You've been saving it for as long as I can remember and it seems funny to give it to me now."

"No, that china has always been meant for you. And I'm so glad you're using it. I've been silly too long, treating it as though it's too good to use." She laid her napkin in her lap. "It's nice to see it here on your grandmother's table."

Ella ran a finger along the flower-strewn edge of her plate. It would have looked at home on the finest mahogany table in the grandest dining room, but she thought it looked equally well here on her grandmother's Formica table with the extra leaf making it almost big enough for all of them. Ella sighed with what occurred to her might be called contentment.

Then she noticed Laura was barely touching her food, though she wore a smile that seemed to light the room. Ella looked from Laura to her brother, who was grinning back at his wife.

"You're pregnant," Ella blurted.

Laura laughed, "Is it that obvious?"

"There's sure something up with the two of you," Ella said. "I'm thinking that's a good guess."

Will raised his glass of iced tea. "We'll have more than new calves to contend with come spring," he said, winning a swat from his wife. He ducked and raised the glass higher, looking at Laura with a tenderness Ella had never seen before. "To my beautiful wife—the mother of my child." Will swiped at a tear as they raised their glasses to the coming blessing.

Ella did her best to savor the joy of becoming an aunt without wallowing in the feeling that she might never have a child of her own. It wasn't as hard as she feared.

31

PERLA LAY IN BED staring up at the ceiling. She was wearing her favorite, somewhat threadbare nightgown that felt so soft against her skin. She laced her fingers across her belly and thought about what joy Will and Laura's announcement brought to them all.

Unlike her own pregnancy all those years ago. She remembered the night she went to Sonny—Arthur—as if it were yesterday. It was not long after he'd confided to her about his wife. She'd been so heartbroken for him, and somehow knowing he was beyond her reach had finally allowed her to admit she loved him. She supposed the hopelessness of the situation left her feeling as though she had nothing to lose.

At dinner that fateful evening, Arthur was quiet with none of his usual joking. Imogene noticed something amiss, but he brushed it off, said he was nothing worse than tired. Perla followed him out onto the porch when he headed out to his room in the barn that evening.

"I wish I could do something to help," she said.

Arthur smiled like an old man who knew it was too late for him to change the trajectory of his life. "You do help. Having you as my friend helps more than you could know." He reached out and touched her cheek.

Even now Perla could feel the electricity of his touch. She'd never experienced anything like it before that night. He seemed to notice it too, because he pulled his hand back and pushed it into his pocket.

"Some things can't be helped," he said before walking out to the barn.

Perla went to bed, but more than an hour later she still lay awake, restless and uneasy. She wanted something she couldn't define—not as young and innocent as she was—but it chafed at her and rubbed her senses raw. Finally she climbed out of bed and slipped outside into the cool night air.

A light burned through the cracks in the barn. Perla crept across the barnyard, pebbles and twigs digging into the bottoms of her bare feet. She paused at the door, open just enough for her to see Arthur sitting on the edge of his cot, head in his hands. She stretched out her own hand and felt the rough wood. She hesitated, then pushed against the door.

Arthur's head jerked up. His eyes were dark, almost liquid in the faint light from a lantern. He stood and cleared his throat.

"Perla." Her name was thick on his tongue. "What are you doing here?"

"I can't stop thinking about how hard this must be for you." She ducked her head. "I can't stop wishing I could help."

Arthur lifted a hand, then let it drop. "You can't. And you oughtn't to be out here in the night like this."

Perla raised her chin. She could feel the cool air slipping under the hem of her nightgown. "It doesn't matter. You're my friend and I care about you." She stepped inside and eased the door closed behind her.

Arthur looked stricken in that moment, but when she reached out to touch his cheek, he groaned and pulled her into his arms. Perla had never known such forbidden bliss.

Of course, as soon as it was over, she realized she'd never

known such guilt and pain, but she determined to hide her agony from Arthur. He was ashamed enough all on his own. She'd kept her chin up and thought she'd fooled Imogene. Although now that Perla was a grandmother and soon to be a great-grandmother, she wondered. Imogene had probably seen right through her.

Perla rolled to her side and curled her knees. She could pull the right one up more easily now and she was grateful for that. She was also grateful Sadie and Ella knew the worst of her story. She lost her innocence to a married man, and although God had forgiven her a long time ago, she finally felt that Sadie had as well. It was a good feeling.

❦

"Ta-da," Ella crowed. Gran and Aunt Sadie looked up from the movie they were watching. "My Appalachian Blessings quilt series is done."

"That's lovely. Now what do you do with them?" Sadie asked.

"Sylvia plans to do a show along with another quilt artist she represents." Ella stood back to study the last piece in the series. "I should probably go, but I never did enjoy those things. Makes me feel funny to see all my work displayed like that for people to pore over. I always feel like the flaws are suddenly really obvious."

"I wouldn't mind going to a show. How about you, Mother?"

"I'd . . . love to." Gran thought a moment. "Where?"

"At Tamarack in Beckley. The opening reception is Saturday afternoon."

"A date," Gran said, clapping her hands.

❦

The drive to Tamarack passed in a whirl of talk and laughter. Gran's ability to speak improved daily, and she seemed livelier than she had in a long time. Ella didn't even have a chance to feel nervous about her work being on display. They parked and walked into the circular building with its odd, spiky roofline.

Once inside, Ella felt the butterflies take flight. Gran, who still used a walker, reached over and squeezed her hand as though she understood. They walked past several display areas with jewelry, fine furniture, and gorgeous scarves before they came to the art gallery. Ella wished they could cruise on by and get some ice cream, but she took a deep breath and turned in at the door.

Her Appalachian Blessings series graced the wall to her left. There were five pieces, and at first glance Ella thought maybe they looked okay. Maybe they even looked pretty great. Sylvia swooped down on her before she could zoom in on any flaws.

"You came," she squealed. "I might have been willing to put cash money on you not showing, but gambling has never been one of my vices." She hugged Ella and kissed her cheek, then gave Gran and Sadie hugs. "Reinforcements—good plan."

Sylvia hooked her arm through Ella's and walked her over to the first quilt piece, a white church on a hill surrounded by a grapes-and-vines border that did seem to rustle in an imaginary breeze, thanks to Aunt Sadie's help. Ella smiled. This might be her favorite. She had half a mind to give it to Gran.

Sylvia released Ella and pulled a piece of paper from her pocket. She slipped a *Sold* sign into the slot displaying what Ella thought was a ridiculous price.

"It sold? But the show only just opened." Ella felt a moment of panic. She wasn't certain she wanted to let this piece go after all.

"Sweetie, they've all sold. We're thirty minutes into the show and they were gone within the first ten. This could make your career." Sylvia made a sweeping gesture at the hangings and the crowd admiring them. "You keep producing like this and we're going to have to increase prices significantly."

Ella swallowed. She was already a little uncomfortable with the prices they'd been charging. She didn't need to charge more. She wasn't sure she wanted the attention her work seemed to be bringing.

Sylvia patted her on the arm. "I can see you're overwhelmed. You and your family enjoy the show. Several other artists have items on display." She cocked her head at Ella and gave her a half smile. "You're talented, my dear. You might want to get used to people appreciating it."

The three women circled the room, admiring some oil paintings on the far wall, pottery displayed on stands in the middle of the room, and finally a series of duck decoys that looked like they might startle and fly at any moment.

Ella glanced at the price on one of the decoys and gasped. "If I start thinking too much of my art, all I have to do is compare myself to this guy. No way will I ever be able to charge that kind of money."

"You never know," said Sadie, peering at the tag. "Hmmm, we know this name."

Ella looked at the placard. *Seth Markley, Hinton, WV.* She jerked her head up and searched the room. There, in a far corner, leaning against the wall, Seth looked back at her, his eyes inscrutable. Ella sort of half waved at him. He peeled away from the wall and walked over to them.

"I didn't know you were an artist." Ella hoped that didn't sound rude. She thought it might have sounded rude.

"Never really thought of myself as an artist. I just like to carve things and decoys have a practical use, so . . ."

"Do people actually put these in the water?" Ella looked back at a carving labeled WOOD DUCK. She wanted to reach out and stroke the feathers, which looked so soft and real.

"They could, but I guess most people buy them to look at. I make them to be used, but sometimes your intent doesn't mat-

ter. People will do what they want no matter what you intend."
He smiled and picked the decoy up. "Go ahead—touch it."

Ella stroked the tail feathers with a tentative finger. While it
wasn't soft, it did have surprising texture and curves that drew
her finger along. "It's beautiful."

Seth's face turned rough. "Thanks."

Ella realized Gran and Sadie had drifted off to look at a
painting. She almost panicked, although she couldn't say why.
Maybe because she now knew Seth was an artist, which made
him more attractive and more intimidating all at once. They
stood looking at the decoys, an uncomfortable silence building.
Finally, Seth cleared his throat.

"Do you hate these things as much as I do?"

"More," said Ella.

"C'mon, they've got bad food in the next room, then we can
go shopping."

"Shopping?" Ella knit her brow and looked around the gallery. She guessed she could afford a piece of art now that she
knew all her quilt hangings had sold. Though not a decoy—she
wasn't doing that well.

"Not in here, out there." Seth pointed to the retail area outside. "I'm thinking you need one of those coal figurines shaped
like the state or maybe a black bear."

Ella laughed and started to say she couldn't since she was
here with Gran and Aunt Sadie, but she spied them chatting
with Sylvia, who caught her eye and made a *go-on* motion. So
Ella did.

Seth walked Ella, Gran, and Sadie to their car an hour later.
He'd offered to buy them dinner, and as tempted as Ella was,
she knew Gran had to be tired. Seth opened Ella's door and
shut it behind her with a heavy click. She lowered the window.

He leaned in, looking at her. "What would you say to a tour of the hunting preserve now that Keith's wrapped up the last details? We can go tomorrow afternoon when no one's hunting."

Ella wasn't sure if he was asking her out or just being nice. "Sure, I'd like that. Now that I know Keith's not the enemy." She laughed to let Seth know she was joking.

"No, Keith was never the enemy," Seth said. "We have met the enemy and he is us."

Ella smiled, though she wasn't entirely sure what Seth meant. He arranged to pick her up the next day and slapped the top of the car as Ella started the engine and pulled out of the lot.

Gran sat in the passenger seat, grinning like a possum. "I like that young man."

Ella sighed. "He is pretty great. So what did you think of the pottery?"

She steered the conversation toward anything but Seth, and thankfully her aunt and grandmother let her. But as she drove, she imagined she could feel the weight of the handblown glass kiss Seth had bought and tucked in her pocket with a wink. Maybe he did like her. Maybe it was time she let him know she liked him.

Sadie cleared her throat, interrupting Ella's thoughts. "I found Arthur Morgan."

Ella felt her grandmother go still in the passenger seat.

Sadie leaned forward and settled a hand on Gran's shoulder. "I found some information about him online."

Gran didn't speak, but Ella, glancing at her aunt in the rearview mirror, couldn't contain herself. "Tell us about him."

"He owns Tug River Natural Resources, a company involved in mining, natural gas, and timber. It would appear he's done quite well for himself. There's very little biographical information about him on the company website, but there is an old photograph, and one of the senior executives looks a lot like Arthur. His name is Christopher Morgan."

Gran squeaked. Ella darted a look at her.

"Yes," Sadie continued. "I feel confident he's my half brother—quite possibly named for you, Mother."

Then it clicked in Ella's mind. Gran's middle name was Christine.

Gran closed her eyes, and Ella could tell she was searching for words. "Will you . . . seek him?"

Sadie eased back into her seat. "I've thought about that a great deal. I found this information a few weeks ago, but chose not to share it until I'd decided what to do."

Ella held her breath and suspected Gran was doing the same.

"I've decided not to contact him. At least not now. Seeing his photograph—knowing where he is—it's enough for the moment." She laughed softly. "He's lost almost all his hair—likely has since that picture was taken. I think it might have been the color of mine. I suspect my brother will lose his, as well. I wonder if he minds."

Ella glanced in the rearview mirror again. Sadie looked wistful and reached forward to squeeze Gran's shoulder once more. "I even discovered a write-up in a company newsletter about how everyone in the organization is expected to pass an annual physical. As proof that not even the owner is exempt, they published Arthur's vitals. It would seem I come from healthy stock on the paternal side." Sadie sat silent a moment. "Mother, you and Papa have been enough for me, and I feel strangely . . . at peace. I feel as though I can rest in the knowing and be satisfied with that."

A tear trickled from Gran's eye and she nodded. "Yes, peace."

32

SETH SAT NEXT TO ELLA in church that Sunday. She thought maybe Richard paused when he saw them together, but she might have been flattering herself. After the service, Sadie took Gran home while Seth and Ella drove over to Laurel Mountain Hunting Preserve. Although the fire damage to the lodge had mostly been repaired, Ella could see the patchwork left behind. It gave her a moment's pause. She'd once wished for worse damage than this, and she almost felt like she should tell Keith she was sorry.

But her regrets were soon forgotten as Seth gave her a tour in what he called a "mule." It was a sort of all-terrain golf cart with nubby tires that traversed the rough terrain with ease. He showed her hunting blinds, two ponds that had been stocked with perch and bass, and miles of trails through the beautiful countryside and lush forests. They traveled across glades where moss grew over stones surrounded by ferns. Rhododendron thickets offered impenetrable mazes, and they passed several creeks that begged them to stop and wade.

As the afternoon waned and dusk fell, Seth took Ella back to the lodge where he'd arranged for dinner. There were plates of sliced tomatoes with mozzarella cheese, sautéed green beans, chicken cordon bleu, fresh bread, white wine, and blueberry pie with vanilla ice cream for dessert.

They settled at a table at the back of the empty dining room. Ella finished her entrée and was eyeing the pie she could see on the server near the kitchen when a group of men—investors, Seth said—came in and sat on the far side of the room. Ella smiled in their direction, and one of the men raised a glass and nodded. She blushed and looked down at her plate. When she looked up, she saw Mark sauntering through the door.

She must have reacted, because Seth reached across the table and touched her hand. She jerked, and he turned to see what had troubled her.

"Isn't that the guy who came to your birthday party?"

"Y-yes. His name is Mark. He and I . . . used to date. A long time ago," she hurried to add. "I've been wondering if maybe Keith hired him to be part of his legal team after meeting him at the party."

"Should we go over?"

"No." Ella realized she sounded abrupt. "I mean, they're probably talking business. We should leave them to it."

A waiter placed a slice of pie in front of each of them as Keith popped around the corner.

"Hey there. I thought I remembered you saying you were bringing Ella out." He nodded at the waiter, who brought over another piece of pie. Keith pulled up a chair. "So, what do you think?"

Ella tried to focus. Mark hadn't even glanced in their direction. Maybe his being here really didn't have anything to do with her.

"I'm impressed," she said. "I don't quite know what I expected when I first heard a hunting preserve was moving in. Maybe something like a paintball course with men in camouflage carrying huge guns." She looked around the room that managed to be impressive and cozy all at once. That was largely thanks to Kristen, although she liked to think her own quilt hangings helped, too. "It's nothing like that."

"I should hope not. Sounds like a good way to get shut down." Keith took a huge bite of pie and swallowed. "No, mainly this is an escape, a getaway where members can step away from all the stress in their lives and reconnect with nature." He set his fork down and pushed the half-eaten pie away. "Maybe even reconnect with God. I've heard men talk about God and nature before, but this is the first time in my life I've really understood what they were talking about."

Seth smiled. "Good for you." He said it again, more softly. "Good for you."

Keith laid a hand on Seth's shoulder. "Thank you, my friend. You preached me the best sermon I ever heard just by . . . being you. I appreciate it." He slapped his hands against his thighs. "Now I'm going to go talk to the bigwigs and the attorneys while you finish your dessert. That's Mavis Sanders's recipe we're using. She let me have it as thanks for the donation to the church." He winked. "Worth every penny."

The two sat in silence, eating their pie. Ella fiddled with her napkin and tried not to look at Mark across the room. He appeared to be completely absorbed in the conversation at his table. Ella thought maybe he hadn't seen her and wondered if she could scoot out through the kitchen and escape. She'd almost decided to do just that when there was a stirring among the men. Mark and an older gentleman stood and looked toward Ella and Seth. She felt her breath catch in her chest as they approached.

"Mr. Ellison, this is Ella Phillips, and this is Seth Markley." He turned to them. "This is Harold Ellison—he's taken over the firm."

Seth stood and shook both men's hands. Ella felt frozen, but finally got her hand out to grasp Mr. Ellison's, almost knocking over her water glass in the process.

"Nice to meet you," she squeaked out.

"The pleasure's all mine. Mark has told me so much about you and your family. Especially what godly people you are. Nothing will see you through tough times like a solid faith." He turned to Mark. "Am I right?"

Mark flushed. "It would seem so."

Ella tried to keep the shock from her expression.

Mr. Ellison slapped Mark on the shoulder. "Mark, my boy, regret is a wasted emotion, but I can see why you might wish you'd seen the light sooner in this instance." He gave Ella a fatherly smile. "Now, I'd better get back to the table before Keith hatches his next plan without me."

Ella stared at Mark. Was this some kind of a joke? A trick?

Seth cleared his throat. "I'm going to step outside for some air while you two talk. Join me whenever you're ready, Ella."

She wanted to grab his sleeve as he passed by her. She didn't feel safe around Mark. She now realized she never had. Why didn't everyone else see him for what he was?

Mark clasped his hands behind his back and rocked on his heels. "So, I'm thinking maybe I owe you an apology." He sighed. "Several, but maybe we can get them all out of the way at once."

"I don't understand."

Mark's face hardened a moment, but then he relaxed. "No. How could you? I haven't been straightforward with you. Can I sit a minute?"

Ella nodded, and Mark sat across from her.

"When Mr. Ellison came on board at the firm, he made it clear that he was a Christian and while he didn't require his attorneys to share his faith, he did expect them to respect it. I didn't even know what that meant, and it seemed like I was falling behind the other guys pretty fast." He ran a hand over his face. "I knew you and your family went to church and talked about God, so I figured if I could get you back and show the old man I had a good Christian girlfriend, it could only work to my advantage. Only you didn't cooperate."

Ella slid back in her chair a notch, deciding it might be worth hearing him out. "Go on."

"So I got pushy. And I worked my way in with Keith and the property up here figuring I could wear you down." He glanced at the men, laughing together across the room. "Only Mr. Ellison got to asking me about what was happening and he got to talking to me about the church and why it was likely important to the people—to your family." Mark hung his head. "I'd never had anyone talk to me like that. Explain God and faith like that. I fought it pretty hard. As a matter of fact, that's about the time I sent your brother that wedding gift." He looked up. "Did they do it?"

A laugh burst from Ella, and she forced herself not to clamp a hand over her mouth. "No, they transferred the passes to some friends who are into all that outdoor adventure stuff."

"I'm glad someone will benefit from my . . . pettiness." He sighed and leaned back in his chair. "My last-ditch effort was to talk Keith out of giving the church back. And I made a very convincing argument if I do say so myself. But Keith was determined to do the right thing. He said it was what God wanted him to do." Mark's face was open and almost . . . innocent. "Just like that. Like it was as simple as that." He looked at Ella. "And all of a sudden I wanted what Keith had. So I went to Mr. Ellison and he explained it all from the beginning and . . . how do you say it? I accepted Christ."

Ella realized her mouth was hanging open. She closed it. "You . . . you're a Christian now?"

Mark shrugged. "I hope so. I'm still working on it. But I'm

pretty sure I'm supposed to ask for your forgiveness. Not just for the last year or so, but for . . . before. I didn't treat you the way I should have."

"I . . . that's . . . okay."

Mark's eyes lit. "You forgive me?"

"I . . . yes, I do."

Mark nodded slowly. "Thanks, I appreciate it." He stood and started back to the table of men, but turned while he was still close. "I'm glad you got to keep the church."

Ella felt tears prickle her eyelids. "Me too."

When she headed out into the cool of the night, Ella found Seth leaning on the porch railing. She joined him and spent a few moments watching fireflies dance in the dusk, grateful that he didn't immediately jump in with questions or conversation.

"I should have talked to him about my faith," Ella said. "He's a Christian now—no thanks to me."

"You mean Mark? Did it never come up?"

"Oh, I suppose I mentioned church a few times, but I didn't really talk about God or what it means to be a believer." She shifted her focus from the sky to the earth. "Maybe I wasn't all that clear on it myself."

"It's good you can admit that." Seth turned and looked at her, and she wished she could settle into his arms, but she didn't know if they were that far along yet in their relationship.

"Mark needed someone to lead him to Christ and it could have been me, but I didn't even think about it."

Seth reached out and drew her to him in a gentle embrace. "Guess you weren't the one God had in mind for the job."

"But—"

Seth cut her off. "The main thing is that Mark found salvation. If God decides to take action, nothing you can do will stop Him. Maybe you missed out on the joy of helping to lead someone else to Christ, but if you'd done that . . . well, you and Mark might still be together." He rested his chin on the top of her head. "And I, for one, am glad that's not the case."

Ella shivered, though not from the cool of the evening. She took a deep breath and moved back a step, instantly missing the warmth of Seth's arms. She wanted to kick this relationship into high gear, but Seth's comments made her realize she needed to let it happen in God's time rather than her own.

"I'm glad too." She tucked her hair behind her ears and leaned on the railing again. "So, about the church. Seems like there's still talk about moving to this new property in town."

Seth grinned. "Changing the subject? Okay." He braced one hip against the rail and crossed his arms over his chest. "I've heard some rumblings to that effect."

"Do you think it matters?" Ella really wanted to know what Seth thought.

"I think everyone should stop making plans to share the gospel and get busy doing it."

Ella's eyebrows shot up, and she propped her own hip so she could face Seth.

"What I mean is, it seems like too many folks are putting a whole lot of time and energy into trying to figure out where the church can have the greatest impact instead of just having an impact wherever it is. As we've been discussing, there's no shortage of souls to save around Laurel Mountain." He made a swirling gesture. "And if the people are the church, then isn't the church already going into town and plenty of other places, too? To work, to the grocery store, to the mall. I think we all need to realize what you just figured out—we have to carry our beliefs past the front door of the church."

Ella surprised herself and Seth by laughing. "You've given this some thought."

Seth ducked his head. "Yeah, I guess I have. You probably weren't interested in hearing that little sermon."

"Actually, what you're saying makes a lot of sense to me. I'm still pretty attached to the building my family's been sitting in for a century or so, but maybe that has more to do with my family than with God. I've been more focused on my own history than anyone else's future." She smiled. "You're an interesting man, Seth. I'm glad we've had some time to get to know each other."

A slow smile spread across his face. "Yeah, me too."

33

IN AUGUST, ELLA AND LAURA went to Clarksville to do some shopping for the nursery. Will insisted he didn't care what they did so long as it wasn't too frilly. They'd opted not to learn the sex of the child, so frills were out anyway.

After several hours of looking at cribs, changing tables, linens, baby clothes, and a dizzying array of supplies that store clerks insisted were indispensable, both women felt frazzled.

"Let's eat," Laura suggested. "This child and I are too hungry to think straight." She patted the baby bump that she could still hide under loose-fitting clothes.

They found a deli that served homemade pepperoni rolls. Once settled at a table near the front, they ordered iced tea and sandwiches with sweet potato chips. They'd get a sack of the rolls to take home.

Laura leaned back in her chair with a sigh. "It's astonishing to me how tired being pregnant makes you. And while I could barely look at food those first few months, now I'm hungry all the time."

"Any weird cravings?"

"Not really—I just want to eat every hour of the day. I even dream about food. Last night I dreamt I was at the hospital for the delivery and insisted on going down to the cafeteria where they had pizza and macaroni and cheese and this huge chocolate cake, and I couldn't find the right line to get into. Every time the line moved, it would suddenly be for the bathroom or the checkout, but I couldn't find . . . hey."

"What's wrong?" Ella asked.

"Isn't that Pastor Goodwin?" Laura pointed to the back of the restaurant with her chin.

Ella twisted in her seat and saw Richard sitting alone at a table. He was turned away from them, but she could see enough of his profile to be sure it was him.

"So it is," Ella said. "Should we go say hi or wait until he passes our table on the way out?"

"Maybe we should invite him to join us," Laura said with a twinkle. "He seems to be alone. Oh."

"Oh?" Ella started to turn again.

"No, don't look." Laura reached across the table to grab Ella's hand. "I think maybe he isn't alone."

"I wonder who it is. The church offices are in town—maybe he's meeting someone from there."

"No," Laura said, shaking her head. "I'm pretty sure that's Tara from church."

Ella felt confused. "Tara? Keith's daughter?"

"Petite. Dark hair that's never frizzy. Skin like marble."

Ella thought about the way Keith's daughter always looked at Richard with admiration and wondered if something might be brewing between them. She couldn't help it; she dropped her napkin and peeked as she leaned over to pick it up.

Laura twirled a strand of hair as Ella resumed her upright position. "Looks kind of cozy, huh?"

"Yes," Ella said.

"You were interested in him once, weren't you?" Laura asked.

Ella considered the question and took a drink of tea. "I guess

I was, but seeing him here with Tara makes me think that's all well behind me."

Their food arrived, and it was every bit as delicious as they expected. Ella ate with relish. The thought that maybe Richard had found someone made her feel . . . free. Laura, as usual, ate as though she hadn't seen food in three days.

"I don't suppose you're planning a Lenten fast next spring."

"Nope," Laura said, sinking her teeth into the thick sandwich. "Maybe I'll give up something else—like television or using credit cards. Food is nonnegotiable at the moment. Hey, here they come."

Laura waved and smiled at the approaching couple. Ella turned and smiled, too. Richard's face was scarlet, and Tara had rosy spots in the centers of her cheeks. Ella found herself thinking no one should look that adorable when embarrassed. She also thought they really didn't have any reason to be embarrassed.

"Laura, E-Ella," Richard said, stuttering a little. "How nice to see you."

"We're out shopping for the baby," Laura said, patting her belly. "How about you?"

Ella was surprised and a little amused by her sister-in-law's direct approach. She'd always thought Laura was a bit on the meek side. Maybe pregnancy had something to do with it.

"Well, I, uh . . ." stammered Richard.

"You probably had some business with the church office," offered Ella.

"Ah, yes," Richard said. "Some paper work to drop off. Thought it would be nice for Tara here—" he stopped to clear his throat—"to get out and have some lunch. She's been . . ." He paused again, seeming to catch himself. "That's for her to share or not." Richard looked deeply uncomfortable.

"Richard has been kind enough to talk to me about a personal issue," Tara said softly, ducking her chin in a way that made Ella want to push her down and put an arm around her all in the same moment. "It was sweet of him to bring me along today." She peered up at him through what Ella would have to describe as luscious lashes. Richard chuckled in an unnatural way.

"Enjoy your day," he said. "See you ladies at church." He hustled Tara toward the door.

Once they were gone, Ella wished she'd been able to put the couple at ease, to reassure them in some way.

Laura looked at Ella's plate and asked, "You going to finish that?"

The phone rang, and after a moment Gran called to let Ella know it was for her. Ella smiled. Six months ago, Gran couldn't have answered the phone if she wanted to.

"Ella? Hey, this is Seth. I was wondering if you'd like to go to a square dance with me?"

"A square dance? Really?"

"Sure, they have them over at the college. It's a mix of locals and students. I've been a few times and it's always fun. Of course, if you'd rather do something else . . ."

"No, a dance sounds like fun. I'd love to go."

Perla watched her granddaughter going about her daily tasks humming and smiling. Perla smiled, too. Ella hadn't hummed when she was seeing Mark. Of course, Ella had changed a great deal since then, anyone could see that.

"Gran, did you ever square dance?"

Perla closed her eyes and remembered. "Yes. Your grandfather carried me home from a barn dance not long after we met."

"Really? Were you dating?" Ella sat down as though settling in for a long chat.

"No, we didn't really 'date' back then." She paused, gathering her next words. "That's the night I told him the truth about Sadie."

Ella's voice sounded almost reverent. "And he didn't mind?"

Perla laughed. "He minded. So much that I was certain there was no . . . future for us. Not that I'd thought there was, but your grandfather was very handsome." She touched her hair. "And I wasn't hard to look at, either."

"So he got over it?"

Perla laughed some more. The way young people talked. "He learned what was important and so did I, thank the good Lord." She brushed at her slacks to give herself a moment to formulate her thoughts. "If we hadn't, we wouldn't have had Henry, and he wouldn't have had you. God has the most wonderful plans."

"So is it hard?"

Perla had to think a moment before she realized what Ella was asking. "Square dancing? Not at all. You just do what the caller tells you to do." She squeezed Ella's hand. "And if you're dancing with someone you like, there's nothing better."

Satisfied, Ella said she was going for a walk. Perla watched her go, grateful to see her granddaughter blossoming. Maybe it was worth having a stroke to draw her family close to her, to learn what really mattered—to her, to Sadie, and to Ella.

She relaxed back in her chair and closed her eyes. Talking was getting easier, but she often felt tired after carrying on a conversation. She smiled, remembering that night when Casewell drove her home from the dance.

She hadn't wanted to go, feeling like it was inappropriate for a single woman with a child to be seen dancing. Her reputation was already fragile, and she feared one misstep would shatter it completely. Looking back on it, she needn't have worried since most of the town had judged her already.

Casewell stood tall on the stage with the other musicians,

playing his mandolin like he didn't care who was listening. She'd watched him play at least a thousand times over the years and she never tired of the way he disappeared into another world where he gave every note his full attention.

And then the musicians took a break, and she tried not to watch him as he made his way down the food table to where she stood dispensing drinks. Even now she could remember the way her hands shook as she poured him a glass of sweet tea. As soon as he took the tea, she braced her hands against the edge of the table so he wouldn't see them quiver.

She only danced once that evening—with her uncle Robert—but she'd wished she could dance with Casewell. She spent far too much time imagining how it would feel. Then he drove her home, and she confessed the truth about Sadie. Early in their marriage she'd offered to tell him the whole story, including Arthur's name.

A tear streaked Perla's cheek and wetted her blouse. Casewell said it didn't matter. As far as he was concerned, Christ's sacrifice on the cross had washed her clean and there was nothing left to confess. He said he'd just as soon not know who the man was, since he preferred to think of little Sadie as his own.

More tears fell, and Perla let them. Casewell had been gone for more than three decades now and there were times when the grief felt as raw as it had that morning when she realized he'd gone from her. She smiled through the tears. Oh, but she'd see him again. She glanced out the window to watch Ella return through the pasture. It looked like she was having a conversation with the birds and the trees. Maybe she was. She always did have a knack for understanding what she loved. And now maybe she was beginning to understand herself.

Perla dried her cheeks and patted her eyes. Yes, she'd see Casewell again, but for now, she had a daughter and a grand-daughter who needed her. And although she wasn't sure she was up to dancing, she was pretty sure she could give Ella a pointer or two before she headed off to her own dance.

⁂

When Seth brought Ella back home that evening, she felt as if she were still whirling around the dance floor. She'd worn a full skirt and cowboy boots, and the sensation of fabric swirling and swishing around her legs as Seth spun and do-si-doed her lingered. Not only had it been nice being out with Seth, the dance had been just plain fun. She was trying not to compare Seth to Mark or even Richard, but honestly she couldn't remember ever having such a good time on a date before.

The September evening had cooled, and the last of the fire-flies flickered over the pasture as Seth helped her down from his truck. Before she could go inside, he grabbed her hand and tugged her up the hill out back, where they could see the moon tangling in the branches of a locust tree.

"Locust trees make the best fence posts," Seth said.

Ella hadn't been expecting a lesson in farm life. "Do they?"

"Yup. The wood is tough to split by hand, but it lasts a long time. Up to a hundred years without rotting." Seth fell silent a moment. "The flowers make for good honey, and if you use it for firewood, it burns slow and hot without a lot of smoke."

"I . . . I didn't know that," Ella said.

Seth turned toward her, his eyes almost black in the twilight. "Some things are harder than others and take a lot of time and effort, but it seems like those are usually the ones that end up being most valuable."

Ella wasn't sure how to respond. Her breath caught in the back of her throat; she couldn't get air in or out.

Seth leaned closer, and when his lips brushed hers, Ella gasped—not in surprise, but in wonder. It was like suddenly

276

understanding something that had puzzled her for years. It was like being able to speak a new language.

Seth straightened and tucked a wisp of her hair behind Ella's ear. "I've waited a long time to do that."

"It was worth it," whispered Ella.

Seth laughed. "For you, or for me?"

Ella blushed and tucked her chin. "I meant for me."

"For me, too," Seth said and kissed her again.

34

ELLA WAS IN LOVE. It was March again, and she gave herself a moment to think over the past few months as she pulled on her boots and a jacket before heading out to the pasture with Dad to check on Will's cows. Will, for his part, preferred to stay close to home as Laura's due date drew nearer.

Zipping up her windbreaker, Ella stood and considered that while she was pretty sure she was in love with Seth, she wasn't quite so sure about what he felt for her. Sometimes, when he spent time with her family, she got the feeling that maybe the Phillips clan was as much a draw for him as she was.

Something Seth said once niggled at her. It was when he first told her he was adopted. He'd said something like, "You're lucky you know your family." Or maybe it was "history." As Ella got to know Seth better, he shared more about his family and the way they'd moved around from ministry to ministry. He longed for roots, and she wondered if deep down he was more attracted to what she represented than to her.

Ella walked with Dad to the gentle pasture on the Rexroad Place. They walked in silence for a while, enjoying the burgeoning warmth of the sun and listening to the symphony of birds welcoming the turn of the season. Ella breathed deeply, loving the smell of moist earth and fresh air. She glanced at her father, who winked at her.

"You're quiet this morning," he said.

"I've been thinking."

"Oh-ho. I learned a long time ago to clear out when your mother gets to thinking, but I guess I'll bite today. What have you been thinking about?"

"I really like Seth. Maybe more than like. I'm just . . . well, I wonder if he likes me for my family and for my history as much as anything else." Ella paused and grabbed a fallen branch, the perfect size for a walking stick. She jabbed it in the mud as they strolled along. "And the funny thing is, he's exactly the sort of man I imagined when I used to dream about living on the farm and being an artist. He'd totally embrace all our traditions, but somehow . . ."

Dad waited a few beats. "But somehow you've realized you want an equal partner—someone who complements you rather than following your lead. Someone who brings his own history and preferences to the equation. Someone who can maybe challenge you and help you grow."

Ella looked at her father wide-eyed. "Well, yeah. I hadn't quite put it into words, but yeah. I think that's it."

Dad threw his head back and laughed. "Favorite daughter, I think you just might be ready to take the next step."

"What's that?" Ella wasn't sure why her father was so amused.

"Oh now, just because I think you're ready, doesn't mean I am." He gave Ella a quick side hug. "Suffice it to say, I don't think you have anything to worry about with Seth. He's enamored of the Phillips clan in general, but as he continues to make our closer acquaintance I have every confidence he'll find his feet. And if I didn't think he was crazy about you in particular, I would have let you know long before this."

Warming to the subject, Ella started to ask another question when her father laid a hand on her arm and pointed to a spot where the dirt road curved behind them. Mom came puffing around the turn like the little engine that could. As soon as she saw them, she waved her arms and tried to speak. Dad reversed directions, stretching his long legs to pick up speed. Ella trotted along behind, worried about what could be wrong.

"They've gone to the hospital," Mom said when they were close enough to hear. "My grandchild is on the way!"

Ella thought if her mother had ever looked happy before, she was ecstatic now.

"We have to hurry," Mom gasped out, turning back toward the house. Dad caught up to her and took her elbow.

"Slow down, woman. You know how long these things can take, and I don't want to have to haul you to the hospital for any reason other than to see our grandbaby."

Soon Ella and her parents were seated in the maternity waiting room at the hospital. It was certainly a cheerier place than the waiting room they sat in when Gran was being treated. There were cartoon characters painted on the walls, toys set up in a corner, and more parenting magazines than Ella knew existed. The other inhabitants of the room ranged from perfectly calm to tense, but even those who seemed anxious had a positive energy about them—a feeling of bursting into song rather than tears. A grandmotherly woman was even knitting tiny pink booties. Ella smiled and admired the fine work.

"This will be my sixth grandchild," she said. "Two by my son and now four by my daughter. It's gotten to the point no one even gets much excited anymore, but I say every child needs some special things of their own. So these"—she indicated the booties—"will go with a baby afghan and the purtiest little sweater and bonnet set I've made yet."

"I take it you know it will be a girl," Ella said, touching the soft yarn. Maybe she could incorporate some knitted pieces into her quilts.

"Yes, I always thought it was kind of nice to be surprised, but you can't tell parents these days anything. My daughter said she needed to know so she could decide which things of the older kids to keep and which things to send to Goodwill. I guess that's practical, though I'd just as soon be surprised."

"My sister-in-law is having her first, and they decided not to find out ahead of time," Ella said. "I'm kind of glad—it adds to the suspense. Although I'm not sure Mom can take much more suspense at this point."

Ella glanced at her mother, who had picked up and discarded four magazines and was now tidying the room—stacking magazines, putting toys back into a box in the corner, and turning tissue boxes so their edges were equidistant from the sides of the tables they sat on.

"Hon, tell your momma to come sit by me," said the woman. Ella gladly did so, and in short order the two women were talking like best friends who hadn't seen each other in years. Ella plopped down next to Dad.

"That was a good idea," he said, looking at the pair with their heads together. "I thought I might have to get her sedated."

Father and daughter sat quietly, waiting. Ella said a silent prayer for the safety of Laura and her child as well as for the sanity of Will.

Richard walked in then and sat down facing Ella and her dad. "What's the word, Henry?"

"She's moving along according to the nurses, but it could be quite a while yet. Fortunately, Margaret made a friend over there, so she's occupied for the time being."

"Would it help if we all prayed together?" asked Richard.

"Probably, but let's leave her be until she notices you're here.

Maybe they'll let you go see Laura and Will, and you can bring us back word."

Richard nodded and headed for the nurses' station. He was gone maybe fifteen minutes before returning through another door. This time Mom spotted him immediately.

"Oh, Richard, you didn't have to come, but it certainly is good to see you." She rushed over to embrace him.

"And it's good to see you," Richard said. "They let me go in and pray with Will and Laura. She's having contractions every two minutes now, so it was a fast prayer."

"Oh, that poor girl," Mom said, tears in her eyes. "And with her parents not able to get here until this evening. A girl wants her mother at a time like this."

"Will seemed to be offering plenty of comfort," Richard said. "And the nurse is great—she joined us in prayer."

"Oh, that's wonderful. Have you spoken to Henry and Ella?"

"Yes, I have," Richard said and moved to bring the three family members together. "And if it's all right with you, I thought we'd pray right here."

After the prayer, Ella raised her head, feeling emotional, and noticed her mother crying and her dad surreptitiously swiping at a few tears of his own. They all sat back down, and Richard moved to the chair beside Ella.

"Excited?" he asked.

"Of course," Ella said. Then she worried she'd sounded curt. "I still can't quite get my head around the idea of Will as a father, but I think he may actually be pretty good at it." She smiled, and Richard smiled back.

It was at that moment Ella realized Richard was just a man who had opted to become a pastor. She'd been holding him up as holier, more special than the rest of them in some way. But really, there wasn't anything more innately religious or godly about him than there was about anyone else. He'd just followed a call that put his faith on display. Maybe she'd do well to be a little more obvious about demonstrating her faith rather than leaving it up to the pastors of the world.

Ella patted Richard on the arm. "Thanks for coming. I think Mom really needed that prayer." She smiled at her mother, who was sitting in a more relaxed posture now, talking to Dad about how they could babyproof the farmhouse. Dad wisely confined himself to nodding and smiling.

"I, uh, I've been seeing a good bit of Tara lately," Richard said. "Could be serious." He shuffled his feet and rubbed his hands down his thighs.

"Tara seems like a great girl. I hope things work out between you." And she did. It would be nice for Richard to have someone. Especially since she had someone as wonderful as Seth.

After a while, they convinced Mom to go down to the cafeteria to get something to eat. They even poked around the gift shop and bought an overpriced bouquet of daisies for the new parents.

"If it were the right time of year, I could pick twice this many for nothing," Mom scoffed. "But Laura needs something to brighten her room."

They returned to the waiting room, where Dad promptly dozed off. Ella was getting desperate enough to consider reading a magazine article, "Sleeping Through the Night: Tips and Techniques," when a nurse swung the door open.

"Phillips family," she called. "Baby Phillips is available for viewing in the nursery."

All three scrambled to their feet, and Dad, though dead asleep as far as Ella could see, beat his wife and daughter to the door. He stopped there and caught himself. Straightening his rumpled shirt, he motioned for the ladies to precede him. Ella poked him in the ribs on the way through, and they shared a smile.

Will met them in the hallway leading to the nursery. "It's a girl! And she's stunning. She's as beautiful as her mother, but with hair so dark it's nearly black. Come see."

Ella hadn't seen Will smile this big since he got his driver's license, and that smile paled in comparison. He trotted to the nursery window and looked frantic for a moment, until he spotted the nurse wheeling his daughter toward the window in her bassinet. Then his earlier smile became like the moon next to the sun. Ella almost couldn't take her eyes off her brother long enough to look at her niece. But she did, joining her parents in beholding the beauty and wonder of this child who was part of them all.

The nurse weighed and measured the baby, who seemed to be peacefully sleeping through it all. Suddenly her dark eyes flew open, and Ella would have sworn the baby looked right at her before her little face scrunched up and she wailed mightily.

Will laughed with delight. "That's my girl! She'll be able to call the cows of an evening."

They all laughed as the nurse swaddled the baby girl, who appeared to have fallen into a deep sleep with her little bow of a mouth making sucking motions. Will turned to wrap his mother in a bear hug. Dad thumped him on the back and blew his nose loudly into his ever-present handkerchief.

"What's her name?" asked Ella, still gazing at the tiny form. Will and Laura had remained tight-lipped about names no matter how much pressure was applied.

"Virginia Anne," Will said. "Virginia after Laura's grandmother, and Anne since that's yours and Mom's middle names."

Ella, who hadn't really cried yet, couldn't stop herself.

Will wrapped an arm around her shoulders and leaned his head over to touch hers. "You see, I don't think you're such a horrible sister after all." They laughed again, and Ella felt as though her insides had been scrubbed clean, like the world was a wonderful place full of love and light, and nothing would ever be really wrong again.

35

RICHARD STEPPED UP TO THE PULPIT. "I have an announcement."

The murmur of conversation settled. Perla looked around to see that some of the folks who came out for the church vote were still attending. Maybe they were hoping for a little more drama, or maybe it was the way Richard had stepped up his sermons lately. Perla wasn't one to critique a preacher—goodness knows it was a hard job—but something had changed in Richard over the last few months. The season of Lent had been filled with meaningful—and useful—sermons. She was looking forward to Easter this year even more than usual.

"I have good news. The elders have met and talked with members of the congregation and we are in agreement. Laurel Mountain Church will stay right where it is."

There was a smattering of applause, and Perla felt happiness radiating off Ella, who was seated beside her. Or maybe that was because Seth was seated on the other side of her granddaughter. Regardless, she found Ella's hand and squeezed it—with her right hand nonetheless.

"But there's more," Richard said, sounding like one of those TV ads. "We've closed on the downtown property and will be using it for Wednesday night Bible study, a new youth group, and a women's group in the evenings. During the day, it will be leased to Wee Care Day Care to provide childcare services. As part of the arrangement there will be five scholarship slots at the day-care center, which will go to needy families in Wise."

This time the applause was downright enthusiastic. Perla thought she might have even heard a whistle from Seth's general direction. Yes indeed, God always had something wonderful up His sleeve. All a person had to do was wait for it.

What Ella had come to think of as the usual crowd gathered at her parents' house after church for Sunday dinner. Mom and Dad, of course, Gran, Will and Laura with Ginny, who was the star every week, and now Seth. Keith came unless Kristen was in town. The two of them were spending more and more time together, and he'd even brought her to church twice. Kristen confided to Ella that there had been a definite change in the man—a good one. The developer had given his blessing to the courtship between Tara and Richard, claiming the pastor kept his creative daughter grounded.

Ella slid into her seat beside Seth and held out her arms to take Ginny from Laura, who was more than happy to eat a meal with both hands free for once. Cuddling the child in her arms, Ella felt a degree of contentment she wouldn't have thought possible two years ago when she was engaged to the wrong man and much too worried about what everyone thought of her.

Seth smoothed his hand over Ginny's downy hair and gave Ella one of his heart-melting smiles. It occurred to Ella that she would marry this man tomorrow if he asked. He was everything she'd been looking for without even knowing it. She leaned over and pecked him on the cheek while Ginny squirmed. Then they said grace and dug into another wonderful meal.

⁂

Easter came early that year, the first Sunday in April. Ella wasn't sure how long she and Seth had been dating. Was it since he took her on the tour of the hunting preserve back in November or since their lunch at the pizza parlor? It didn't really matter. The main thing was that they were dating, and the time they spent together made Ella realize how much energy it had taken to be with the wrong person. Spending time with Seth was almost effortless, especially as she became more confident that his attraction was to her and not just to her family.

"I was hoping you'd let me escort you to Easter services," Seth said as they strolled through the pasture on a sunny day at the end of March. "Good Friday and Easter Sunday, if you're up for it. I expect you planned to go with your family, but I'd be honored if you'd let me pick you up and take you."

Ella was charmed that he would even ask. "I'd love to. And of course you'll have to come to dinner after church Sunday and do your part to put a dent in the feast Mom's planning."

"Is Will going to be there?"

"He'd better be, unless he wants to deal with Mom."

"Oh well, I guess I'll come anyway." Seth laughed. "Seriously, I can't think of anything I'd like better than to sit in church with my sweetheart followed by some of the best cooking in the county."

Ella laughed too, and it felt like birds singing.

⁂

Seth picked her up at dusk for the Good Friday service. He wore khakis and a soft chamois shirt open at the collar. Ella was amazed at how appealing chamois could look on a man.

"Why do they call it good when it's the saddest service of the year?" she asked as Seth opened the door of his truck for her.

"Actually I've been reading up on the Lenten season," he said, sliding behind the wheel. "It might be a variation on 'God's Friday,' but I think it's mostly because as terrible as Christ's death was, it's the best thing that ever happened to mankind." He gave Ella's hand a squeeze before starting the engine and driving them to church.

During the service, Ella was surprised to feel a lump in her throat and tears prickling her eyes. The pulpit had a black cloth over it, and the cross mounted high on the front wall was draped with a black swag. There were no candles, no bright lights, and just before they left, Richard turned out even the few dim lights, leaving them in total darkness. Ella felt a sob rise in her throat, but swallowed it down, telling herself she was being silly. Of course this was sad, but she knew how it all turned out. She knew Jesus rose again and all was well not only for Him, but for her. Like Seth said, all of this was a good thing. So why did she want to hang her head and cry?

Seth dropped Ella off at her front door. He seemed touched by the service. It had been a quiet ride home. He hugged her and kissed her cheek. Ella shivered, and he rubbed her shoulders through her baby-blue sweater.

"I'll see you Sunday morning," he said, and his words sounded like a promise.

⁂

Feeling the need for quiet, Ella grabbed a windbreaker from the coatrack and headed back out to walk and clear her head. She ignored the chill creeping up her spine from the hem of her coat as she scuffed along the gravel road, head down, puzzling over how the Good Friday service had affected her this year. Maybe it was experiencing it with Seth. She didn't try to put too many labels on their relationship, but what she felt was deeper and more meaningful than anything she'd experienced before.

Of course, the story of the crucifixion and death of Jesus was difficult to hear. He'd been beaten, tortured, taunted, and denied by the people He loved most. It was truly awful what He went through, but hey, He was God, right? Wholly God and wholly man. So while it must have been painful, He knew it would be okay in the end. It wasn't like a regular person going through all that.

Then Ella remembered the part of the story in the Garden of Gethsemane where Jesus's agony became so great that His sweat was like drops of blood falling to the ground as He begged God to let Him off the hook. That was the man talking, right? Any man would prefer not to be tortured and crucified. But again He knew it would be okay, so why was Jesus so distraught?

Occasionally when Ella prayed, ideas popped into her head that were so wonderful and so to the point, she could only conclude they came straight from God. She had never heard Him speak in an audible voice, but she thought of those times as God speaking to her. On this night, as she circled back toward the house and the brilliance of the porch light, she thought she heard an actual voice.

Whirling around, Ella peered into the dark, but couldn't see anything. The moonlight made the world look frosted, and if anyone were close enough for her to hear them speak, she would surely be able to see them. Then she heard it again, but this time she was certain the voice was welling up from the depths of her own fear and insecurity.

"Father, why have you forsaken me?"

Like kindling catching fire, Ella finally understood. Jesus hadn't asked to be spared the desertion of his friends, the unjust accusations of others, the beating, the torture, or even death. He dreaded separation from His Father. Now that she'd gotten into the habit of talking to God, Ella couldn't imagine what she did before. How had she hammered out problems? How had she found peace in difficult situations? How had she known what to do? Well, obviously, she hadn't.

And here was Jesus—not simply praying to God, but knowing God, being God. Talk about close communication, about the deepest possible understanding. And that was severed utterly with nothing but the hope that Sunday morning would dawn. Going to the cross had been the greatest leap of faith of all time.

Tears washed over Ella's cheeks. For the first time in her life she thought she understood what it was Jesus had done. What it was God had arranged for the benefit of all mankind. And she was broken.

On Sunday morning, Ella hesitated before putting on her Easter finery. Was she showing off? Did it look like she cared more about how she looked than what Easter was all about? She thought about Friday night and the moment when she realized what it was Jesus had sacrificed for her. No, she decided, this was a celebration and she should wear her very best.

Seth arrived right on time. Ella admired his gray slacks with a pale blue shirt and a tie that had . . . pink stripes.

He saw her eyeing the tie. "The clerk at the store said it was just the thing for Easter Sunday." He shrugged. "So I bought it."

"It's perfect." Ella reached out and adjusted the knot, then smoothed the tie down. Touching him like that felt good, sort of proprietary. Seth smiled as though he liked it, too.

The service was gorgeous, and Ella wished she were wearing an evening gown, a tiara, or maybe the crown jewels—nothing would be too fine this morning. There were a few ladies wearing hats, and they looked grand dotting the packed pews like a watercolor painting all in pastels. Ella longed to make a quilt hanging of it.

Seth held Ella's hand through most of the service, wrapping

it in both of his when they prayed. Ella realized Seth was the first boyfriend she'd ever worshiped with. Maybe if she and Mark . . . well, that didn't matter now. She looked at Seth out of the corner of her eye. He was so attentive to the service, and his face was lit up like . . . like it was when he looked at her sometimes. She shivered, and he tucked her arm closer to his side.

After church they all headed back to the farmhouse, where Mom served a ham studded with pineapple and maraschino cherries. Ella scooped Ginny into her arms, looked around the table, and was humbled and abashed by what she saw.

The day Gran had her first stroke, she'd come home partly out of duty and partly to escape Mark. She might have even had some notion of fulfilling her dream of moving back—which had come true, but certainly not in the way she imagined it. Now here she was surrounded by her family as well as people who would have been strangers two years ago. Keith sat at the end of the table next to her father, deep in conversation about spring gobbler season. Richard and Tara chatted with Will and Laura. Ella thought she heard something about a double date now that the Easter season was ending. Gran, Aunt Sadie, and Mom had gotten a letter from Delilah's niece, inviting them all down for a birthday party, so they were making plans for a mother-daughter beach trip that would include Ella.

Seth rubbed Ella's shoulder, and she handed Ginny off to Mom. She counted all the well-loved faces around the table and realized there were eleven adults, the same as the number of apostles who rejoiced when Jesus rose on the third day.

Ella thought about how Jesus told His followers again and again that He would be back. But they didn't understand. Ella sympathized with them. She might have a knack for understanding people, yet she knew how easy it was to miss hearing God's voice when blinded by the world.

She thought about how she'd run away from Mark, using her

grandmother's illness as an excuse. How Aunt Sadie pretended not to care who her father was for fear she might hurt those she loved most. How Gran spent sixty years carrying Arthur Morgan's secret because she thought it might do more harm than good. They'd all robbed themselves of peace because they didn't have faith in one another. Because they didn't trust the truth.

After they ate, Seth motioned for Ella to follow him into the living room, where she settled on the sofa. Seth sat next to her, wrapping an arm around her shoulders. It was so perfect, Ella almost panicked. What if she were focused on the wrong thing again? What if Seth distracted her from what was really important?

She laughed under her breath. No wonder the disciples had such a hard time. They were human, too. She rested her head on Seth's shoulder and sighed. Gran came into the room and slipped into an armchair with admirable grace for a woman her age who'd suffered two strokes. Ella realized her grandmother was still beautiful and wondered if she might not find love again, as well.

Gran picked up a stack of books on the coffee table and sorted through them. "Ah-ha. I think this belonged to you . . . and Will," she said, holding up a copy of *The Velveteen Rabbit* that was newer than her own back at the little gray house.

She flipped it open and smiled, smoothing the page, then began to read. She could do so smoothly now, with only a little hesitation.

"'Generally, by the time you are Real, most of your hair has been loved off, and your eyes drop out and you get loose in the j-joints and very shabby. But these things don't matter at all, because once you are Real you can't be . . . ugly, except to people who don't understand.'"

Gran closed the book and pressed it to her heart. "I felt so very shabby after Sadie was born—ugly even. But your grandfather . . . in-invited me to be Real." She paused, and Ella thought it was one of those moments when she'd lost the next word. But then Gran smiled, the right side of her mouth lifting almost as high as the left. "No, that's not right. God invited the two of us to be Real together, to know each other through Him." She looked at Seth's hand on Ella's arm, and Ella's head resting on Seth's shoulder. "There's nothing better."

Gran stood. "Now, if you'll excuse me, Laura said I could give Ginny her bottle, and I'm thinking that's almost as close to heaven as I can get here on earth." She reached out and cupped Ella's cheek, smiled, and left the room.

Seth sat forward and faced Ella. "Your dad and I talked last week."

Ella was thinking about the lines Gran read, about being Real, so she just nodded. Seth and Dad talked all the time, and she'd learned not to be jealous, finally trusting that Seth loved her for herself more than for her family.

Seth slid off the sofa and got down on one knee. He took Ella's hand and got her full attention. She felt her pulse begin to do crazier things than usual.

"It may be too soon, and if it is, say so. But I'm really hoping . . . what I mean to say is . . . will you? Will you?" He swallowed convulsively, and Ella held her breath. "I know you had a bad experience before, but I'm really hoping you'll be my . . . wife."

Ella remembered when Mark asked her to marry him. He'd thrown the idea out on the spur of the moment. *"Hey, what if we got married?"* Thinking back on it now, she realized he'd never actually asked her. He'd just wondered what if . . . ? And now she thought she had a pretty good idea what would have happened if they'd gotten married. She shuddered, then realized she was keeping Seth waiting.

"Are you sure it's me you want?" she asked with a sly smile.

He moved to sit beside her and pulled a ring box out of his pocket. "I've been praying about it pretty much since you got after me for tearing down the chicken house. For a long time." He grinned. "Well, it felt like a long time—I had the notion God was telling me to wait. But here lately . . ." He flipped open the box to expose a sapphire and diamond ring. "I feel like I have the go-ahead."

Ella looked deep into his eyes and saw nothing but hope and love there. Speechless, she nodded her head because she couldn't form the words she wanted. She thought this must be how Gran felt when she'd had her strokes—overflowing with emotion and unable to utter a single coherent word.

But Seth knew. He understood her perfectly. He eased the ring out of its velvet slot and slipped it onto Ella's left hand where it fit like suddenly recognizing you're on the road home.

Acknowledgments

READERS AND FRIENDS OFTEN ASK ME how long it takes to write a book. Turns out it depends on the book.

THIS one took more than a decade. And if you looked back at that first draft (which I'd thank you to burn) you'd recognize little beyond the names of characters and the setting. Because this was my first book, and while it might not have been absolutely awful, it certainly wasn't very good.

But I was determined to save it—felt I was *meant* to save it.

There was a point when I seriously considered scrapping the whole story and starting over, but I'm stubborn (just ask my family) and not a little determined. So, bit by bit, Ella found her way and so did I.

Both of us want to thank everyone who kept the story alive, starting with those early readers—Meg Barbour, Christy Bennett, Anne Riddell, Judy Ross, and Anne Smith—to my last beta reader, Brandy Heineman. Thank you all.

I especially appreciate my agent, Wendy Lawton, who agreed that resuscitation was possible, and my editor, Dave Long, who believed me when I said I could save the story. I hope ya'll aren't sorry you let me pull out the paddles and give it one more shock.

Mostly, though, I want to thank my husband and my parents, who loved this story from the day I first wrote THE END, little knowing how far off that actually was. Jim is my best friend, and when he tells me he's proud of me—well, I tear up just thinking about it. Mom and Dad are my biggest cheerleaders and the ones who helped build the foundation all my stories are built upon.

Of course, when it's all said and done, like Ella, all I can do is claim to have been obedient (eventually, grudgingly, haltingly) to what I'd been called to do. If I did it well, the credit is entirely vertical.

Sarah Loudin Thomas is a fund-raiser for a children's ministry who has also published freelance writing for *Now & Then* magazine, as well as the *Asheville Citizen-Times* and *The Journey Christian Newspaper*. She holds a bachelor's degree in English from Coastal Carolina University and is the author of the acclaimed novels *Until the Harvest* and *Miracle in a Dry Season*. She and her husband reside in Asheville, North Carolina. Learn more at www.sarahloudinthomas.com.

If you enjoyed *A Tapestry of Secrets*, you may also like . . .

In small-town West Virginia, 1954, one newcomer's special gift with food produces both gratitude and censure. Will she and her daughter find a home in Wise—or leave brokenhearted?

Miracle in a Dry Season by Sarah Loudin Thomas
sarahloudinthomas.com

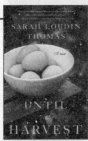

When a family tragedy derails his college studies, Henry Phillips returns home to the family farm, feeling lost and abandoned. Can he and local Margaret Hoffman move beyond their first impressions and find a way to help each other?

Until the Harvest by Sarah Loudin Thomas
sarahloudinthomas.com

When a wedding-planning gig brings single mom Julia Dare to the Caliente Springs resort, she's shocked to discover that her college sweetheart, Zeke Monroe, is the manager. As they work together, Zeke and Julia are pushed to their limits both personally and professionally.

Someone Like You by Victoria Bylin
victoriabylin.com

More Fiction From Bethany House

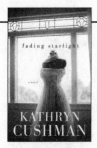

After a red carpet accident leaves her blackballed, Lauren Summers would do almost anything for another chance at her dream of a career in fashion. Does that include making a deal with a reporter to befriend a former Hollywood star, learn her secrets—and then betray her trust?

Fading Starlight by Kathryn Cushman
kathryncushman.com

Stella West has quit the art world and moved to Boston to solve the mysterious death of her sister, but she is in need of a well-connected ally. Fortunately, magazine owner Romulus White has been trying to hire her for years. Sparks fly when Stella and Romulus join forces, but will their investigation cost them everything?

From This Moment by Elizabeth Camden
elizabethcamden.com

Still reeling from her father's death, Lucinda Pennyworth arrives in New York seeking a fresh start. As she begins to establish a new life for herself, she dares to hope that a handsome West Point cadet may have a role in her future.

Flirtation Walk by Siri Mitchell
sirimitchell.com

⟡ BETHANYHOUSE